The above is a small sampling of the extraordinary praise given to the triumphant film,
Rain Man. Now its immense power is expanded
beyond the limits of the screen in a novelization
that does full artistic justice to its remarkable
cast of characters, its complex plot, and its richly
reverberating meaning.

RAIN MAN

RAIN MAN

A NOVEL BY
LEONORE FLEISCHER

BASED ON A SCREENPLAY BY
RONALD BASS AND BARRY MORROW
AND A STORY BY BARRY MORROW

Ⓞ

A SIGNET BOOK

NEW AMERICAN LIBRARY

A DIVISION OF PENGUIN BOOKS USA INC.

Acknowledgments

"I Saw Her Standing There" by John Lennon and Paul McCartney
Copyright © 1963, 1964 NORTHERN SONGS LTD, London, England
All rights for the United States of America, its territories
and possessions and Canada assigned to and controlled
GIL MUSIC CORP., 1650 Broadway, New York, N.Y. 10019
International Copyright Secured   Made in USA
All rights reserved

A Penguin Book Distributed by New American Library

SIGNET TRADEMARK REG. U.S. PAT. OFF. AND FOREIGN COUNTRIES
REGISTERED TRADEMARK—MARCA REGISTRADA
HECHO EN DRESDEN TN

SIGNET, SIGNET CLASSIC, MENTOR, ONYX, PLUME, MERIDIAN
and NAL BOOKS are published by New American Library, a division
of Penguin Books USA Inc., 1633 Broadway, New York, New York 10019

First Signet Printing, February, 1989

1 2 3 4 5 6 7 8 9

PRINTED IN THE UNITED STATES OF AMERICA

CHAPTER ONE

It was perfect. Nothing could possibly go wrong. This was the sweetest deal that Charlie Babbitt had ever come up with, and it was made up of all the elements he valued most in life. Flash and class, a big profit on zero investment, a fast turnover, plus it was legal. Not exactly Fortune 500, but legit none the less. And there was no risk. At least, that's what Charlie Babbitt had to keep telling himself. No risk.

Of course, it was a deal that had required some fast talking and even faster juggling, but that was what Charlie liked best about it. He was a master at both, and the fancy-dance master was at work here. It had taken him weeks to pull it together, but it would be worth it.

Raising the money had been the hardest part. Two hundred thousand dollars, two hundred really big ones. Most of the juggling had gone into finding a bankroll, a money man. Bert Wyatt had been cagey, sniffing a rat. But there was no rat, not even a mouse. The collateral was there, gleaming on the dock, six gorgeous classic Lamborghinis just arrived from the motherland, the *mamma-mia*-land, and each one worth close to eighty grand. They were his, all his, at least for now. He could see them, touch them, run his hands along their sleek and gleaming flanks, open the hoods and examine the perfect mechanisms of their superb motors, sniff the newly oiled leather and the fresh tyres. They smelled better than a woman.

'I've got the papers right here,' Charlie Babbitt had told the customs inspector proudly, taking the declarations out of his slender attaché case of genuine ostrich-skin. 'Six late-model Lamborghini Countachs, one silver, two black, one white and two red with red interiors.

Ignoring Charlie's rapturous patter, the inspector had taken the papers and studied them carefully before signing and stamping them. Then and only then had he looked at Charlie. 'You enterin' them in a demolition derby?' he asked with a sarcastic grin.

'No, man, in the Miss America pageant,' Charlie had grinned back. He was so pleased with himself he was ready to bust.

All the way back to the office he'd thought about the deal, going over it again and again in his head, searching for flaws and finding none. This was his masterpiece, the culmination of close to ten years of dealing and hustling and scrabbling to make a few bucks. This would take him out of the class of used-car dealers and start him on the road to being up there with the big ones, the dealers with the top franchises and the fancy showrooms. Goodbye, San Pedro. Hello, Bel Air.

Okay. It was supposed to work like this. Two hundred thousand from Wyatt on a short-term note, four weeks at 17 per cent per month interest (the greedy bastard!) with the Lamborghinis themselves used as collateral. The two hundred grand, plus the sizeable deposits from the six customers Lenny Barish had lined up and waiting – a syndicate of lawyers – had paid for the cars. And for Charlie Babbitt's *con*-siderable expenses. Charlie didn't come cheap.

He'd managed, after a stint of hard bargaining with his overseas supplier, to get six classic vintage Lamborghini sports cars, no two alike, in mint condition at $40,000 apiece. Three years ago Charlie would have paid less, but the lira versus the dollar was killing him. Still, he was lucky to get these at this price. He was selling them at $75,000, minus the discount, 10 per cent off on each car, to sweeten the deal and make the customers happy. The cars were just sitting there waiting on the pier at San Pedro, having cleared customs. Charlie had gone down to the docks himself to watch them being unloaded from the Italian freighter and to make sure that none of those beautiful bodies was scratched. Their ownership papers were tucked safely into his briefcase.

Now all Charlie had to do was take possession of the beautiful sports cars, squirrel them away where nobody could find them but himself, obtain their California registration papers, collect the rest of the money from the buyers – who were getting a real bargain with a final purchase price of $67,500 – deliver the Lamborghinis, pay off the swing loan, and he was looking at a fast profit, and a big six-figure one, all without dirtying his hands or setting a wrinkle into his close-fitting Giorgio Armani suit. And all without putting in a penny of his own.

And everybody would be happy. Six Beverly Hills divorce attorneys would be driving mint-condition luxury cars at a discount; the bankroll would get his money back plus his 17 per cent vigorish. Charlie Babbitt would be counting his profit in a condo in Palm Springs. He was a little sorry, though, that he had to sell every Lamborghini because with a little more forethought the white one might have been his own.

Charlie thought for one split-second of keeping it for himself; his profit would be big enough on the other five. That classic little baby just might be his baby, his to love, his to drive. But never mind. Plenty of those left in Italy; one of them was bound to have his name on it.

The deal was supposed to go down almost overnight, but Charlie had allowed himself a good wide margin of time – four whole weeks, plenty of time to get the cars registered, even with the Environmental Protection Agency looking over his shoulder with their sonofa-bitchin' emission-control laws.

It was the sweetheart deal of the century; not a cent of his own money was at risk, and the profit would all be his – well, his and Lenny's. He'd promised Lenny twenty-five thou just for coming up with the buyers. But Lenny wasn't a full partner, getting half; no way, not with Charlie Babbitt doing all the masterminding.

So, if it was such a pussycat of a deal, why was the whole damn thing unravelling under his very eyes? Why was it coming apart, falling down around Charlie Babbitt's ears?

The transaction had been planned for speed; after all, four weeks' interest on $200,000 at 17 per cent was a fat $34,000, too many bucks to just flush down the toilet. The sooner Charlie paid back the note, the more money he'd be able to keep for himself. But now it was almost six weeks later, and the deal hadn't gone down *yet*. The meter was running on the loan, and the national debt was piling up. Suddenly it was looking suspiciously like Charlie Babbitt would soon be pricing a condo not in Palm Springs but in Hard-Case City.

God *damn* that Environmental Protection Agency anyway! Why the hell couldn't they go save the whales or chase after nuclear-power-plant melt-downs instead of bugging a businessman's behind about state laws and fuel emissions? Didn't the EPA have any idea how hard it was to lay your hands on six available emission-control fuel-injector nozzles that could be adapted to vintage Lamborghinis? Chevys, sure. Jeep Cherokees, no problem. But *Lamborghinis*? Weeks had dragged by, and his mechanic had come up empty. Charlie had even upped the ante on the adaptors to twenty-five hundred bucks apiece, highway robbery, but still nothing.

'They didn't come up with adaptors. They didn't *make* adaptors for vintage Lamborghinis. Those Eye-talians don't care *what* kind of air they breathe.' Charlie's mechanic, a hulking guy named Eldorf, had been emphatic.

Without the adaptors, the EPA had said no three separate times to the resale of the cars in three separate inspections. And without the EPA's stamp of approval on the registration papers, the cars could not be sold in the state of California. Period. He might be able to shlep them up to Oregon and register them there, but it was already too late for that. Where would he find the right freighter at the right price at the eleventh hour?

Charlie was too damn close to being dead in the water. He'd already blown the down payments from that lawyers' syndicate; it was part of his rightful profits and he'd spent it in advance. A man in his position had to look good. Looking good and living high didn't come cheap these days with a decent haircut costing two hundred and fifty bucks, and non-prescription sunglasses with the right designer label and retro look at $400 the pop. And don't forget how the American dollar was taking a nosedive overseas. An Italian custom-made suit that had cost maybe thirteen hundred bucks two years ago was up to two thou today. The deal that was supposed to happen overnight, no risk, had dragged on so long that all the parties involved were getting very, very anxious.

And, in endless demanding telephone calls, they were passing that anxiety along to Charlie Babbitt, who didn't take all that well to anxiety.

Susanna Palmieri parked her Volvo in the space next to Charlie Babbitt's sleek little silver Ferrari. It was eleven thirty Friday morning when she stepped out and surveyed her surroundings, the place where she had worked these last three weeks. The sign might read 'Babbitt Collectibles', but there was nothing worth collecting about the rusting quonset hut except maybe the sleaze. The hut stood at the end of a long street of junkyards and warehouses. Its corrugated roof was fast losing paint in long, peeling strips. Erected as a temporary building in 1946, the quonset had hosted a long succession of temporary businesses, of which Babbitt Collectibles might be not only the latest but also the most temporary.

How could she, a beautiful, intelligent girl with a strong moral upbringing from an Italian Catholic home, a graduate of a strict convent school, have let herself get involved with a man who did business out of an oversize shed in the ass-end of nowhere?

Why did Susanna Palmieri, who was obviously destined for something better in life – such as marrying a guy with a decent job and a steady income, a guy who might just tell her he loved her every once in a while – get so tangled up with somebody like Charlie Babbitt that she was actually going to Palm Springs for the weekend with the owner of Babbitt Collectibles? She shook her lovely head as she picked up her little overnight bag, opened the quonset door and stepped inside the crummy little office she knew so well. Why? she asked herself again.

Ah, *now* she remembered, she thought, as her eyes fell on the owner of Babbitt Collectibles shouting angrily into a telephone. Charlie. Charlie Babbitt. That's why.

Susanna stood for a long moment watching him. No question, he was the most beautiful man she'd ever laid eyes or hands on. Tall and well-muscled, yet with a lean, flexible twenty-six-year-old body, Charlie had thick, dark hair that always threatened to curl no matter how hard it was brushed. His eyes were long and wide, a brilliant hazel shadowed by heavy lashes. His lips were full, almost a girl's lips until he smiled. When Charlie Babbitt smiled . . . oh, who couldn't fall for that smile, those thirty-two gleaming white teeth, that overkill cleft in his chin?

Yet Susanna was no airhead to be conquered by a man's good looks alone, even though Charlie Babbitt's looks were irresistible. Beauty may be exciting to go to bed with at night and wonderful to wake up with in the morning. But to spend the rest of the day with, beauty gets boring unless there's something solid to go with it.

With Charlie, the something solid was a ferocious, angry intelligence. An explosive, dangerous temperament under those slick, expensive threads but, at the same time, a good brain that saw instantly to the heart of any problem and could come up with a fast, workable solution. If only he would harness that intelligence and make it into something useful and important instead of chasing blue-sky 'deals', Charlie Babbitt could be a force for the world to reckon with, young as he was.

Taking a deep drag of the Lucky Strike between his lips, Charlie waved one hand at Susanna, gesturing for her to get to work, but his real attention was fixed on his furious telephone call. Susanna went to her desk and picked up the telephone. With quick small fingers, she tapped out the long string of digits for an overseas call, put the receiver to her ear and said, '*Pronto? Qui* Babbitt Collectibles.'

Despite its grandiose name, Babbitt Collectibles was a pathetic affair. The whole place stank of stale cigarette butts; overflowing ashtrays stood on every available surface. There were three metal desks, which had been acquired fifth-hand at a liquidation sale, three wooden chairs and a filing cabinet. One of the desks was Charlie's; one belonged to the 'secretary', who did not at present exist, had never existed and probably never would exist.

This desk had been awarded to Susanna Palmieri shortly after Charlie met her and had fallen for her petite beauty, her tight little body, her fiery Roman quality and that charming Italian accent. As soon as he'd learned that Susanna was fluent in Italian, *lingua toscana in bocca romana*, he'd put the moves to her. They became lovers in the same week she went to work for Babbitt Collectibles, and she had been invaluable in putting the deal with the Lamborghini people together.

At the third desk sat Charlie's 'partner', actually an employee. Lenny Barish was twenty years old, but he had spent the last three years of his life selling over the telephone. He was on the telephone. Only he wasn't shouting; he was whining. On the far wall crude maps of West Germany and Italy were thumb-tacked to the wall. For all his Italian custom clothing and bench-made English shoes, for all his vaunted 'class', Charlie

Babbitt was nothing more than a used-car salesman operating on a borrowed shoestring.

While he listened to the voice at the other end, Charlie's shouting died down for a moment. But his thick black eyebrows were drawn together in a heavy scowl, and he looked ready to explode again at any second. He puffed furiously on his cigarette.

'No, sir,' Lenny was whimpering, 'I spoke with Mr Babbitt on that very subject just this morning . . .' His eyes pleaded with Charlie to help him out here, and he waved one imploring hand, but Charlie Babbitt had troubles of his own, and they were boiling over.

'Yeah, well, it's been five and a half *weeks!*' he yelled into the receiver. '*Weeks!* How the hell can you wash out with the E P A *three* times?'

Lenny looked up in unhappy surprise from his own hassling phone call with one of the anxious buyers of the Lamborghinis, the silver '85. This third rejection by the E P A was news to him, and not welcome news.

'Uh, yes, sir,' he said miserably into the phone. 'They're finally clearing E P A. Just one . . . or two more days . . .'

'You're really on a roll here,' Charlie was snarling. '*Six* cars, three times *each!* *Zip* for eighteen – not a great batting average, wouldn't you agree? What are you, a mechanic or a N A S A engineer? We've got to *move* those goddamn cars. This isn't some lousy auto museum we're running here! I'm *dying!* Help me out, damn it!'

Now Lenny had broken out into a sweat as the buyer on the other end of the line increased the pressure. 'Well, sir, I th-think that's hardly n-necessary,' he stammered, his waving hand begging for Charlie to intervene.

But Charlie paid Lenny no attention. 'Yeah, so what

do I tell my swing loan? I'm into him two hundred thou, okay? *Thou!* Three zeros!' Angrily, he ground his cigarette out into a full ashtray, immediately lighting another.

Susanna finished her call, said, '*Ciao, grazie,*' and hung up. Glancing at the watch on the slender wrist, she frowned impatiently. She held out her arm to Charlie, tapping significantly at the watch. They had to be on their way pretty soon; it was going on eleven o'clock, and it would take them for ever to get out of town, with the freeways crowded with Friday weekend traffic. Palm Springs was a very long drive, and Susanna was apprehensive about crossing the desert at night. Charlie had promised her a three-day celebratory weekend. That was a week ago, while he still had something to celebrate.

Charlie threw Susanna a quick glance and a nod that said, 'Just cool it a sec. I'm in trouble here. Be patient for just a little while longer.' He went back at once to the call that was making him so angry.

'He could have *taken* the cars eleven days ago! They're *collateral*, for chrissakes! I'm holding him off with a whip and a chair!' Susanna could see the panic beginning to grow behind Charlie's eyes.

The phone rang, the third phone on Susanna's desk. Charlie flicked a glance over at Susanna, his eyes telling her to answer it. Removing her gold hoop earring, Susanna picked up the receiver and announced brightly, 'Babbitt Collectibles.' An irate voice began yelling at her.

'Yes, sir,' Lenny was babbling into his phone, 'I know the agreement was four weeks . . .' He waved wildly, desperately, to get Charlie's attention, but Charlie continued to ignore him, fighting his own battle out of his own trench.

'Look, have you tried *cash*?' Charlie was demanding into *his* phone. 'How much can an EPA guy *earn* a week, for chris—' He broke off, aware that Susanna was signalling him frantically. She'd placed her own call on hold, but the expression on her face told Charlie that this was urgent.

'It's Wyatt,' she informed him as she got his attention. 'About your swing loan.' She looked at Charlie quizzically.

Charlie didn't answer, but his face grew suddenly very cold and very still, his eyes hazel stones in his head.

'If he doesn't have his money by five thirty,' continued Susanna, 'he's going to seize – he definitely said "seize" – all the –'

'Call you back,' Charlie barked into his own receiver, hanging up before the mechanic could answer.

'Cars,' finished Susanna.

A boyish grin spread over Charlie Babbitt's handsome features. Boyish yet manly, a winning, convincing smile. Instantly suspicious, Susanna took one step backward, shaking her head vehemently, no. Whatever it was, she wanted no part of it. Her immortal soul was in enough danger just being with Charlie Babbitt.

Charlie placed his right hand gently on the girl's waist. His voice was low and controlled, as though nothing at all was wrong, as though all of this was just everyday routine.

'Tell him . . . you don't understand. I signed the cheque on Tuesday. You watched me sign it with all the others. And personally gave it to the mail girl.'

Susanna continued to shake her head firmly. She wasn't sure what any of this was about, but she knew a huge lie when she heard one. For three weeks she'd been overhearing something of what Charlie Babbitt was up to – how could she help it when all three desks were so close together and Charlie shouted so loudly on the phone? – but she didn't want to be a part of it, didn't even want to *know* about it. She'd been hired to deal with Italy because she was Italian and spoke the language fluently, but that was *it* as far as Susanna Palmieri was concerned. Even so, deep in her bones she knew that *it* wasn't really *it*, not as long as she and Charlie Babbitt were involved so deeply on a personal level. She was his girlfriend now, and he had a claim on her, a claim he rarely hesitated to press.

Charlie caressed Susanna's thick, curly black hair with unhurried fingers, and his voice dropped even lower. 'Please. I need this,' he told her softly.

In the place where Charlie always melted her, Susanna felt herself beginning to melt. Hating herself for agreeing, angry with Charlie, she nevertheless turned to the phone and picked it up. She punched the hold button again.

'Sir, I don't understand this,' she echoed. 'Mr Babbitt signed the cheque on Tuesday. I watched him sign it with all the others. And I personally gave it to the mail girl.' Behind her she could hear Charlie's pent-up sigh of relief come spilling out. 'Just a second. My other line . . .' She put the call back on hold.

'"Five thirty."' She repeated Wyatt's words. '"No dicking around."'

Charlie Babbitt began pacing, his brain running eighty miles an hour, his body instinctively moving nervously to catch up. 'Could he please ask his book-keeper to check her records just once more? As a personal favour to you. It'll be your ass – say "job" – if there's a problem.'

Susanna frowned, but she turned to the phone again. 'Could you please ask your bookkeeper to check her records just once more? As a personal favour to me. I'm afraid it'll be my job if there's a –'

Before Susanna could even finish the sentence, the sound of loud banging interrupted her. She and Charlie turned to see Lenny, desperate to get Charlie's attention, pounding hard on the side of his metal desk. His eyes were two large saucers of pleading, and sweat rolled down his cheeks and into his collar. Lenny's voice was hoarse now as he almost wept into his receiver. 'Yes, sir, just as soon as Mr Babbitt gets back from his meeting . . .'

Finally realizing the extent of the boy's desperation, Charlie moved quickly towards Lenny's desk to coach him. But Susanna called to him, and her voice was also urgent. He stopped, torn between them.

'Charlie. Watch my lips. Five thirty,' she reported verbatim.

Charlie Babbitt remained frozen in his tracks and closed his eyes for an instant. He drew in one long, ragged breath, while his speeding mind, like a frantic laboratory rat, raced through the maze, looking for an escape hole. And, of course, he soon came up with a narrow one, only big enough for a lab rat to shinny through.

'Okay,' he snapped impatiently. 'Listen up. I'm on a plane to Atlanta. You'll have a replacement cheque on my desk to sign first thing Monday. It's the best you can do. "Please, please, don't kill me with Mr Babbitt on this . . . I really need the job." Okay?'

The girl scowled, stung not only by her conscience but also by Charlie's impatience with her. Sometimes the careless way he spoke to her made Susanna's blood boil. Nevertheless, she turned again to the telephone.

Charlie's attention immediately focused on Lenny, who was fighting for his life with the customer. 'Well, I wouldn't do that, sir,' he was croaking desperately. 'Not until you've talked with Mr Babbitt personally . . . Uh, you want a number for him? Well . . .' Lenny shot a glance over at Charlie, who shook his head emphatically. 'No, sir, he's on the road just now, and . . .'

'Charlie!' called Susanna.

He whirled on her, his face darkening, his eyes as cold as the Bering Sea. 'You wanna put your brain in gear, baby?' he snarled. 'Just one time?'

Susanna flinched as though he'd struck her, but she pressed her lips together, taking into consideration the pressure he was under from all sides. 'You have to call him when you land.'

'Charlie!' bawled Lenny Barish.

Charlie Babbitt had been in the pressure cooker so long that the valve snapped, sending everything boiling over. Here he was, trying to hold everything together single-handed, living precariously on borrowed money, on borrowed time. The sound of his own name being bleated by the helpless Lenny triggered the explosion. He spun around, with a single, wide movement of his right arm sweeping everything off Lenny's desk – phone books, files, notes, all came crashing to the floor – as the boy watched stunned.

'You . . . have . . . a . . . problem?' demanded Charlie through gritted teeth, with dangerous enunciation.

Lenny's Adam's apple bobbed as he gulped for air. 'Mr Bateman wants to back out on his car. And take Mr Webb with him. They . . . uh . . . they want their down payments back.' He almost whispered the latter part of the sentence, aware that the down payments were history, only the wisp of a memory, never to be resurrected.

Charlie closed his eyes, saying nothing.

'They've found two cars at Valley Motors,' continued Lenny. 'And they want to go that way.'

'Charlie, please,' Susanna insisted.

Quietly he turned to her, his emotion nearly spent by the violence of his blow-up at Lenny.

'Wyatt wants to know where the cars are.'

He nodded. Sure he does. That'll be the day. 'Tell him the truth. You don't know.' Nobody knew except Charlie; the cars were all he had to gamble with, his last chip, his ace in the hole. Turning back to Lenny, his voice calmer, he instructed, 'Tell Bateman that was me on your other line. I just settled out with EPA. And . . .' He hesitated, struggling with himself, then gave in with a sigh. 'Tell them I'm knocking five grand off both their deals. Because I appreciate their patience.'

Lenny nodded gratefully and went back to his call. Susanna hung up the phone and looked over at Charlie. Monday,' she said. Wyatt had agreed to wait until Monday.

Monday. And this was only Friday. He had the entire weekend to come up with something, golden time, a reprieve. Charlie let his breath out in relief, and the tension went out of his muscles, leaving his neck and shoulders aching like hell.

He looked over at Susanna, seeing her for the first time today. His girl. She had stood by him when he'd needed her, and he was grateful. He'd show her a great time this weekend to pay her back. She was so pretty; Charlie's eyes ran over her small body in appreciation. She was adorable, a pocket-size Italian spitfire with a mop of curling black hair and two eyes like flashing jet and a petite delicacy that never failed to arouse him. He reached for her, clasping her thin shoulders, pulling her towards him, kissing her tempting red mouth.

'So. Ready for Palm Springs?'

Susanna's large black eyes widened in surprise. 'We're still going?'

Charlie nodded. What was the problem? 'This is all a . . . minor glitch. Nothing more.'

'Nothing more?' echoed Susanna. That explosion, the desperate telephone calls, the frantic singing and dancing, the lies . . . minor?

Charlie's shoulders shrugged expressively. 'Eldorf will come up with those six nozzles,' he answered with confidence. 'For the fuel injection. Then I pass EPA, deliver the cars, pay back the loan . . . and . . .' He paused for dramatic effect. 'Clear eighty grand. Even.' He gave her his second-best dazzling smile, the cocky one. 'Not bad . . . for a couple of phone calls.'

The sun was setting over the western mountains as the silver Ferrari, doing eighty miles an hour, ate up the distance across the desert. The sky was a darkening dome, still lit from above by the glowing tops of the clouds as they held the last of the sun's rays. Stars in their recognizable constellations began to fill the bowl of oncoming night.

Susanna Palmieri shivered a little; the almost infinite size of the sky over the desert always caught at her soul, making her feel tiny and insignificant.

Susanna had almost given up expecting a commitment of any kind from Charlie Babbitt. He was an enigma wrapped in a riddle and tied with a puzzle. Were his feelings for her equal, or nearly equal, to hers for him? He never talked about them, never discussed feelings of any kind except impatience. Did he care for her? Did he care for anybody except himself?

When they were alone together, making love, Susanna could often have sworn that he did. Charlie was ardent, even tender; he held her closely against him, kissing her with passion and meaning. Susanna knew that she was beautiful to him; she could read it in his eyes and his eager smile as he appeared to devour the sight of her.

But once his trousers were back on, it was a very different Charlie Babbitt, a Charlie Babbitt with his eye on the main chance, always looking for that opening, that weakness in others that he could turn to his own advantage. Where other men dreamed, Charlie schemed. Susanna loved him, but she wasn't so sure she always *liked* him.

For the last ten miles she had sat silent, appraising him with her eyes, unable to read anything from the expression on his face. Charlie kept both hands on the wheel and stared straight ahead, lost in his own thoughts, not sharing them, never sharing them. Yet Susanna knew that he wasn't as cocky or as confident about the deal as he'd appeared. Something was definitely troubling Charlie; even in the short time they'd been lovers, she had learned how to read the signs.

'I don't want to be demanding here, but do you think you could say maybe ten, twelve, words to me?' she asked finally. 'Before we get to the hotel.'

Charlie glanced over at Susanna, who met his look with an upraised eyebrow. 'Consider it foreplay,' she told him drily.

Charlie grinned in appreciation. This was some lady, this earthy little girl who wasn't afraid of him or of anything else.

'I'm glad we decided to take off Friday,' he replied lightly. 'Gives you three whole days to bitch at me.'

'Look,' Susanna said pragmatically, 'if you're so damn worried, call your service and get your messages. I know it's just . . . a real minor glitch, but –'

'That's what's on my mind, huh?' laughed Charlie, but there was tension in his laugh and behind his eyes.

'God, I hope it's not another woman!' Susanna rolled her eyes in mock concern.

'Maybe it's three other women,' Charlie teased.

'Well, maybe they called you.' Susanna punched the service number into the car phone.

'Three-oh-one-nine,' came the voice of the operator.

'Babbitt.' Charlie identified himself tersely. Susanna watched him rather anxiously, worried for him.

'Two calls from a Mr Bateman. You want the number?'

'No,' said Charlie, without looking at Susanna.

'Okay,' said the service operator. 'And then there's . . . oh . . .' Her voice broke a little. 'Oh, shit,' she whispered softly.

Charlie and Susanna exchanged glances. What the hell?

'There's this, uh, Mr John Mooney. The message says he's your father's lawyer. In Cincinnati. And . . . your father died, sir.'

Susanna gasped, her eyes on Charlie. But his face didn't change, and he didn't say a word.

'The, uh, the funeral's Sunday,' the operator continued, flustered. 'He had some trouble tracking you down. I've . . . got . . . his number –'

But Charlie had clicked off. His foot stayed glued to the gas pedal, still doing eighty, and his eyes stared straight ahead at the highway, but there was a tension about him that made Susanna ache with pity. The girl's eyes filled with sympathetic tears. His father. How awful.

'Oh, Charlie,' she whispered. 'Are you all right?'

He didn't answer, but he took his foot off the gas, and the car began to slow. Pulling over to the shoulder, Charlie braked, and the Ferrari stopped. But Charlie still sat, staring ahead of him, encased in silence like a fly trapped in amber.

Susanna reached out her hand and gently touched his shoulder, just to remind him that she was there for him.

He turned to her. 'Sorry about the weekend, hon.'

'The *weekend*?' Charlie's response was so inappropriate that Susanna could scarcely believe her ears. 'Charlie –' She pulled his face towards her with the tips of her gentle fingers, seeking his eyes with her own.

But Charlie evaded her glance. 'Look,' he mumbled, keeping his eyes turned away from hers, 'we . . . uh . . . we hated each other. Actual . . . *hate*.'

But it wasn't hatred that Susanna heard in his voice; it was pain. Hurting for him, hurting with him, she stroked his hair, soothing him like a mother soothes a child, with loving hands.

'My mom died when I was two. And it was just . . . me and him.'

Susanna gnawed at her lip. 'He . . . beat you?'

Charlie hesitated. 'Inside,' he said finally, drawing the word out from deep inside his guts. 'Nothing I did . . . was good enough. A few Bs on a report card and the As were forgotten. All-league football shoulda been all-city.' He gave Susanna a faint, bitter smile. 'See, I had this po-tential . . .'

They fell silent for a moment, each of them locked away with private thoughts.

'I'm going with you,' Susanna said suddenly.

Charlie shook his head. 'That's sweet.' He smiled at her. 'But there's no point in it.'

'I want to,' retorted Susanna stubbornly. 'That's the point.'

But Charlie kept shaking his head, as stubborn as she was. 'Don't sweat it,' he told her shortly.

Hurt, Susanna pulled back, her hand dropping from his hair. Once again, the shallow Charlie had made a stranger of her, pushed her at a distance. Yet, not quite. The feel of her hand in his hair had been the only thing keeping him together. Now, vulnerable and alone, Charlie reached out to Susanna.

'I keep forgetting who I'm talking to,' he whispered, with a small, sad smile.

Susanna pulled his head down to her breast and laid her cheek on his hair. Sad as she was in the circumstances, a bright pang of gladness nevertheless pierced her heart and went through to her soul, lighting it up. Charlie needed her.

CHAPTER TWO

On the fast drive back across the desert Charlie was nervous and moody, but Susanna accepted it as a natural reaction to the sudden and unexpected news of his father's death. As they speeded west, he outlined his plan to her in short, staccato sentences. He'd drop her at her apartment to pack, pick up her Volvo and drive it to his place to get a suit for the funeral. With those financial dogs of creditors barking at his heels, Charlie wasn't comfortable about being seen driving around LA in his Ferrari, or even turning up at his apartment, so he'd come back as soon as possible and make the travel arrangements over Susanna's telephone. They'd spend Friday night at Susanna's place, leave for the airport early in the morning, reach Cincinnati in time for dinner and to spend the night at a hotel, make the funeral and fly back home immediately afterwards. As for the Palm Springs weekend, he'd make it up to her, he promised.

Susanna was all packed by the time Charlie showed up, and he went straight to the phone with his AmEx Gold in his hand. He booked two first-class seats, then called the Broadham in Cincinnati and ordered a double room.

'No, just for tomorrow night. We'll be checking out first thing Sunday morning.'

As soon as the jet cleared the runway at LAX, Charlie downed two Chivas in rapid succession, turned over in his seat, his face to the window, and went to sleep. Alone, Susanna nibbled at caviare on crackers and sipped at stale champagne. She felt as flat as the wine; all the bubble had gone out of her. Once more Charlie Babbitt had shut her out of his life.

Charlie didn't wake up when the dinner trolley rolled around, and Susanna didn't rouse him. He must be exhausted, with the heavy load he was carrying. Resigned to her loneliness, she picked at some lobster salad and ate only half her Cornish hen.

Just as they were beginning their descent Charlie opened his eyes, famished. When the shapely red-headed flight attendant explained unhappily that the galley was closed and all the trays and food had already been stored away for landing, Charlie gave her his Number One smile, the Destroyer, and said in a soft purr, 'Gee, I'm sorry to cause you so much trouble. It's just that I haven't eaten all day and I'm starving . . .'

Within six minutes the stew was back with a loaded tray – cold shrimp, filet mignon with mushroom caps (*I didn't get filet mignon,* Susanna noted, fuming), duchesse potatoes, Cobb salad, hot rolls, a chocolate parfait, fresh coffee and a cognac.

'Will this be all right?' she asked breathlessly.

This time the Destroyer spread ever so slowly across Charlie's face until it surfaced in his eyes. 'You saved my life,' he murmured. 'I don't know how to thank you.'

I bet, thought Susanna in Italian, watching him wolfing down his food with gusto. *I just bet.*

The hotel itself was a surprise to Susanna. The Broadham was large and must once have been elegant, but it was old. There was still a sleepy, crumbling dignity to its cracked marbled lobby and dusty, broken crystal chandeliers that spoke more of nineteenth-century opulence than of efficient modernity. Charlie Babbitt usually went for everything new . . . sleek, shiny, flashy and contemporary. This was very different.

By the time they'd checked in and were shown to their shabby room Susanna felt the burden of fatigue weighing her down. All she wanted to do was sleep; tomorrow, starting with the funeral, would be a heavy day, and today had been no lightweight either. She had a blurred impression of high ceilings with cracked plaster, broken gilded mouldings and tattered velvet draperies, but the only thing that called to her was the deep old bathtub and the double bed. After a long, soaking bath, she fell asleep almost immediately.

At her side, Charlie lay awake for hours, smoking one Lucky after another and staring into the darkness.

Sunday morning was even more of a surprise. When Susanna emerged from the suite's dressing room in a modest two-piece black dress and dark stockings, she found Charlie adjusting his sober necktie in front of the mirror. He looked . . . different. She tried to put her finger on the difference.

Charlie was wearing a suit she'd never seen before, and something about it – the conservative cut, perhaps, or the dark pinstriped fabric – transformed him from a flashy Angeleno in hot imported threads to a young Eastern businessman whose probity and sobriety could never be called into question. No Hollywood used-car salesman ever looked like this. It was only when he put on his ever-present sunglasses that Susanna recognized something of the old Charlie Babbitt.

Yet the strangest thing about it was that this new dignity didn't seem to be an act or just one more facile facet of his multifarious personality. To Susanna it looked very real.

The car he'd hired was waiting outside the hotel's gilded revolving doors. It was a handsome black Lincoln town car, very suited to the occasion, but another surprise – although on reflection Susanna had never really expected Charlie to barrel up to the cemetery in a red Caddie convertible.

Side by side they sat without speaking as the car purred silently through the downtown streets of Cincinnati and out to the suburbs. Concrete, brick and steel soon gave way to grass and trees, small identical tract houses and, further out, large, well-kept homes widely spaced behind electrified gates until, finally, the Lincoln turned in through the stone walls of the cemetery. Memorial Park, established in 1835, was a picture-pretty place of rolling hills and green sweeping lawns, dotted with cypress and willow, and populated by prosperous souls waiting patiently in marble crypts or beneath granite markers for Judgement Day.

At the top of a knoll, in one of the choicest spots in the park, a funeral gathering was assembling. About a dozen solemn-faced, white-haired men and women in black garments were gathered around an open grave. Apart from the hot, bright blue of the summer sky, the only touch of colour in the scene was the purple in the Episcopal minister's robes and the deep red of a huge wreath of scarlet roses, on which appeared in golden letters the simple legend 'Sanford Babbitt'.

As the car stopped, Charlie got out, smoothing the wrinkles from his suit. All eyes turned to stare at him.

'I think you're expected,' said Susanna quietly.

Charlie squared his shoulders and walked slowly up the hill, encapsulated in silence. Susanna followed at a short distance. They stood to one side as the simple burial service began and didn't participate in the responses or the singing of the hymn, although Susanna could not prevent herself from crossing herself when the minister spoke the words, 'I am the Resurrection and the Life.' The reaction was ingrained.

It was a short service, soon over. Charlie threw a handful of earth on his father's costly bronze coffin without blinking an eye or shedding a tear. At a nod from him, Susanna walked slowly down the hill to the car, but Charlie approached one of the mourners, and the two shook hands. This had to be John Mooney, old Mr Babbitt's attorney. She couldn't hear what the two men were saying, but she watched Mooney take out a ring of keys, remove a couple and give them to Charlie, who slipped them into his breast pocket.

Charlie Babbitt came down the hill from his father's grave site without once looking back. Getting into the car beside Susanna, he said only, 'Change of plans, okay? We're gonna stay in Cincinnati another night. There's something I gotta do before we go.'

'Where are we going now?' Susanna asked, as Charlie put the key in the ignition.

'You'll see when we get there.'

'Where's "there?"' she persisted.

'East Walnut Hills.'

Walnut Hills is a section of Cincinnati where there are few visitors and little traffic. The homes are imposing, as close to mansions as the definition fits. Each one sits on at least ten acres, and neighbours don't chat over back fences or run back and forth between one another's kitchens. It's not that kind of place; it's the kind of place that whispers, 'Money', because it's beneath one's dignity to shout it.

'This is it: home, sweet home,' said Charlie sarcastically.

Impressed, Susanna got out of the car in front of Sanford Babbitt's huge, stone-columned manor home, the house where Charlie had been raised until that mysterious and awful day he'd left home, still a boy.

Charlie climbed out of the Lincoln and carried the suitcases up the front steps.

'I had no idea ... you came ... from all this,' breathed Susanna. She was still drinking in the newness and strangeness, trying to fit it all together in her head – all this and a Charlie Babbitt she didn't know.

'Thanks,' Charlie said shortly.

'I didn't mean it like that.'

But Charlie wasn't listening. He'd set the suitcases down and was moving towards two cars that were parked side by side under the *porte-cochère* that led from the house to the garage. One of the cars was a maroon-and-silver Rolls-Royce town car, but it was the other car on which Charlie's eyes were glued.

It was a 1949 Buick Roadmaster convertible, the last good year before the Brontosaurus-with-tail-fins designs came out. Painted a rich cream, the convertible boasted a gleaming finish that had been patiently hand-waxed and hand-rubbed to a high gloss. Everything about her was perfect, from her jaunty polished chrome work to her vivid-red leather seats, from her predatory fenders to the sabre-toothed front grille, from the trademark Buick portholes in the hood to the dashing backward slant of her windscreen. She was a beauty, special, and Charlie's face reflected his special appreciation of her.

The sight of the two-tone Rolls stunned Susanna. 'He was a stockbroker?'

'Investment banker,' answered Charlie, never taking his eyes off the Buick convertible. 'They dress better.' He ran his hand lovingly over the car's hood.

Susanna pulled her awed attention away from the Rolls and became pleasantly aware of the Buick. 'Some car,' she approved.

'I've known this car all my life,' said Charlie softly, adding, 'Only drove it one time.'

Something in the way he said that made Susanna look sharply at him. But he didn't meet her glance and said no more.

In a large flower bed encircled by stones was a magnificent collection of rose bushes. Susanna, who loved flowers, recognized the rarity of some of the varieties. But they were drooping, their leaves dusty, their petals turning brown at the tips.

'Somebody should be watering these. They're all dying.'

Charlie threw a glance of contempt at the roses, so withering that it might have killed the bushes off on the spot. 'Don't worry about it,' he snapped. Another surprise. What grudge could he possibly be holding against rose bushes?

Susanna followed Charlie up the steps to the front door and waited while he fished out the keys that Mooney had given him. When they walked in, she gasped at the splendour. A tall entrance foyer, leading to a grand staircase at the rear, held an impressive pair of nine-foot-high mirrors in gilded baroque frames, which hung across from each other, reflecting Charlie and Susanna over and over into infinity, like a mirror in a Renaissance painting. The house was deserted; it was Sunday, and even the skeleton staff of servants had been given the day off in Sanford Babbitt's memory.

Charlie pushed open the door to the living room. A strong odour wafted towards them, a smell compounded of lemon-oil furniture polish, the stale air that disuse and unopened windows bring to a room and the dust that collects in the folds of draperies no matter how often they're vacuumed. The room was vast, a broad ocean of costly oriental carpeting on which ponderous and heavy pieces of antique mahogany furniture sailed majestically like Cunard luxury liners.

On the walls a collection of oil paintings were solemnly hung in giltwood frames; they had no special merit and were painted by academicians of no daring or originality. Yet the whole effect was one of impressive power and opulence, of old money and of deep, black silence. You couldn't imagine laughter in a room like that, or angrily raised voices, or words of passion and love. It was a room for occasions, not emotions. Yet emotions there had been, and harsh ones.

Charlie Babbitt stood in the doorway for a long moment, his eyes checking the room out inch by inch. His expression was unreadable, prompting Susanna to ask, 'What?'

He didn't look at her, speaking more to himself than to the girl. 'When I told him I was leaving . . . I was standing . . . here. He sat . . . in that chair.' He shook his head as though to clear it, then, taking Susanna's hand, he led her around the house, showing her everything: the huge kitchens (there were two of them, and both had been manned by servants); the dining room with its wall sconces and low-hanging chandelier over a long table that could seat twenty people; the impressive library lined with tall bookcases and leather-bound volumes with gilded page-tops; the endless series of second-floor master bedrooms, all large, all with marble-manteled fireplaces and four-poster beds, all with marble-tiled bathrooms.

Even so, Susanna's favourite room was the simple third-floor one that Charlie had had as a boy. It was a boy's room taken from a movie set – bunk beds, baseball pennants on the walls, shiny fighter-plane models like Migs and F-14s, Beaver Cleaver stuff. Everything had been kept exactly as it was when Charlie had left home, even down to the scruffy clothes in his closet.

It was difficult for Susanna to associate the Charlie Babbitt she knew, fast-talking, fast-lane and cool, with bunk beds and a battered old bookcase filled with classics like *Treasure Island* and *Robin Hood*. Difficult but charming and somehow touching. Here was a side of Charlie Babbitt that nobody else in Los Angeles knew except for her.

Rummaging around in Charlie's closet, Susanna pulled out old cartons of assorted junk and sat down on the floor to browse through them. Photographs, autograph albums, a Kiss poster, old singles. This was fun, taking a private trip through her lover's past. She looked up to see Charlie grinning down at her fondly.

'Well, that's a funny look.'

'For a crazy lady, you have nice ears,' he remarked.

'I'm not crazy, I'm just interested. You were his only child. You came along when he was ... what? Forty-five or something. He probably thought he was never going to have a son.' Susanna bit her lip, hesitating, then continued. 'So he *had* to love you ...'

Bending over, Charlie began to caress the tips of her ears.

'So why did he hate you?' she demanded bluntly.

'Pink ears ... and they're a little pointy ... right

there.' A moist nibble followed the trail of his finger, and Susanna knew what it was that Charlie wanted. He wanted not to talk about his father or about their relationship. He wanted to take off his funeral clothes. He wanted to make love to her, here in his boyhood room, on his old bed, the bottom bunk, so that the ghost of the boy he used to be could see the man he had become.

And suddenly that's what Susanna wanted too.

Afterwards she wrapped herself in an old sweatshirt of Charlie's and belted on a pair of his jeans with the legs rolled up. None of his clothes fitted him any more, so Charlie went shirtless, wearing only the trousers of his pin-striped suit. Together, they ran through every inch of the house, pigging out in the kitchen on what they could find in the freezer and on the pantry shelves – tins of pickled oysters, packages of cracked crab, Louis Sherry French Vanilla ice cream. They were like two children let loose in the largest, most expensive playhouse in the world.

At last, the house below explored, the two of them went up to the attic, a vast, dusty storage space but well lit and relatively neat. Most of the Babbitt lives were documented up here, locked up and preserved in iron-bound wooden trunks from out of the past, filled with historical memories. More of Charlie's life too. An old baby's highchair – strange, he didn't remember ever sitting in that – boxes of toys, private papers in tin document cases, cartons of personal belongings.

They sat on the attic floor, idly looking through some ancient magazines, tired but not unhappy and feeling closer than they'd ever been. Then, out of the blue . . .

'Y'know that convertible out front?' Charlie asked.

Susanna nodded, sensing something important coming.

'His baby. That and the goddamn roses.' There was a raspy, bitter edge to his voice. 'That car was off-limits to me. "That's a classic," he'd say. "It commands respect. Not for children."' He sounded authoritarian, and Susanna heard the echo of Sanford Babbitt's words.

'Tenth grade. I'm sixteen. And, for once, I bring home a report card and it's all As.'

Susanna looked impressed.

'Don't look so damned surprised.'

'How about blown away?'

'Yeah. Try that.' Susanna made a blown-away face, and they exchanged grins. 'So I go to my dad,' Charlie continued. '"Can I take the guys out in the Buick?" Sort of a victory drive. He says no. But I go anyway. Steal the keys. Sneak it out.'

'Why then? Why that time?' Susanna's eyes were fixed on his face, wanting to know.

'Because I deserved it!' Charlie's voice rose until it shook. 'I'd done something wonderful! In his own terms. And' – Charlie's voice dropped – 'he wasn't man enough to do right.'

Even then, Susanna thought sadly. *Even then there was a hole in Charlie Babbitt's moral fabric.* She said nothing, only listened intently.

'So we're on Columbia Parkway. Four kids. And we get pulled over. He'd called in a report of a stolen car. Not his son took the car without permission. Just stolen.' Charlie's boyish face grew tight, remembering. 'Central Station. The other guys' dads bailed 'em out in an hour. He left me there two days.'

'Jesus,' whispered Susanna, deeply shocked.

'Drunks throwing up.' He shuddered, reliving those awful forty-eight hours. 'That's the only time in my life I was gut-scared. Shit-your-pants, can't-catch-your-breath scared . . . I left home. I never came back.'

That was it, the whole story. The story of a boy who ran away from an implacable, domineering father for whom the son was never good enough, a boy who was spending his valuable life trying to prove to that father that he *was* good enough, only now it was too late. His father would never recognize his successes now, nor any more judge his failures. His father would never be proud of him.

Charlie smiled at Susanna, a tough, I-don't-give-a-shit smile, but the hurt was so plain that he couldn't stand to see the love and caring in her face. It made him too vulnerable. He stood up, glancing once more around his room at all his former possessions.

'Look at all this junk. Cowboy hats, and trains, and . . .' He shook his head in a mixture of amusement and disgust. 'I'm hungry again. Let's go raid the fridge.' He gave one hand to Susanna, pulling her to her feet.

As they walked towards the door, something caught Charlie's eye, and he stopped dead, looking at the floppy corner of something sticking out of a box. Frozen, he stared at it, while somewhere in the dark recesses of his memory something stirred . . .

'Christ,' he whispered. Out of the mist-filled labyrinth of his baby memories a fragment of music . . . the Beatles . . . floated up, swirled round his brain . . . then evaporated.

Reaching down to the carton, Charlie pulled the memory out. It was a blanket, an ancient, threadbare baby blanket, faded from a thousand washings. He held it in his hand, staring at it.

'That's yours?' asked Susanna, although it was obvious that it had to be.

But Charlie didn't answer, only studied the blanket under the light, poring over it as though it were the treasure map of his past. His fingers rubbed the worn-out fabric; he lifted it to his nose and smelled it, lost in a reverie.

'Charlie,' Susanna prompted gently.

The spell broke. 'Damn, I just had this flash of something. You know how, when you're a kid, you have these sort of . . . pretend friends?'

Susanna nodded. Her 'pretend friend' had been the Holy Virgin; she still told secrets to her sometimes, speaking familiarly as though Mary was in the same room with her.

'Well, mine was named – what the hell was his name?' Charlie scanned his memory. 'Rain Man. That's it. The Rain Man. Anyway, if I got scared or anything, I'd just wrap up in this blanket and the Rain Man would sing to me.' He grinned. 'Now that I think of it, I must have been scared a lot. God, that was a long time ago.'

'So when did he disappear?' smiled Susanna, touched. 'Your friend.'

Charlie shook his head. 'I don't know,' he admitted. 'I just . . . grew up, I guess.' He turned the baby blanket around in his hands for a few seconds longer, then tossed it casually back in the box, deliberately shutting the door on his earliest memory.

'Let's eat.'

That evening, while Susanna sat cuddled in Charlie's bed upstairs, going over a photograph album of Charlie's baby and boyhood pictures, Charlie Babbitt and his father's attorney John Mooney met in the dining room below, legal papers strewn over the polished mahogany table. The will: Sanford Babbitt's last will and testament. Charlie, as sole heir apparent to the considerable estate, had a vested interest in the proceedings, so he listened intently to Mooney, but so far he wasn't happy with what he was hearing.

All Mooney had to say was, 'It's all yours, kid,' yet those words had not crossed his lips.

Still, Charlie stayed cool; in the poker game of life you don't tip your hand or show your cards until the other guy pays to see them.

'Now we'll get to the actual reading of the will in a moment, but first I have this statement which your father requested I read to you. Do you have any objections?' John Mooney peered over his bifocals at Charlie.

'Why should I?' shrugged Charlie. Thank God, it was a letter and not one of those ghoulish from-beyond-the-grave videotapes. At least he didn't have to look at the old man. All he had to do was listen. Even so, a pang of uneasiness hit him smack in the gut.

Mooney nodded briefly, then picked up a sealed envelope and deftly slit it open. He removed a couple of sheets of stiff, expensive stationery and carefully unfolded them. Charlie recognized the embossing – his father's letterhead.

'"To my son, Charles Babbitt. Dear Charles,"' began the lawyer in a dry voice. '"Today I turned seventy. I am an old man but not too old to remember vividly the day we brought you home from the hospital, your late mother and I. You were the perfect child, so full of life . . . and promise."'

Charlie winced inwardly. There was that goddamn

38

word again, promise. His father's favourite pair of syllables.

"'And I remember too,'" Mooney continued reading, "'the day you left home, so full of bitterness and grandiose ideas. So full of yourself . . .'"

The lawyer broke off reading, looking up to see Charlie's reaction. But Charlie kept his poker face, revealing nothing.

"'I can understand and forgive your rejection of the life I offered you. College and the other advantages so eagerly accepted by your peers . . .'"

'He wrote it,' Charlie remarked with a bland smile. 'I hear his voice.'

"'And, being raised without a mother,'" Mooney went on without lifting his eyes from the letter, "'the hardness of your heart is understandable as well. Your refusal to pretend that you loved or even respected me. All these I forgive. But your failure to write, to telephone, to re-enter my life in any way, has left me without a son. I wish you all I ever wanted for you. I wish you the best.'"

John Mooney stopped reading and folded the letter as carefully as he'd opened it, replacing it in its envelope. It was evident that the elderly lawyer was moved by the words he'd read. He coughed a genteel cough, but Charlie didn't utter a sound. He just sat there waiting for the bottom line to be revealed.

Now the attorney picked up the will, a many-paged document in crisp blue covers. Without a glance at Charlie, he began to read.

"'To Charles Sanford Babbitt, I bequeath that certain Buick convertible which, like my son, entered my life in 1962. It has served me long and faithfully without complaint. May it bring him pleasant memories of me.

Also outright title to my prize-winning rose bushes. May they remind him of the value of excellence and the possibility of perfection."'

The general uneasiness in Charlie's guts began to take on a menacing shape. All of his instincts were on red alert.

"'As for my home and all other property, real and personal, these shall be placed in trust in accordance with the terms of that certain instrument executed concurrently herewith."'

Mooney looked up, finished, and began to fold the will.

'Trust'? 'That certain instrument'? What 'certain instrument'? What the hell was going on here? 'Uh . . . what does that mean?' asked Charlie quietly. 'That last part?'

'It means the estate, in excess of three million dollars after taxes and expenses, goes into a trust fund for an unnamed beneficiary.'

'And who is that?' Although the tension was rising so high in Charlie it was beginning to get to his shoulders and neck, he kept his voice even. No sense in pissing the lawyer off before Mooney told him what he needed to know.

John Mooney put the papers neatly back into his briefcase. 'Unnamed means I can't tell you,' he said efficiently. As far as he was concerned, this reading was over, and his work here was done.

'Who . . . uh . . . who controls all this money? You?'

Mooney shook his head. 'He's called a trustee. I am not permitted to tell you his name.' He got to his feet and reached for his homburg.

'So . . . how does it all work?' persisted Charlie. In the dry factuality of the attorney's words he could hear an iron door clanging shut, leaving him, Charlie Babbitt, out in the cold.

'Forgive me.' Mooney shook his head with finality. 'There's nothing more I can say.' He started for the door, with Charlie staring after him. At the dining-room door, the lawyer turned. 'I'm sorry, son. I can see that you're disappointed, but –'

'*Disappointed?*' Charlie came shooting out of his chair with a furious roar. 'Why should I be *disappointed*? I got a used *car*, didn't I? And how about the *rose bushes*? Shit, let's not forget the damn *rose bushes!*'

Witnessing the boy's rage, the elderly lawyer flinched a little. But Charlie was caught up in his anger and didn't notice.

'Some . . . what did you call him? "Benefactor"?'

'Beneficiary,' said Mooney quietly.

'Some *asshole* beneficiary gets over three million dollars! But did he get the ROSE BUSHES? Hell, no! The *rose bushes* got saved for Daddy's only son! Boy, I bet that other schmuck is crying his eyes out!'

'Charles –'

'I mean, *shit!*' Charlie was too far gone in indignation to listen. 'Those are bitchin' rose bushes, man.'

'There's really no need to –'

'Screwed from the grave!' ranted Charlie. '*Screwed!* SCREWED! From the goddamn GRAVE!' He forced himself to gulp down some air; he could hardly breathe. 'He is sitting down there in hell, Mr Mooney. Looking up. Laughing his ass off.' He started to shake his head, hard, while Mooney watched him anxiously.

'Sanford Babbitt. You wanna be that asshole's kid for five *minutes?*' he demanded. 'Did you *hear* that fucking letter? Were you *listening?*' Charlie broke off, unable to go on. His hands were clenched into fists and he was breathing hard, almost panting.

'Yes, sir, I was,' replied John Mooney, looking Charlie straight in the eye. 'Were you?'

When the lawyer left, Charlie paced the dining room like a caged animal for about two minutes, then ran out of the front door. Air! He had to have some fresh air! He was choking on his emotions, and bitter bile rose up in his throat. Hurt, indignation, frustration and a terrible feeling of being lost and alone threatened to overwhelm Charlie, and he fought to regain control of himself. He felt as though he'd been beaten, cruelly, viciously beaten, and left for dead.

Those damn rose bushes! Charlie recognized the perfect irony in Sanford Babbitt's bequest. Those bushes had meant more to him than Charlie, his only child, had ever meant. Charlie could remember the long weekends when his old man, instead of taking him out somewhere – to a ball game or a circus or even just for a drive in the Buick convertible – had spent hours fussing around those goddamn roses. Pruning, weeding, spraying, mulching, staking. Whatever affection might have been hidden away in an investment banker's cold and mercenary heart poured out on flowers, not people. Not even his own flesh and blood. But then, those rose bushes had never disappointed him. They'd brought Sanford Babbitt many blue ribbons, while his son Charlie had never won a prize.

No wonder Charlie hated those rose bushes. Now he felt their thorns piercing him, reminding him of their perfection and his own defects. Well, let them die!

Unnamed beneficiary. The words reverberated in his head, blocking off all rational thought. *Unnamed beneficiary.* But who? Who the hell was robbing him of more than three million dollars that was rightfully his?

Who was laughing at him, mocking him as a used-car salesman and nothing more, never to be anything more? No, they weren't going to get away with it. There had to be a way out of this. Think, he had to think!

Somewhere out there was a person – man? woman? child? – who would inherit a fortune, Charlie's fortune. He had to find this person before he could put up a fight. Even Charlie Babbitt couldn't struggle with someone he couldn't see. He had to find this person, *now*. Before too much time passed, before the waters got too muddy with lawyers, probate, trustees. But how to locate him? Where to start looking?

By the time Susanna found him, standing by the empty swimming pool, smoking a Lucky, Charlie had calmed down enough to be formulating the skeleton of a plan.

'I was looking everywhere for you,' she told him, concerned. 'How did it go?'

He gave her his most confident smile. 'Got what I expected,' was all he said.

CHAPTER THREE

Charlie slept fitfully, tossing in his narrow bed, and his dreams came tumbling over him in dream-waves, both vivid and bad. In some of them something was chasing after him; in others he was chasing after something. But he never did know what that something was, or whether it would be good for him or would hurt him, or what he would do if it caught up with him or he caught up with it.

He opened his eyes finally around six thirty in the morning; it would be a couple of hours earlier in Los Angeles. The dream-feeling of being pursued by something ominous was still with him. Thirsty and disoriented, he wasn't sure where he was for a minute, then it all came back to him. He was at home. In his old room. In his father's house in Cincinnati. And his father was dead.

Now he replayed yesterday's events in his head. His father's funeral. The will. The goddamn rose bushes. Sanford Babbitt's ghostly laughter from the far side of the grave. *Shit!* He sat on the edge of his bunk bed, coughing a deep, hacking, Lucky Strike cough. Still coughing, he lit up the first cigarette of the day. Behind him Susanna stirred, and he touched her gently, soothing her so that she'd go back to sleep. He needed to be left alone for a while to think. This was probably the most important day of his life.

Wearing only his briefs, Charlie padded silently into the kitchen, where he set a flame under a saucepan of water for instant coffee. Opening the refrigerator door, he found a half-full container of orange juice and drank it down straight from the carton. He lit another cigarette, then sat down at the kitchen table, going over his plan.

Step number one, the one without which the other steps would be impossible, was to find out what so-called 'trustee' was playing fast and loose with Charlie's money and who in hell the 'unnamed beneficiary' might be. After that he'd play it by ear. Something would occur to him; something always did.

This was Monday morning. Seven a.m. Banks opened at nine; the servants would probably be here by eight. He had to get moving. He managed to get the worst wrinkles out of his funeral suit by hanging it in the bathroom for the hot shower to steam-press. Having showered, Charlie shaved very carefully, smoothing his cheeks with aftershave from the medicine cabinet. Sanford Babbitt's aftershave. Except for the old man's cigars, he smelled just like his father now. Then, dressed, he went to wake up Susanna with a cup of hot, black instant coffee laced with sugar.

'Time to get going, sweetheart. I've got a few fish I have to fry. Let's roll.'

When the cream convertible pulled up in front of the Midwest America–Republic bank in downtown Cincinnati, Susanna looked puzzled. 'What are we doing here?'

'Something I gotta look into,' Charlie answered blandly. 'Won't take a minute. You stay here.'

It took him forty seconds to case the bank, looking for his pigeon. He spotted her sitting at the third desk back, in the row of lowest-echelon executives who were authorized to handle the transactions that the tellers couldn't make on their own – the transfers of funds, Keogh deposits, overdrawn current-account inquiries. She was not too young and not too pretty but wearing lots of make-up and sporting an elaborate ash-blonde hairstyle that spoke of long hours under the hands of a colourist with a set of hot rollers. In short, she was vain and she was approachable. Five minutes with the Destroyer smile and a plausible story ought to do it.

Five minutes later, Charlie Babbitt emerged from the Midwest America–Republic Bank with the name of his father's trustee in his pocket. A Dr Walter Bruner. And an address somewhere out in the country. And a good set of directions for getting there.

Even behind the wheel of a classic Buick convertible open to the air, a hot July sun bathing his head, Susanna at his side, Charlie was unaware of the day, the girl or the car. All he could think of was Bruner, whoever the hell he was. And what he could say to him to get him to turn over more than three million dollars that were rightfully Charlie Babbitt's. He kept going over scenarios in his mind, writing and rewriting them.

They'd long ago left the suburbs and were now driving down a country road through the summer-green hills of the Ohio countryside. But Charlie had no eyes for the scenery, although Susanna was moved to murmur, 'This is so beautiful. You used to come here?'

'Actually, no.'

The girl's small face looked puzzled. 'So why are we –?'

Before she could finish the sentence, she was pitched forward in the car, narrowly avoiding hitting the windshield with her nose. Charlie had put his foot on the brake, hard.

'Missed it,' he muttered, backing up to the turn-off, which was easy to miss. Half-concealed by the trees in full leaf was a narrow driveway and a sign: PRIVATE DRIVE.

Starting up the narrow road that was shadowed by a verdant arch of overhanging chestnut trees, Charlie glanced apologetically at Susanna. 'Just some stuff I have to wrap up for my dad's estate,' he told her a little too casually, 'Won't take long.' Behind his designer shades, his hazel eyes were unreadable.

They drove slowly, the Buick carefully navigating the stony and winding road, not much more than a path. Then, after about a quarter of a mile, the road widened, rose and took a broad turn. It crested a hill and suddenly a large white building came into view. Handsome and well-proportioned, set in beautifully kept grounds with lawns like green velvet, it wore the look of a fine old hotel or resort. Perhaps it was even some wealthy man's huge estate.

Where are we? wondered Susanna.

They drove past a very pretty little pond, with ducks swimming busily on it and wild flowers growing along its mossy banks. At the side of the road a man in a smock was painting at an easel, facing the pond, his back to the car. Charlie slowed down.

'Excuse me. That place up there – isn't that Wallbrook?'

But the man kept his back to them, ignoring the car and its passengers.

''Scuse me,' said Charlie more loudly.

Without a word the man turned suddenly, and Susanna gasped. Even Charlie's cool deserted him for a minute. The man's hands and face were smeared with brightly coloured paints; blotches of wet colour covered his clothing. And, on the easel, not a landscape of the pond and the ducks or a picture of the lovely house. Instead an unholy mess, a formless daub done by finger-painting. The man wore a vacant smile like that of a mindless child. Charlie looked at the painter and his painting for a frozen moment, then put the car in gear and took it up the driveway to the front door.

Next to the entrance a neat bronze plaque bore the lettering: WALLBROOK HOME FOR THE DEVELOPMENTALLY DISABLED.

Climbing out of the car, Charlie walked to the front door and knocked hard, using the brass knocker. An attractive middle-aged woman, neatly dressed and efficient, opened the door to them.

'I'd like to see Dr Bruner, please.'

The woman nodded, leading Charlie and Susanna to a large, comfortable reception room filled with chintz-covered chairs, sofas, a fireplace covered by a brass screen and a table covered by expensive magazines. A waiting room. It might be furnished in the best of taste with expensive antiques, but it was still a hospital waiting room. The woman escorted Susanna and Charlie to a pair of adjacent chairs and waited while they seated themselves.

'Dr Bruner is still in conference. Will you be comfortable here for a while?'

Charlie nodded, flashing her his third-best smile, the Polite Young Man number, and the woman smiled back and left. Instantly Charlie sprang out of his chair and went to the doorway, peering down the corridor. He looked both ways, then took a step out of the door.

'Charlie,' Susanna called nervously, 'I don't think we should poke around here.'

'Then don't,' he snapped over his shoulder. With

that he was out the door and heading down the hallway. Anxiously, Susanna ran to catch up with him. She didn't want to be left behind sitting there by herself.

Further along the corridor the place began to look very different. The antiques and the flowered wallpaper were giving way to plain, solid, utilitarian furniture and coats of institutional green paint. It was looking a lot more like a hospital. With Susanna clinging to his arm, Charlie explored his surroundings.

Oh, yes, Wallbrook was definitely a hospital for sick people. But the patients were developmentally, not physically, ill. Not violent, at least not in the public recreation rooms they looked into, but each was locked away in a private world of his or her own creation. Many of them watched television without really seeing or understanding the little video dramas on the screen. Others sat at tables, shuffling children's blocks or large wooden puzzle pieces around, or even down on the floor, playing with toys. One grey-haired old woman clutched a tattered doll tightly in her withered arms, crooning wordlessly to it. Each was alone; there was no sharing with others, no communicating between them.

Or they ate snacks, like pudding cups or apple sauce – baby food. A handful of uniformed attendants took care of their more obvious physical needs – washing chocolate pudding off lips or spittle off chins, or escorting one or another of the patients to the bathroom.

It was very quiet; no screaming or hallucinating, no rage, not even fear. Tranquillizers took care of all that. A few nice pills when the schedule called for medication, washed down by canned orange juice, and Attila the Hun becomes Morris the Cat. Better living through chemistry.

The private rooms, the ones in which the patients

lived and slept when they weren't out 'socializing', were far more disturbing. Susanna and Charlie looked into only a couple. Most of them were empty, the patients having been shuffled like cards into a series of 'activities'. But a few remained behind in their own little cubicles because no amount of 'socialization' would break through the heavy walls of madness that kept them prisoners.

In one little room they saw a young man sitting on the edge of his single bed, his hands hanging empty at his sides. Then, as Susanna and Charlie passed, he saw them, and the young man began to pound violently at his temples with his clenched fists. His eyes rolled wildly in their sockets, and he moaned without words, pummelling himself.

'No more, Charlie, please,' Susanna begged. 'Let's go back to the waiting room.'

But Charlie wasn't ready to go back yet. He wanted to see it all, all of this place in which Sanford Babbitt had tied up his millions. So this was Wallbrook Home. The laughing academy. The ha-ha hotel. Kindergarten for kooks. The farm for the chronically funny. *Shit!* This was gonna be harder than he thought.

He was up against an entire institution here, and it would be armed to the teeth to keep some nameless person, maybe even a loony, in millions of dollars of loot just so it could rake in its annual percentage. He'd have to get a crowbar to pry his money loose. And now he'd seen enough; taking a grateful Susanna by the hand, Charlie went back to the waiting room.

When Dr Bruner was free to see him Charlie squared his shoulders and slipped his sunglasses on. In any kind of dealing Charlie Babbitt kept his eyes hidden so that nobody could read in his face what was going on behind it. *Cool*, he told himself. *Very cool, Charlie. No sudden moves, and watch every word. These guys are not your friends.*

The psychiatrist's office was plush to the point of opulence. Tall windows, looking out over the lawn, reached from the high ceiling to the polished floor. Bookshelves lined the walls; they were overflowing with fat volumes of medical and psychiatric data. The doctor was sitting in a high-backed leather swivel chair behind a large Victorian oak partner's desk. He stood up to shake Charlie's hand and motioned for the boy to sit in a chair opposite the desk.

Charlie sized up his opponent carefully. Dr Bruner was an imposing man of about fifty-six, with a thick lion's mane of greying hair and a calm, pleasant face. But his eyes, behind his tortoise-framed glasses, were keen and intelligent. He could easily guess why Charlie was here, but he allowed the young man to state it for himself.

Charlie Babbitt wanted the name of the unnamed beneficiary. He asked for it politely.

'I'm sorry. I am not empowered to tell you that.' Just like Mooney.

Then who the hell is? The words rose angrily to Charlie's lips, but he choked them back. Polite and respectful, that had to be his cover, at least for now.

'I don't see the point of secrecy, sir.' Leaving his chair, Charlie went over to stand by the window. 'If this patient were . . . an old girlfriend of Dad's . . . something like that –'

In his line of sight was the Buick convertible with Susanna sitting in the back seat, just waiting for him and enjoying the sunshine. As Charlie watched, an obvious patient, a small man wearing a backpack, shuffled clumsily up the path towards the car. Charlie paid him no attention; the crazies here were only lawn furniture.

'Mr Babbitt, I knew your father from the time you were two years old,' said Dr Bruner gently.

Charlie turned. 'The year my mother died,' he said quickly.

Bruner nodded. 'Now, I am trustee of the fund. But this hospital and I receive nothing from that.'

Yeah, right, thought Charlie. Out loud, he said, 'Hardly seems fair. Maybe that's something . . . we could discuss . . .' His words suggested sympathy and possibility in equal measure. They hinted at a deal, with money changing hands.

But Dr Bruner didn't nibble at the bait. 'This is a burden I took on out of loyalty to your father,' he replied firmly. 'And that's where my loyalty remains.'

Anger surged through Charlie's veins. *Cool*, he reminded himself, turning back again to the window to hide his impatience. That patient with the backpack was now standing at the Buick's side, staring at it. 'And you think I should . . . feel a little of that . . . loyalty,' said Charlie with some difficulty.

'I think you feel cheated out of your birthright,' replied Bruner gently, 'by a man who had difficulty showing love.'

This was so true, so to the point, that Charlie stiffened a little in surprise. He felt a sudden physical pain, as though pierced by the thorns of a hundred rose bushes. *This shrink is no dummy*. Outside, the patient had taken a small notebook out of his backpack and was writing furiously in it. Scribble, scribble. Then another long look at the car. Scribble, scribble. As though he were taking notes.

'And I think,' continued Dr Bruner, 'that if I were in your shoes, I'd feel the same.'

An opening? Charlie turned back to the doctor and took his shades off, looking Bruner straight in the eye. Sincerity time.

'I was hoping we could talk. That you would . . . explain . . . Dad's side of it. Help me to see the right of what he did. Because, failing that, I have responsibilities of my own, sir. And I have to meet them.' Charlie paused for effect, to let his next words sink in. 'Even if that means a fight.'

Dr Bruner sat back in his chair and laced the tips of his fingers together. Something very much like a smile tugged at the corners of his lips. *There it was. The opening gun. Intimidation. The law-suit threat.* He'd been expecting it, waiting for it, watching this handsome young Charlie Babbitt dissemble and hide his anger behind dark glasses and under a transparent veneer of phoney politeness. Yet there was still something attractive about this boy, the hint of a deep intelligence, of strongly developed instincts for survival in a bestial world. He could be dangerous, but even so he was likeable, an opponent worthy of respect.

'Well, I'll bet you are a fighter, Mr Babbitt,' Dr Bruner said mildly. 'And, y'know, as director of this institution, why, I've been pushed and poked and kicked at by the best.' The psychiatrist looked hard at Charlie. 'Somehow or other, I'm still here.'

His words held a finality. The interview was over. Charlie had come away with nothing. If he'd thought to drive a wedge into Trustee Bruner, he'd failed. The unnamed beneficiary was still unnamed. But Charlie wasn't licked yet. This was only round one, and they were still dancing around each other. As yet, neither had so much as laid a glove on the other. It might take more time than he'd thought, but Charlie Babbitt was resourceful and could even be patient when he saw the necessity for patience.

Dr Bruner walked him out through the front door. The day was getting hotter, but it was still beautiful, rich in summer sunshine and the many-noted singing of birds.

The patient with the backpack was still standing by the Buick, still writing furiously in his little notebook, as though he were taking notes for an accident report. He kept looking from the car back to the book, never once glancing at Susanna, who was staring at him in fascination.

'Raymond,' said Dr Bruner, his tone tinged with urgency, 'you're not supposed to be here. Go back inside.'

The patient with the backpack paid no attention. His pencil kept flying across the notebook page. Charlie walked rapidly by him without really seeing him and reached down for the door handle.

'Pitiful,' said Raymond.

Charlie looked up. *You talkin' to me?*

But Raymond wasn't even looking in Charlie Babbitt's direction. All his attention was on his notebook, and he was talking to its pages.

''Course, those seats are *not* real leather . . . Those are *pitiful* seats . . . not . . . *brownish* leather . . . These are red.'

For the first time, Charlie looked at Raymond. He saw a small man of indeterminate age but probably in his early forties. He looked completely harmless. Like all the patients, he was neatly dressed in simple, freshly laundered clothing, a short-sleeved cotton shirt and cotton trousers, belted up high above his waist, almost to his armpits. In his shirt pocket was one of those plastic pen-holders, filled with pencils and ballpoint pens. Raymond's hair was cut in an institutional chop; it stuck up at odd angles in some places and was plastered down with water in other places. Otherwise he appeared clean and well cared for.

His features were totally unremarkable, two rather small black eyes set closely together on either side of a large, fleshy nose. What distinguished Raymond's face was a total absence of expression. There was no light in those eyes, no laugh creases around them, no frown lines between them. It was the kind of face a child might draw, flat and possessing no life, a face that had never known life.

Charlie smiled and shook his head a little. 'Y'know,' he told Susanna, amused by this crazy, 'my dad *did* have brown leather in this thing. When I was real little.'

'And, and,' Raymond continued rapidly and tone-lessly, to himself, 'you *use* the ashtray, because . . . because that's what . . . what it's *there* for. That's *real* leather, and it's . . . it cost an *arm* and a *leg*.'

The smile faded from Charlie's face, replaced by a look of astonishment.

'Jesus,' he whispered. 'He used to say that. "Arm and a leg" and "ashtrays" . . .'

He looked hard at the patient, who looked hard at his notebook. Then, suddenly, Raymond looked up for a second and their eyes met, Raymond's gaze expressionless, Charlie's hidden behind his sunglasses. But only for a second because Raymond's attention went immediately back to his written pages.

'You come with me, Raymond,' said Dr Bruner urgently. 'These people have to go.'

The hair at the nape of Charlie's neck prickled, and something tugged keenly at his gut. Some instinct . . .

'Do you know this car?' he asked Raymond sharply.

Instantly Raymond's hands clasped together and made strange wringing motions, impeded by the pad and the pencil. A look of fear came over his dull features, and he looked desperately over to Dr Bruner for help. But the psychiatrist's answering look was so withering that he dropped his terrified gaze to the ground.

'You!' said Charlie more vehemently. 'Why do you know this car?' He whipped off his sunglasses so that Raymond would be forced to look him in the eye.

Now Raymond's thin body began to jerk spasmodically, as though a current of low-level voltage was passing through his bone marrow. His eyes shifted from side to side in his head, avoiding Charlie's direct glare.

'I . . . don't . . . know,' he managed to mumble, the words barely audible.

'Bull*shit*, you don't know!' Charlie snapped. '*Why* do you know?' He took a step towards Raymond, who backed away in terror.

'That's enough, Mr Babbitt,' Dr Bruner intervened. 'You're upsetting him. You're –'

'Charlie, please,' put in Susanna.

Now Raymond looked from Susanna to Dr Bruner to Charlie as a fact seemed to register in his head. He pulled his hands apart and began to write furiously again in his notebook, mumbling away as he set down the words.

'Babbitt Charlie. Charlie . . . Babbitt. Charlie Babbitt one-oh-nine-six-one. Beechcrest Avenue.'

Charlie stopped stone-dead. 'How do you know that address?' he demanded, dumbfounded.

Raymond hung his head, and his voice was so soft they could scarcely make out what he was saying. 'I know because. That's why.'

Not good enough. Every feral instinct in Charlie was thrumming away on high as he stalked his almost paralysed prey. 'Because . . . that's why *what*?' he pressed.

Raymond's head jerked up as though Charlie had pulled a string, and he looked Charlie in the eye. There was nothing in Raymond's expression except agitation – no recognition, no response. No connection between them at all.

Dr Bruner spoke quietly, his voice resigned. 'Because he's your brother,' he said.

A little gasp from Susanna, then silence. Raymond stopped his mumbling, and Charlie shook his head in total disbelief. Then he gave a little bark of laughter. 'What does that mean?'

'Brothers have . . . the same daddy. And mommy,' supplied Raymond. Then he said, as if he were a child reciting what he had been taught for his own protection, 'Sanford Babbitt. His house is one-oh-nine-six-one Beechcrest Avenue. Cincinnati. Ohio. The United States of America.'

Charlie's jaw dropped, and his eyebrows shot up to his hairline.

'Our mommy is Eleanor Babbitt,' droned Raymond. 'Her house is with the angels.'

'Charlie, oh, my God,' whispered Susanna, struck with realization and pity. It was the truth. This patient was Charlie's brother.

But Charlie wasn't yet ready to accept this. He wheeled around and stalked off, as though physically distancing himself from Raymond would make any supposed relationship between them null and void. But after a few paces he turned back, his face a study of the mixed emotions of anger and astonishment. His voice was anguished.

'That can't . . . How can that be?' he demanded of Dr Bruner. 'I don't *have* a brother! I *never* had a brother!'

Agitated, Raymond cast his eyes towards Bruner, but the psychiatrist was focused on Charlie. So Raymond fixed his eyes on the watch strapped to his wrist and began to speak to it, his words tumbling out rapidly.

''Course, thirteen *minutes* is Wapner . . . and these are . . . they're not *actors* . . . and *real* cases filed . . . in the . . . the . . . *municipal* court. Court of Califor*ni*a.'

Raymond Babbitt turned, and without a backward glance at Charlie, Susanna, Dr Bruner or the Buick he shuffled rapidly and clumsily away up the path towards the main building. He had an objective firmly in mind. Wapner.

''Course, now it's *twelve* minutes . . .'

CHAPTER FOUR

So there you had it. The unnamed beneficiary now had a name, Raymond. Charlie Babbitt, who went out looking for a beneficiary, had found instead a brother, Raymond Babbitt. Raymond Babbitt might be locked away in a private hospital for the developmentally disabled, but he was not your average, ordinary crazy person. No, Raymond Babbitt was your crazy person with three million dollars. And why not? Why shouldn't he have it? Wasn't he the elder son of Sanford Babbitt, investment banker, rose fancier, doting father? And doesn't the oldest son inherit? Even if he is a feeb, a mental defective, a retard? Sure, made sense. Maybe to Sanford Babbitt it made sense, but not to Charlie Babbitt.

Of course, Raymond Babbitt wasn't going to get a helluva lot of enjoyment out of that three million. How much could pencils and notebooks cost? What else did he want? Not for Raymond the fast cars and faster women, the slick, expensive Italian suits and the beach-front condos. Not for Raymond skiing in Aspen or Carnival in Rio. He wouldn't be throwing *his* money away on crap like the good life and a wonderful time. Even the most expensive private sanatorium with the biggest-name doctors, the most up-to-date facilities and medication every hour on the hour wouldn't put that big a dent in the annual interest on three million dollars.

'We have to talk,' Charlie said firmly to Dr Walter Bruner.

The doctor nodded. 'Let's go inside and have some lunch. After, I'll tell you anything you want to know.'

Lunch was sandwiches, salad and coffee for three in the psychiatrist's office. Charlie ate quickly without saying anything; Susanna and Dr Bruner made polite conversation, mostly about Wallbrook's extensive gardens. Like Sanford Babbitt, Dr Bruner was a flower-lover.

The lengthening rays of the afternoon sun were just beginning to slant over the sloping lawn when they came back outside. The *People's Court* television programme was over, and the latest real-life judicial decisions of Judge Wapner had been duly recorded in the correct notebook, so Raymond was back outside, taking one of his shuffling ambles around the grounds, his backpack strapped firmly to his shoulders.

Susanna went to join him, and they sat down on one of the stone benches together, side by side. But Raymond paid the girl no attention at all; instead he kept scribbling in a notebook. Charlie and Dr Bruner walked through the flower garden, talking together but keeping Raymond in sight.

'What can I tell you?' the psychiatrist asked.

Where to begin? 'What's he writing?'

'Lists, mostly. He has . . . uh . . . he has one he calls the Ominous Events List. Obituaries. Bad-weather reports. He tries to control dangerous things. By putting them safely in a book.'

Charlie thought this over a minute. 'We all do things like that, don't we? Magic stuff?'

Dr Bruner nodded appreciatively at Charlie, and his respect for the young man's intelligence deepened. 'Ritualistic behaviour used as an apotropaic to ward off private demons, yes. Except to Raymond there's danger everywhere. And routines, rituals, are all he's got to protect himself.'

'Rituals?' echoed Charlie, wanting explanation. Never mind 'apotropaic', whatever the hell that was. He didn't even want to *deal* with that.

'The way he eats. Dresses. Sleeps. Uses the bathroom. Walks, talks ... everything. And any break in that routine is terrifying. But –' the doctor broke off, hesitating. How much could Charlie really understand about an illness like Raymond's? 'But he's a person, your brother. A gentle and, in some ways, a highly intelligent person.'

'Intelligent?' Charlie's eyebrows sh~ up in surprise. He glanced over to where Raymond was sitting scribbling.

Dr Bruner nodded. 'He's a savant. He has certain deficiencies, certain disabilities. But he also possesses abilities. Some rather startling abilities.'

Raymond? This was a little much for Charlie to swallow. He looked over to where Raymond was devoting his full attention to his scribblings. 'But he's retarded,' he protested.

'No, he's not. He's autistic. Actually, a high-functioning autistic, probably as a result of damage to the cerebellum or the frontal lobes in the fetal stage. What's important for you to understand is that Raymond doesn't relate to the world or to other people. You and I and other normally functioning people, we relate every minute of our lives. We constantly gather pieces of information and process them into some kind of worldvision, an outlook on life. Whenever we receive new information, we fit it in with what we already know; we evaluate it to see if it's true or important enough to process. And, most important, we connect – with events, with one another. We react. We interact. We possess a wide range of emotions – sadness, happiness, love, hatred, dislike, pity, passion, dedication, contempt, sympathy, desire, joy. We experience a whole spectrum of emotions every day we live.

'Not Raymond. He gathers in pieces of information and files them away in his brain and his notebooks. But they're just individual facts without reference points or context. He's unable to evaluate them; they're all alike to him. Today's weather report is as important to write down and keep as a great thought from a great thinker. He can't perceive any connection between facts, just as he sees no connection between himself and any other person. That's the salient thing to remember about an autistic person. He can't have a relationship of any kind with you, or you with him. It's an impossibility. The mechanism just isn't there. He was born with a piece missing.

'And the most important thing is that Raymond cannot *feel*. He possesses only two emotions – fear and something that I can only describe as "not-fear". It's not a feeling of security; it's simply the temporary absence of fear. Something in his mind turns in on itself. It shuts the world out.'

Dr Bruner stopped speaking and looked sharply at Charlie to see if he understood and how he was taking this. Charlie was nibbling at his lower lip, and his eyes were narrowed as he looked across the lawn at his brother. Whatever he was thinking he kept hidden.

'What he did with you today . . . that was very open,'

said Dr Bruner gently. 'Very. For a stranger. And that could be good for him.'

Charlie shook his dark head, marvelling. 'The world is weird, y'know. Three million dollars. And he's wearing a backpack.' He looked at the psychiatrist. 'What the hell is he gonna spend it on?'

Susanna and Raymond had left the garden. When Charlie Babbitt came looking for them, he found them in Raymond's little room, building a house of cards. That is, Susanna was sitting on the floor building the house, while Raymond sat at the foot of his bed watching her intently. Next to the bed stood Vernon, a tall black man in a green hospital uniform. Vernon was Raymond's attendant.

There were only three pieces of furniture in the room, but the room was overcrowded with Raymond's possessions, mostly books. Books were everywhere, overflowing the small bookcase, stacked on top of it and beside it in piles on the floor. There were books on the bureau and even books tucked into the shade of the ceiling light fixture. Apart from books, there were baseball memorabilia of all kinds – pennants on the walls, pictures of players and teams, posters advertising games. Even the cards that Susanna was using to build the little house were baseball cards, each one with a different player.

'Okay, now, hold your breath,' Susanna was saying as Charlie appeared in the doorway. She was just getting ready to put a card roof on the one-storey card house.

Raymond drew in a deep breath as the card was placed gingerly on top. The walls wobbled a little but held firm. Success.

'You can breathe now.'

Raymond exhaled noisily.

Charlie nodded at the baseball cards. 'You got any Fernando Valenzuelas there?'

'These are all old guys,' Susanna answered. 'I never heard of them.'

'Reds. Cincinnati. 1955,' said Raymond.

'I know,' smiled Susanna. 'You said.' She picked up a card. 'This one next?'

When he saw the card she was holding, Raymond began to tremble, agitated, shaking his head fearfully. Not right. Not the right card.

'Ted Kluszewski is first base. First base . . . first base is next . . .' His teeth were almost chattering. The effect of the wrong card on him was astonishing in its severity.

Susanna reached out and touched his arm very gently. Raymond stiffened, and she drew her hand away. 'First base,' she said gently. 'He's right here, see? Ted Kluszewski.'

'Big Klu,' said Raymond, relaxing. The routine was restored. He was fine now – for the moment.

Charlie felt a malicious impulse of curiosity. 'Whattya think, Ray? Wouldn't it be fun to just . . . knock it all down?' He made a move towards the baseball card house.

Raymond glared at him as though he'd suggested murder, and the two brothers stared at one another. Charlie could see genuine terror in Raymond's eyes. Relenting, he changed his tack.

'I see you've got all those great books there. You read, huh?'

'Reads and remembers,' put in Vernon. 'Whatever he gets his hands on.'

Going over to the bookcase, Charlie railed his hand

along the spines, reading the titles, touching each book in turn. Raymond got jerkily to his feet and began to twitch spasmodically, that low-voltage tic again. He was like a little bird trying to perch on a hot wire, lifting one foot and then the other without moving from its place.

'You don't like him touching your books, huh?' Vernon asked him.

'I don't know,' replied Raymond, backing towards the door. He didn't know. This had never happened to him before; he had never written it into any of his notebooks, so how could he possibly know?

Vernon smiled reassuringly at his patient. 'He won't hurt any,' he told Raymond cheerfully.

But Raymond was busy scanning his inner databank for a piece of protective precedent. ''Course, this is an *un*announced visit,' he croaked. 'This is not a *weekend* visit!' He had backed out of the door now and peered around the jamb in time to see, to his horror, Charlie Babbitt pulling a thick volume off one of the book-shelves.

'V-E-R-N . . . V-E-R-N . . . ,' called Raymond, trembling with fear.

'That's my name.' The black man turned to Charlie. 'He's scared.'

'Charlie, put the book back,' protested Susanna.

But Charlie wasn't ready to do that yet. The malicious little boy in him was still operating. Besides, he wanted to see how far Raymond could be pushed and which buttons did the pushing. But perhaps more than any of these, he genuinely wanted to discover what Dr Bruner had meant when he called Raymond Babbitt an autistic savant.

'*The Complete Works of William Shakespeare.*' Charlie announced the title. 'You read all this?'

'Yes,' answered Raymond in a near-whimper.

'You know all of it?'

'Yes.'

Charlie opened the cover of the leather-bound volume. There was an inscription written on the flyleaf. 'Happy birthday, Raymond. With fondest wishes, Father.' The inscription was in Sanford Babbitt's handwriting. The sight of it gave him a strange pang, like a sudden punch in the chest.

Charlie leafed through the pages, stopping at the beginning of a play. 'How about . . . *Twelfth Night*?'

Immediately Raymond began to recite the Duke's opening speech that begins the play. His voice was flat and expressionless, and the words came out by rote, without punctuation or emphasis, without beauty or poetry or meaning.

'If music be the food of love play on give me excess of it that surfeiting the appetite may sicken and so die that strain again it had a dying –'

Charlie snapped the cover shut and immediately Raymond stopped reciting, as though the cover had been snapped on him too. *Cute*, Charlie thought. *Useless, but cute.*

'Aw right, my man!' giggled Vernon.

'That was wonderful, Raymond,' Susanna said encouragingly.

But Raymond kept his eyes fixed only on Charlie. They stared at each other, a room and a world apart.

'What else can you do, Ray?' asked Charlie.

It was not a question Raymond had an answer for because it didn't involve memorizing anything and reciting it on command. The little jerky bird movements started up again.

''Course, what else *can* you do? So do I.'

This was a real conversation-stopper. 'So do I what?' asked Charlie.

'So do I what,' echoed Raymond flatly. And, almost as an afterthought, '*Ha!*'

To this last, of course, Charlie had no answer except for a blank stare. This appeared to give Raymond a sense of triumph, if he could have experienced such a sense, which, in fact, he couldn't.

'*Ha! Ha! Ha! Ha!*'

'Raymond –' Susanna put her hand out.

But Raymond ignored it. He was too busy taunting Charlie and finding it hard to stop.

'*Ha! Ha! Ha! Ha! Ha! Ha!*'

'Raymond, is this the next one?' Susanna's excellent instincts led her to the right path to reach Raymond. She held the baseball card out where he could see it. 'Johnny Temple?'

Raymond shut his mouth in the same second, now intent only on the card. Charlie Babbitt was forgotten. Scanning his databank, he came up with Johnny Temple. Second base.

He shuffled over to Susanna and knelt down beside her on the floor, taking the card gently from her hand. Then, slowly and very carefully, he placed the card against the roof of the house. It shivered, but it didn't fall.

'You can breathe now,' Raymond told Susanna.

The girl laughed, but Raymond didn't crack a smile.

'He likes you, ma'am,' said Vernon. 'I can tell.'

Susanna turned eagerly to Raymond, but the connection – if there had actually been one – was broken. He was holding the next card up to his face, inspecting it minutely, searching for micro-organisms. He paid no attention to Susanna at all.

The girl's face fell. 'When I touched him before, he pulled away,' she said sadly to Vernon.

'Don't take it personal,' the black man answered kindly. 'I'd guess I'm closer to him than anybody in the world. And he's never hugged me. Never touched me. It's not in him.' Vernon smiled. 'Shoot, if I left town tomorrow and didn't say goodbye, he'd never even notice.'

Raymond was still totally preoccupied with the baseball card, turning it this way and that, experiencing it totally.

Mesmerized, Charlie asked Vernon, 'Can he . . . hear us? When he's like that?'

'Hey, my man!' Vernon called out to Raymond. 'You want to show your brother your ducks?'

Raymond didn't take his eyes off the card. 'I don't know.'

'It's that pond you passed on your way in,' Vernon explained. 'He sits there half the day.'

Now Charlie turned to Susanna. 'Maybe you should drive back to town,' he said easily, 'so I can be alone with Ray. We can get to know each other better. Then come back tonight and pick me up. Whatta ya say? Could you do that for me?' He grinned at her lovingly.

Susanna felt a stab of disappointment and also annoyance. He was using her again – how, she wasn't sure. But she could sense it. Charlie was up to his old manipulative tricks.

'I suppose so,' she said reluctantly. 'If you want.'

Charlie's grin widened. 'C'mon, Ray,' he said cheerfully to his brother. 'Let's walk the lady to the car.'

He started to get up, but Raymond's hand shot out stiffly, barring his way. Raymond's body was rigid, and he didn't look at Charlie. It was several seconds before

Charlie followed his brother's eyes and realized that what Raymond was doing was protecting the little house of cards. Charlie nodded and edged his way gingerly around the house, careful not to touch it. After all, wasn't it Raymond's and Susanna's masterpiece? See? He might be autistic, but Raymond wasn't so hard to read.

They waited while Raymond slowly put his backpack on and adjusted the straps, one after the other, in the precise and proper order. He never took a step out of doors without the pack on.

The afternoon shadows had lengthened noticeably when the three of them walked out into the Wallbrook grounds, Charlie with Susanna, Raymond trailing a few steps behind them. As they drew close to the Buick convertible Charlie turned to his brother.

'Ray, I just want to say goodbye to Susanna alone for a second. Okay? Be right back.'

Raymond nodded his assent, but as Charlie began to walk towards the Buick again Raymond followed behind, like a dog at heel. Charlie stopped, frowning, but he kept his voice very patient.

'No. Alone means without you. You stand here. We go there. Okay? Susanna, say goodbye.'

Susanna scowled a little; a young woman of enormous warmth and empathy, she hated the way Charlie talked to his poor brother, ordering him around as if he were some kind of dumb animal. Nevertheless, she complied. 'Bye-bye, Raymond. See you soon.' She smiled and waved at him.

Raymond didn't smile back, but his hand came up and did an eerily perfect imitation of Susanna's wave.

Charlie took a step, and behind him Raymond took another. Charlie's hand shot up like a dog trainer's.

'Stay!' he ordered, stopping Raymond in his tracks. This time Raymond stayed. Taking her hand, Charlie pulled Susanna urgently out of Raymond's earshot and over to the car. There was a look on his face Susanna had never seen before, a tension around his mouth.

'Listen, change of plan,' he said swiftly in a low, urgent voice. 'This is what I want you to do . . .'

Susanna listened in confusion. What exactly was Charlie up to, and why couldn't he be straight and upfront with her about it?

'If you'd just tell me why,' she complained. 'First you say, "Go to town." Then –'

'Just *do* it,' argued Charlie a little desperately. 'Please. It won't be long. It's really for Ray.' Charlie was clever; he knew all her weak spots, and one of them was sympathy for poor Raymond.

Susanna glanced over to where Raymond was standing, watching them anxiously. He was pacing back and forth, never taking his eyes off them. He craned his head forward as far as it would go, obviously to see and hear them better. His anxiety and obvious misery touched Susanna.

'Okay, whatever,' she sighed. 'Go. He's waiting for you.' Charlie wrapped his arms around her in gratitude and gave her a long, deep kiss. Then Susanna climbed into the Buick and drove off.

Charlie made a beckoning gesture, and Raymond trotted over obediently. Ready to show Charlie his ducks.

They sat side by side on the damp bank of the pond, watching the ducks swim by on the mosquito-laden waters. That is, Charlie watched the ducks while Raymond kept writing in a notebook, a green one this time. Occasionally he looked up to check the progress of the ducks, but never did he look at Charlie.

'What are you writing?' asked Charlie.

'I don't know.' Raymond kept his expressionless gaze fixed firmly on the notebook page.

'Looks like the Ominous Events List to me,' commented Charlie.

''Course, rain was 1.17 inches. 'Course that's 1.74 inches of rain below normal in Cincinnati,' recited Raymond tonelessly. 'That's the driest September since 1960. Very little rain.' The fact seemed to agitate him, and he squirmed a little as he kept jerking his head between the ducks and his notes.

'So that's the Ominous Events List.'

'No,' said Raymond.

'Raymond,' Charlie said quietly. 'Raymond, look at me. I want to tell you something.' Raymond trembled but kept his face turned away from Charlie's. 'Listen. Dad is . . . uh . . . Dad is dead, Ray. He died last week. Did they tell you?'

Raymond didn't answer, but the tension in his small body spelled acute anxiety.

'Do you know what . . . "dead" is?' asked Charlie quietly.

Hesitantly, Raymond nodded. But it was evident to Charlie that his brother had no concept of death.

'It means Dad is gone.'

'Can I see him?' asked Raymond.

Charlie gnawed at his lip.

'I want to see him,' Raymond said with more force than Charlie had heard in his voice so far.

Charlie thought a minute. 'Sure, Ray, you can see him. We'll go see him together. Let's do it right now.'

'Right now,' agreed Raymond, for whom 'right now' meant getting up very slowly, putting his green notebook in exactly the right place in his knapsack and his pencil back in the plastic pocket holder in the same position he had taken it from. 'Right now' meant putting his backpack on left strap first, then right strap, then tightening the straps in the correct order. Only then was he ready. Charlie watched these rituals with barely concealed impatience.

Nodding for him to follow, Charlie led Raymond along the path away from the hospital. Behind them Wallbrook faded in the distance and disappeared entirely as they rounded a bend in the road. A few yards further along, almost hidden behind the chestnut trees, sat the Buick, and behind the wheel Susanna was waiting.

'Slide over,' said Charlie, opening the door on the driver's side. Seeing Raymond, Susanna's eyes widened in surprise, and she looked questioningly at Charlie. But he said nothing, only nodded to Raymond to get in beside Susanna, while Charlie himself took the wheel.

'This is Daddy's car,' said Raymond. 'Pitiful seats on the inside. Blue on the outside. The licence plate used to say "3021" in red.'

'Charlie, wait a minute!' protested Susanna. 'Where are we taking him?'

'Field trip,' he replied shortly, firing the engine and peeling out with a squeal of tyres. As they drove away, Raymond looked back over his shoulder in the direction of Wallbrook. His face showed nothing, but his body language expressed nervous anxiety.

'Don't worry, you're coming back,' Susanna told him reassuringly.

Charlie said nothing.

'You said I could see him,' Raymond said. His words were accusing, but his tone was flat, without emotion.

'He's in the ground,' answered Charlie.

Putting one hand out tentatively, Raymond almost touched the cold marble headstone but pulled his hand back at the last minute. He read the carved inscription once more.

SANFORD BABBITT 1918–1988
BELOVED HUSBAND AND FATHER

In the ground. Daddy's in the ground. Raymond looked down between his feet; he was sitting cross-legged on Sanford Babbitt's grave. But he could see nothing, only grass. No Daddy. He reached out his hand again and pulled hesitantly at a tuft, then looked over to Charlie, who lay on his back on the lawn near the grave.

'You can talk to him,' Charlie told Raymond. 'He can't talk back. But maybe he'll hear you.'

A pause, while Raymond thought that over for a moment or two. Then, in a voice loud enough to pierce the earth, loud enough to make Charlie jump, he yelled, '*Daddy, this is Raymond!*'

No answer. Bending over clumsily, Raymond put his ear to the ground, listening.

'I told you, he can't talk back. But don't yell any more, okay? He can hear you better if you whisper.'

Raymond looked doubtfully at Charlie. Whisper? How could that be? But Charlie nodded; he seemed to be serious. So Raymond bent over again, putting his mouth very close to the grave, and whispered hoarsely, 'Daddy. I'm here with my brother. Charlie Babbitt.'

Again he glanced over to Charlie, the authority, for confirmation. His eyes asked the question, did Daddy hear me? And Charlie's nod answered, yes.

'Ray, I was thinking. Would you like to go to a ball game? A real one?'

But Charlie's question bounced off a blank wall. 'Like' and 'dislike' were not in Raymond's frame of reference.

'We'll sit behind first base. At Dodger Stadium. And we'll watch Fernando pitch. And I'll buy you a beer.'

This brought a reaction, although not the one Charlie expected. Raymond began to squirm.

''Course, I'll be going *all* the way there. *All* the way alone. All the way to Cali*forn*ia, just . . . alone, and I'm not *allowed* to –'

'You won't go alone,' said Charlie lightly. 'You'll go with me.' He kept his voice casual, not wanting to spook Raymond any more than he had to.

Go. Go with Charlie Babbitt. Go to California with Charlie Babbitt to see a baseball game and drink beer. The concept was so new to Raymond that he literally froze, just staring at Charlie. He struggled to put the words together, to make a usable, memorable, writable fact of them, but they didn't fit. Oddly enough, though, he felt no fear.

CHAPTER FIVE

On a country road back to Cincinnati, zipping along in the Buick convertible, doing seventy, Raymond now in the back seat, watching the road go by, taking note of every tree, every signpost, every billboard. His eyes darting back and forth, his brain recording without making sense of any of it. Who knew what was going on inside that damaged brain?

They didn't go back to the house at one-oh-nine-six-one Beechcrest Avenue. They didn't go back to the Hotel Broadham. Instead they drove to a downtown motel and signed in for a double room for Charlie and Susanna, also a single connecting room next door for Raymond.

'Okay, killer,' said Charlie cheerfully, unlocking the door to his room and putting the suitcases down on the double bed, 'Here comes the presidential suite.'

Naturally, Raymond didn't understand a word of that but stood firmly in place in the exact centre of the faded carpet, his eyes fixed on Charlie. Charlie beckoned to him; time for Raymond to go to his own room. Again, no response, just the empty suspicious stare. Charlie gestured again, more vehemently this time, and Raymond finally moved. He took a clumsy step or two forward and bumped into a lamp table he hadn't noticed. The table went over with a crash, taking the lamp with it. Raymond froze in terror. This was one for the Serious Injury List. A genuine disaster.

Then he did something he'd never done before. He bent down and snatched up the lamp. Miraculously, it wasn't broken. He clutched it tightly, then, impulsively, he held it out to Susanna. A gift.

Surprised, Susanna hesitated. Their eyes met, and her hand came out to accept it. She smiled at him warmly, aware of the dark and private struggle he must be going through.

'Thank you, Raymond.'

He stared gravely back, not returning the smile. A smile was entirely beyond his abilities.

Charlie was getting impatient. His own pace, the workings of his sharp mind, were so rapid that it was nearly impossible for him to slow down enough to accommodate the snail's pace of Raymond's functioning.

'C'mon!' He unlocked the connecting door between the two rooms and motioned Raymond forward. With his shuffling gait, Raymond went slowly into the next room.

'Your room, Ray,' said Charlie breezily. Mistake.

Instantly a look of fear crossed Raymond's face. His eyes went skittering around, shifting back and forth anxiously, as he gazed about himself, terrified.

'This is . . . is *not* my room. This . . . is *definitely* not my room,' he jittered.

'Just for tonight, that's all,' Charlie assured him easily.

'Until we take you back home,' added Susanna.

But Raymond was beyond hearing reassuring words. He was locked away somewhere else, on a roll now, all his elaborate defence mechanisms doing ninety miles an hour. His monotone speeded up, the words tumbling out in a rush.

''Course, I'm going to be here a *long* time. A *very* long time. It's going to be . . . the *longest* time, and I'm . . .'

'No, Raymond, really!' Susanna tried to interrupt the babble of flowing fear.

'*Gone*. I'm *gone* for good. Gone for good from my home.'

'*No*, Raymond. It's just for tonight. I promise, Raymond.'

Susanna's tone was so forceful, so authoritative, that it immediately stemmed Raymond's babbling. For the first time he appeared to hear her, and it calmed him down a little. But not entirely.

''Course, they moved my *bed*.'

'Hey, that's right,' said Charlie. 'You like it under the window, huh? No problem, bro.' He started pushing the bed into its new position, with Raymond anxiously watching him. Now the bed was under the window, and it seemed to make Raymond feel a little better, a little less disoriented. But not for long.

'They took . . . they took the books. They took *all* the books,' he jittered.

'Not all of 'em, Ray.' Pulling open the dresser drawer, Charlie pulled out the Holy Bible that the Gideon Society places in every hotel room in America for the spiritual solace of the lonely traveller. 'Here.'

Raymond reached out both hands for the book, but he held it awkwardly, at arm's length, while his black shoe-button eyes kept shifting around the room. His problems were multiplying by the second. 'They took the shelves.'

'Y'don't *need* shelves,' Charlie said a little impatiently. 'That's why they put the book in a *drawer*.'

Logic could make no impact on Raymond, unless it was the secret logic of his own devising. His darting eyes were drawn to the overhanging light fixture, and 'light fixture' meant book-storage space to him. Back home in Wallbrook he kept books stashed in the ceiling fixture. Ergo, that's where they belonged. It never occurred to him – how could it? – that this fixture and the one back in Wallbrook differed in size and shape; this one was smaller and more shallow. You put books into it; that was all he knew. Reaching up, he tucked the Bible into the fixture. It hovered there for a minute, then tipped out and came crashing to the floor. Another disaster, and definitely one for the notebook.

The catastrophe was overwhelming. This wasn't supposed to happen. Numb with fear, Raymond stared at the fallen Bible, his body twitching as he whispered to the floor rapidly under his breath. Whisper, whisper, whisperwhisperwhisperwhisper. Neither Susanna nor Charlie could make out a word of it.

'What are you saying, Ray?' asked Charlie. 'I can't understand.'

But Raymond was outside their reach, locked away firmly in his own world. Whisperwhisperwhisperwhisper. Twitch, twitch, jerk. Susanna felt a chill running up her back. She was really concerned now. Raymond appeared totally flipped out, past the point of no return. She had been afraid that something like this might happen. All of it was too much for Raymond, too new and threatening. They never should have brought him here; if only Charlie would listen to her sometimes.

Walking straight up to his brother, Charlie stepped so close to Raymond that their faces were only inches apart. His proximity practically forced Raymond to look at him, to hear him.

'I can't help you if I can't hear you,' said Charlie firmly. 'What ... the ... hell ... are ... you ... saying?'

Slowly, Raymond focused, raising his eyes from the book on the floor. But he still continued to jerk and twitch, a puppet on tangled strings. His eyes glued to Charlie, he began backing away, rubbing his hands together nervously and shaking his head spasmodically from side to side.

'Charlie, let's take him home,' begged Susanna, her heart aching at the sight of so much terror. She knelt to pick up the Bible from the floor.

'He's okay.' Charlie shook his head dismissively. 'You like pizza, Ray?'

'You like pizza, Charlie Babbitt,' answered Raymond blankly. But his anxiety appeared to have abated somewhat. 'Pizza' was a word he understood, a familiar Wallbrook word.

Susanna took a step towards Charlie. 'I think he means –'

'I know what he means. We're brothers. He likes pizza. I like pizza. *We* like pizza. We like pepperoni and onion, right, Ray?'

Like? Pepperoni? Like? Raymond couldn't begin to answer that.

Charlie headed back for his room to make the call. 'I'll order up a large. You want a beer with that, Ray?' he called over his shoulder. 'Maybe a milk?'

Now Raymond and Susanna were alone together, but it was as if the girl didn't exist. All of Raymond was focused on his bed. It wasn't ... right ... Something ... wasn't right. Something wrong, disturbingly wrong. He moved it a few inches to the right and studied it. Another couple of inches. Still not right. Raymond began to panic.

'V-E-R-N . . . V-E-R-N . . .,' he called anxiously. He pushed his bed to the left about a foot and looked at it hard. Wrong. It was still all wrong. The panic increased, spread, threatened to engulf him.

'V-E-R-N . . . my *man*!' Raymond hollered. 'V-E-R-N, my *man*!' But there was no Vern to come and make things right again. Only strangers.

'Charlie, he's scared,' breathed Susanna. 'We'd better–'

Suddenly, as abruptly as it had started, the hollering stopped. Raymond had finally got the bed right, the way it was supposed to be, the way it *had* to be, and the panic went away as quickly as it had come. Charlie came from his own room and checked out the bed.

'Hey, that's nice, Ray,' he approved. 'When you're finished in here, you can come and do mine.'

Do?

'So what's on TV?' Charlie asked affably. '*People's Court*? Judge Wapner? C'mon, look at your watch.'

Raymond looked at his watch, then spoke to it. '*Wheel of Fortune*,' he told the dialface. 'Today's . . . today's contestants . . . will win . . . will win *fabulous* prizes . . .'

'Great. Sit down. I'll put it on.'

Obeying Charlie, Raymond sat right down on the edge of the bed, perching there uncomfortably, ignoring the chair. Charlie nodded and switched on the set, turned the dial. There it was, just as Raymond had foretold. *Wheel of Fortune*.

'Amazing,' laughed Charlie. 'You're gonna save me a fortune in TV guides, Ray.'

Restored to calm, Raymond sat watching the game show, which was more real to him than anything beyond the perimeters of the little screen. Charlie grinned cockily at Susanna. See? He was right. He knew exactly how to handle Raymond. Nothing could be easier. Taking the Bible out of her hands, he knelt down in front of Raymond and put the book into his lap.

'You've got your TV. You've got your book. Pizza's coming. Life is good, huh?'

Raymond and Charlie looked at each, Raymond with that unblinking stare out of dull black eyes.

'You ever smile?' Charlie asked.

'I ever smile,' answered Raymond, continuing to stare.

'Prove it,' challenged Charlie. He grinned at his brother, showing all his teeth, one of his best charming smiles. Raymond looked at him for a moment, then grinned back. It wasn't a real smile; it was a physical imitation, like his mimicry of Susanna's wave. It resembled the smile of a window-dressing dummy, but it was a smile after all. Raymond Babbitt's first smile.

'The man has po-tential.' Charlie laughed.

Sitting on the edge of his bed, Raymond watched *Wheel of Fortune, The Price is Right, Let's Make a Deal, People's Court, Hollywood Squares.* The pizza arrived, and Raymond ate three slices of it. He didn't eat it in any of the traditional ways, not from crust in, not from the centre out, not flopping the sides of the slice over the middle to keep the cheese inside. He didn't eat it at all until Charlie had cut up the slices into tiny squares for him, each one exactly the same size as all the others, and each tiny square had been skewered on a toothpick. Then he ate the squares slowly and methodically, in some predetermined order, nibbling them off the toothpicks one at a time. He didn't seem to mind that the pizza was stone-cold, the sauce congealed, the cheese rock-hard, the slimy pepperoni slices curling drily at the edges.

The pizza finished, Raymond started on a bag of Cheez Doodles, eating them one at a time, at the same rate, his hand rising from the bag to his mouth like an assembly-line robot. The hour grew late; Charlie and Susanna had long ago retired to their own room to eat pizza, watch TV and make passionate love, but Raymond kept on watching the set, continued to munch his Doodles.

The Late Movie was on, an oldie that Raymond didn't recognize, but he watched it anyway. It was right under his nose, and that was all that was important. On the screen a little boy was watching cartoons on *his* TV set. His mother came into the room.

'Johnny Peters!' she scolded. 'You told your father you were doing your homework! Now shut that set off, young man! Right NOW!'

At the voice of command Raymond rose obediently and went to his television set and shut it off. The room was dark. He went back to his bed and sat on the edge, exactly where he had been sitting without moving for hours. He stared at the set. The screen was blank.

There was nothing to do but read, so Raymond read for a while, then closed the book. He needed TV.

From the next room came muffled noises, panting and gasping, occasional moaning. Raymond didn't understand the erotic noises, but they didn't worry him because there was another sound from Charlie's room, the sound of a television set, switched on and forgotten when the lovemaking began. Charlie has TV. Raymond has no TV. He picked up the bag of Cheez Doodles and opened the door connecting the rooms.

Tangled under the covers on the double bed, Charlie and Susanna were locked in mortal venal combat, their lips and loins hotly joined. They were so deep into their lovemaking, they didn't hear Raymond come in. As for Raymond, he didn't so much as glance in their direction because on the mesmerizing screen David Letterman was talking to a guest. David Letterman, a viewing must for late-night TV enjoyment.

Raymond sat down at the edge of the bed and put his bag of Cheez Doodles beside him on the writhing covers. The bag started jumping around, but Raymond was too intent on Letterman to notice. Rhythmically he reached into the bag and took out one crisp cheesey morsel after another, all without taking his eyes off the TV screen. He didn't hear the other sounds in the room take on a new urgency as the lovers speeded towards their climax.

Without looking, Raymond reached behind him for another bite and grabbed a human leg instead. Susanna's leg.

There was a gasp and Susanna froze. Slowly she looked over her shoulder to find Raymond munching away beside her on the bed, staring back at her with a totally blank expression.

'Uh . . . hi!' Susanna said nervously and gave him a wide smile so that he wouldn't think she was angry at him and freak out again. Raymond answered her with the new thing he'd learned, the mockery of a smile. They show their teeth to you, you show your teeth to them.

Charlie's voice came out muffled from under the covers. 'Ray, are you in here?'

'I'm in here,' answered Raymond.

Charlie drew a deep breath, trying to keep calm. 'Well, get out.'

Raymond stood up obediently and reached for his bag of snacks. His eyes met Susanna's, but he said nothing and shuffled out of Charlie's room back to his own. The door closed behind him.

'Go in there,' Susanna said tightly.

'What for?'

The girl reached over and switched on the lamp by the bed. Yelping in protest, Charlie put his hands over his eyes to shut out the painful light.

'I said, go in there, Charlie.' Her voice was urgent, and her dark eyes, drilling into him, were brilliant in their intensity. 'He's scared. He's never been away before. Besides, you've hurt his feelings.'

Shit. Stung by the justice of her words, Charlie knew he had to give in, but that didn't make him feel any better about it. The interrupted sex had been wonderful. He'd been . . . *this* close. Grumbling, he rolled out of bed and pulled on his jeans, then stalked to Raymond's room through the connecting door. Susanna too got up from the bed, went into the bathroom and began running a hot bath.

'I thought I told you to watch TV.' Charlie glowered at his brother.

'Mine went off. I'm watching yours,' explained Raymond.

'Well, you can't. I'm busy.' He rummaged around, finding the Bible. 'Here, read your book.'

'I did already,' said Raymond.

Charlie sighed, and his hazel eyes searched the room, lighting on a stack of motel literature. 'You read this yet?'

Raymond nodded. Now Charlie was fast running out of patience. He couldn't believe that Raymond had actually read everything in the room; he assumed that his brother had simply turned all the pages, reading bits and pieces. But Charlie was damned if he was going to babysit a forty-year-old man with Susanna temptingly naked in the next room. Desperate, he grabbed up the Cincinnati telephone directory.

'How about this, then?' He waved the phone book under Raymond's nose.

'No,' Raymond admitted quietly.

'Good.' Charlie dropped the directory into Raymond's lap. 'Do whatever you want. Just stay in here. Understand?'

There was no reply. Raymond looked at his lap, at the wall, at the floor, everywhere, in fact, but at Charlie.

'Well, don't just sit there like an asshole!' thundered Charlie. 'Answer me! Do you understand or not?'

Raymond's words were mumbled, barely audible. 'I understand or not.'

'All right, then.' Mollified, Charlie opened the door between their two rooms, leaving it ajar, and went back to his own room, looking for Susanna. He found her in the bathtub, her dark curly hair scooped up and pinned loosely on the top of her head, her shoulders and neck sweetly pink from the steam. But the look on her face was anything but inviting.

'You go right back in there, Charlie,' she demanded, her eyes flashing fire, 'and you apologize!'

Charlie gaped at her incredulously. 'What was I supposed to do?' he yelled indignantly. 'Tuck him in like a baby? I'm not his mother, for chrissakes!'

'No!' retorted Susanna. 'You're his brother. His *kid* brother, as a matter of fact.'

'And what's that supposed to mean?'

'You could show him some respect!'

Respect? For an idiot like Raymond? Was she real? Italians with their loony ideas! Charlie looked at Susanna closely. No mistake, she had some kind of bug up her ass about Raymond.

'Whatever's wrong with him, Charlie, it's not his fault. And that's more than I can say for some of us.'

Charlie fought to hold on to his temper. He knew Susanna was digging at him, and it pissed him off. He wasn't used to taking heat from women.

'You see what a mind he has, Charlie,' Susanna continued earnestly. 'When he uses it. He could have been a brilliant person. An extraordinary person!' Her voice softened with pity. 'He could have been your big brother, someone to look up to, to teach you things –'

Charlie put up his hands, palms first, to cut her off. In a conciliatory tone he said, 'Let's take it easy, babe. You're getting all worked up about nothing.'

Nothing! Hadn't he been listening to a word she said? Her hot Mediterranean temper flared up. 'Where the hell do you get off, calling your brother an asshole?' she demanded, glaring at Charlie. 'If you brought him out here just to insult him, you might just as well take him back right now.'

Charlie drew his breath while his mind went racing. This was the opening he'd been waiting for, but now he didn't know whether or not to take it. At last he decided and plunged in head first.

'What if . . . what if he's not going back?'

'What the hell does that mean?' gasped Susanna, her eyes getting wide.

'It means. . . .' He looked her straight in the eye. 'It means I took him, and I'm keeping him.'

Charlie's sudden declaration, coming out of the blue, stunned Susanna. She was mystified. 'Why in the world would you do that?' she wanted to know.

'I don't know,' confessed Charlie. 'I was . . . pissed at him.'

'At Raymond?'

'At my dad.'

Now Susanna was totally confused. Charlie wasn't making any sense here. 'You're mad at your father, so you're keeping Raymond?'

Charlie nibbled his lip, and his eyes avoided hers. 'Just until I get what's . . .' He hesitated, then finished in a low voice, 'What's mine.'

Susanna's eyes widened, then narrowed as Charlie's words began to take on meaning.

'What's yours?' she repeated. 'What *is* yours?'

'Well, Dad left Ray . . . He left him some money.'

Ah, money! Now she was beginning to understand. To understand and to get mad. 'Really? How much?' she asked him frostily.

Charlie looked away, said nothing.

'Charlie. How much money . . . did . . . your . . . father . . . leave?' demanded Susanna very slowly and clearly.

Charlie drew a deep breath, then faced the music. 'Three million. All of it. Every last dime.'

There was an explosion in the bathtub as Susanna rose up in fury. Water cascaded everywhere, dripping from the ceiling, pouring off the walls. Charlie was drenched. Wringing wet, Susanna reached for her shirt and pulled it on, her damp fingers struggling with the buttons.

'Shit!' yelled Charlie. 'What do you think you're —'

But Susanna pushed past him, storming into the bedroom, grabbing up her clothing and pulling it over her wet body. She jammed her feet into her shoes, fuming. Shaking the water off him like a wet dog, Charlie stumbled unhappily after her into the bedroom.

'Honey, look. This is ridic— What the hell are you doing?' He broke off in dismay.

What Susanna was doing was packing. She'd dragged

her suitcase out of the closet and was throwing her clothing into it helter-skelter.

'What? You're running off in the middle of the night?' He laughed, hoping to get her to laugh with him, to see how absurd this all was. What the hell did she care if he held on to his mental defective of a brother an extra couple of days? No skin off her pretty ass, right? Besides, when he got hold of the money, there'd be some great times in store for the two of them. Charlie Babbitt was no miser. He knew how to show a girl a good time. All Charlie had to do was to get Susanna to calm down just long enough to listen, and he was sure she'd agree. She'd go along with him.

But Susanna was in no mood to calm down and listen, let alone to go along with Charlie Babbitt's plans for Raymond. Furiously she continued her packing, dumping her cosmetics bag on top of everything and snapping the suitcase locks shut with a click of finality.

'Hey, c'mon!' protested Charlie. 'I need you!'

The girl whirled on him, her eyes flashing dangerously. 'For what?' she yelled. 'Baby-sitting? Pussy? I don't have three million bucks, Charlie! Your date's in there!' She pointed to the doorway of Raymond's room, through which Raymond could be seen sitting on his bed, scribbling away in terror in one of his notebooks, stealing frightened glances at the yelling couple.

Seeing him, Susanna's heart gave a wrench of pity. But although it slowed her down, she didn't let it stop her. She grabbed her suitcase and reached for her bag, but Charlie got to it first. He held the bag out beyond her reach; the two of them grappled for it.

'What did I do?' demanded Charlie. 'Wait a minute – '

'Give . . . me . . . that . . . bag!' said Susanna through clenched teeth.

'What did I do here? What's my goddam crime?'

He loosened his grip a bit, and Susanna was able to wrench the bag out of Charlie's fingers. 'You're *using* Raymond!' she shouted. 'You're using *me*! You use *everybody*!'

That stung; it hit Charlie right where he lived. 'Am I using you?' he demanded of Raymond.

'Yes,' answered Raymond.

'Shut up!' Charlie yelled back furiously. He turned to Susanna. 'He's answering a question from a half-hour ago!' Rushing to the connecting door, he flung it wide open. Now it was his turn to be boiling mad. His temper was terrible, and he'd been trying hard to contain it, but it was getting away from him.

'Look at him!' he yelled at Susanna, while Raymond, in abject terror, clapped both hands over his ears and began to whisper desperately. 'What good is three million dollars to him? He's got nothing to spend it on! He doesn't even know what it is!'

Susanna put her suitcase down and tried to get to Raymond to comfort him, but Charlie barred the way, his hazel eyes blazing, his full lips working in fury.

'That money would just sit there, with that goddamn doctor, for the rest of Ray's life!'

That stopped Susanna right in her tracks. She shot Charlie a glare so icy it would freeze a chilli pepper. 'So it's hardly like stealing, huh?' she demanded in a cold, quiet voice.

Trapped. Charlie shut his mouth, finding nothing to say. The accusation had some truth to it, and the truth hurt. Susanna brushed by him into Raymond's room, with Charlie trailing after her.

'And when it's over, what happens to Raymond?' asked Susanna in the same dangerously quiet tone.

Charlie's eyes dropped. 'Well ... he'll ... just go back to Wallbrook. Or some place even better. He'll be just ... the same.' Even to his own ears, the words sounded lame and flimsy.

Susanna's eyebrow shot up. 'Only *you*'ll have his money.'

'Whattya mean, *his* money?' Charlie exploded. All of his careful dissembling, his meticulously preserved cool, was blown to the winds. He lost his cool and his temper completely. 'Whattya mean *his* fucking money? That bastard was my father too. Did he leave me half? *Did he leave me half?* Where's *my* fucking half?'

'Raymond, you're coming with me,' Susanna said decisively, reaching for him.

But Charlie grabbed hold of Raymond's arm and gave it a savage yank, pulling him away from Susanna. At the same time, he raised his left hand in a fist, brandishing it threateningly at the girl.

Susanna stopped, frozen. She looked from Charlie's eyes to his fist, then back again. This told her everything she needed to know. That did it; she couldn't stay here another minute, not even to rescue Raymond from his rotten brother. Turning on her heel, Susanna grabbed up her suitcase and headed for the door without another word. Charlie let go of Raymond's arm and ran after her.

'Goddamn it, I'm entitled to that money! It's mine!' he howled.

Reaching the door, Susanna wheeled on Charlie. 'You're crazy!' she accused. 'You have kidnapped this man! Do you understand that?'

Astounded, Charlie came to a halt. 'How can I kidnap him? He's my brother!'

'You think this guy Bruner is just gonna roll over and take it?'

But Charlie wasn't interested in Dr Bruner and what he would or would not take. All he wanted was to justify himself to Susanna, so that he wouldn't lose her. He wanted her to see his side. Cleverly he aimed for her weak spot, her pity. 'My father has stuck it to me all my life! Now, what do you want from me?'

Susanna opened the hotel-room door. 'Out,' she said, and with that she was gone.

For a moment Charlie just stood there, staring at the door, unable to believe what had just happened here. Then, in rage and frustration, he viciously pulled the door open and slammed it again, hard enough to shake and splinter the jamb. His whole body was trembling, and he was panting.

Damn broad! This was no good, no damn good at all. He had to pull himself together. He went over to the night table and picked up his package of unfiltered Lucky Strikes. Pulling one out with difficulty, he lit it up with trembling fingers and took a deep drag, getting the smoke way down there into the bottom of his lungs, waiting for the calming effect to begin. In a few seconds Charlie felt a little better.

So. So, that's the way it was going to be. Susanna was out. Great. It was just him and Raymond now; he was on his own. He was better off this way, he lied to himself, already missing Susanna ferociously, aching for her. But with a massive effort of will he pulled himself together until he could breathe normally again.

Raymond. He'd better find Raymond, see if he was okay or if he'd wigged out again in some weird way. This must have been pretty traumatic for him. A real disturbance of the routine. Charlie went back to Raymond's room, a big smile on his face, ready to be nice to his brother. What he saw made Charlie stop in his tracks and just stare.

In the centre of the room Raymond Babbitt was standing on a non-existent pitcher's mound, winding up to throw to a non-existent hitter. He had retreated completely from the here and now into a ritualistic fantasy that would protect him. It was a device not unlike Charlie's cigarette, but to Raymond it was a matter of life and death. To survive, he had to get away. Now he was away, in a world where he was a major-league pitcher. His face was grim, his eyes paranoid, small and squinting.

'The wind-up,' muttered Raymond. He suited the action to the word, but his coordination was poor and his actions slow and jerky. His lips were clenched in concentration as he let the imaginary ball go. At the crack of the imaginary bat Raymond started towards the plate but returned.

'Foul ball.'

Charlie stood watching him, realizing that Raymond had gone some place where he couldn't follow.

'Kidnap, huh?' He spoke softly, aware that Raymond wouldn't hear him even if he shouted. 'Be a lot easier, Ray, if you'd just write me a cheque.'

Raymond checked the bases. This was a scary situation for a major-league pitcher, men on first and third. Two strikes, three balls on the batter. It was up to him, Raymond Babbitt, star pitcher of the 1955 Cincinnati Reds. He had to keep it together . . . keep it together . . .

'Full count,' whispered Raymond, terrified.

CHAPTER SIX

At what time Raymond might have won (or lost) his major-league game Charlie would never know because he fell asleep, exhausted, less than an hour after Susanna had stormed out. There was no sound from Raymond's room, however, so Charlie presumed he must have got at least some sleep. Either that, or he pitched thirty innings.

When Charlie went in to see him early in the morning, Raymond was already sitting there, waiting, on the edge of his bed. He was fully dressed, his hair slicked down with water and sticking out in all directions. He seemed to be calm enough, although he was holding his head at a stiff, awkward angle, tilted sideways on his neck. Charlie made a mental note that Raymond could use a clean shirt and some underwear, a comb and a toothbrush. But what the hell for? He'd soon be back at Wallbrook, maybe even later today if everything went as planned. Charlie was waiting only until the switchboard at Wallbrook opened and the psychiatrist was at his desk before he phoned for the showdown with Dr Bruner.

He didn't expect to be here in Cincinnati more than a day or so, only long enough to cut a deal with the psychiatrist trustee, turn over Raymond and get his ass back to Los Angeles where it belonged. Too many strings had been left untied back there for Charlie Babbitt to waste time here. By now his creditors would be out looking for him with a posse.

But first things first, and the first thing on the agenda was breakfast. A couple of easy blocks down from the hotel was an ordinary greasy-spoon diner, catering mostly to the downtown breakfast and lunch trade. Raymond followed Charlie inside with his usual molasses-in-January shuffle, and they sat down at a clean table by the window. It was still early, and the place was nearly deserted. At the counter sat a couple of truckers dunking doughnuts into black coffee.

'Good morning,' said a pretty blonde waitress, coming to their table with napkins and silverware. Her big blue eyes were fixed with interest on handsome Charlie Babbitt.

Charlie looked up. She was *very* pretty, young and buxom. For openers, he gave her his Number Four, the boyish smile.

'Actually, it's a beautiful morning,' he grinned, with a significant lift of his eyebrow.

The waitress almost purred as she stuck her shapely bosom out for Charlie to study while she bent over him to hand out the menus.

Raymond studied her chest too, his eyes squinting to see better. Her attention on Charlie, the blonde didn't notice.

Charlie accepted the menu with a broader smile. 'Thank you.' He gave the two simple words a spin of hidden meaning. 'So, uh, what's fresh today?'

'That would be me,' the girl answered with a giggle, and her blue eyes sparkled.

'Uh-huh,' Charlie's eyes travelled up and down the girl's slender body, and he asked with a wicked grin, 'In fact, we were wondering what's exciting around here? After dark?'

'Sally Dibbs,' said Raymond suddenly. He was reading the waitress's name off the little plastic nameplate pinned to her chest over the handkerchief pocket. 'Four-six-one-oh-one-nine-two.'

The girl's eyes widened in amazement, and she stared at Raymond in disbelief. 'How . . . how could you know my phone number?' she stammered.

Charlie looked in astonishment from Sally to Raymond. What the hell? Catching his look, Raymond tensed up, certain he'd done something wrong. His eyes fell to his lap.

'The telephone book,' he mumbled to Charlie. 'You said read it.'

The waitress's fluffy blonde head was turning from Charlie to Raymond, from Raymond to Charlie, not knowing what to think. Charlie uttered a laugh that he hoped was light.

'He . . . uh . . . he remembers things.'

'I'll be right back,' the waitress told them nervously and fled with a hurried shake of the apron bow tied over her behind. That little man was definitely *weird*.

And now Charlie Babbitt was remembering things. 'Remarkable abilities', Dr Bruner had said about Raymond. And 'autistic savant'. Back in Wallbrook, when Raymond had displayed his phenomenal memory over Shakespeare's *Twelfth Night*, Charlie had dismissed it as cute. Freakish, maybe, but useless. But that was Shakespeare.

This was different. This was numbers. Memorizing numbers could be useful, very useful. Numbers had potential. Charlie lit up a Lucky and took a long, deep, thoughtful drag, his eyes sizing up Raymond, seeing him in a new light. A light with potential.

'How could you do that?'

'I do it,' Raymond answered softly. He was still afraid, still thinking that his brother was angry at him, that he'd done something really wrong. He couldn't meet Charlie's gaze, his eyes shifting from the saltshaker to the silverware, anywhere but Charlie's face.

And Charlie understood that. For the first time he had an inkling of what might be going on in Raymond Babbitt's head. He spoke gently, approvingly.

'That was good. I liked that. Did you memorize the whole phone book?'

'No,' said Raymond, which Charlie recognized as Raymond's way of saying yes. Charlie was making progress here. He treated his brother to a big smile. Raymond grimaced back in that travesty of a smile that Charlie had taught him. You do it to me, I do it to you. The panic was over. He'd been forgiven.

'Hungry?' asked Charlie, opening the menu.

Raymond nodded.

'What do you want?'

Want? 'Want' was in the category of 'like' or 'dislike'. It implied choice, preference. Preference is a category that holds no meaning for an autistic. Raymond didn't know how to *want* consciously; the mechanism just wasn't there. The only things he ever 'wanted' were things necessary to his immediate survival, as building blocks for the walls of his defences, like his TV programmes or his bed positioned just so, but he could never conceive of, or express, these things as 'wants'. Without an answer in his complex but limited arsenal of weapons, he could only sit dumb.

'Ray,' said Charlie patiently. 'What do you want?' He still had a lot to learn.

'This is Tuesday,' recited Raymond, calling on his

memory of his old Wallbrook routine. 'Breakfast is pancakes . . . with maple syrup.'

'Bet your butt,' laughed Charlie.

Raymond liked the sound of that. 'Bet your butt,' he echoed. A fear came at him suddenly, washing over him, and he looked around the table, his features starting to crumple. 'They took . . . they took the toothpicks,' he panicked.

'Look, that was okay in the motel. With the pizza. But in a restaurant you eat with a fork.' Charlie's lecture on table manners went unheeded.

'They took the toothpicks,' Raymond said again, and it was evident that another crisis was on its way. Charlie moved fast to avert it.

'You don't need toothpicks for pancakes,' he insisted. 'They keep sliding off.'

But Raymond wasn't easily diverted from crisis. He changed his tack. 'I do *not* have my maple syrup,' he announced in his nasal monotone.

'Relax,' replied Charlie. 'You don't see any pancakes yet, do you?'

He hadn't yet learned that ordinary logic was always the incorrect approach, that Raymond operated on an extraordinary logic of his own. 'The . . . the *promised* maple syrup . . . is . . .' Raymond began to stammer, starting one of his paranoid monologues.

Charlie was beginning to lose his cool. 'We haven't fucking *ordered* yet,' he snapped. 'You weirded out the waitress.'

''Course, we're gonna be here the *entire* morning, with *no* maple syrup and *no* –'

Something snapped in Charlie. This was slick Charlie Babbitt here, and he was about to be humiliated in a fucking diner, for chrissakes! He was trapped in Cincinnati with this crazy he couldn't get through to, and all the while the meter was running up a tab on his life. Susanna had walked out on him; he didn't have a dime; his life in LA was swirling down the old toilet bowl, and for all he knew Dr Bruner didn't *want* Raymond back.

Suddenly he hated his brother, really hated him, resenting him for everything that was going wrong in his own life, for the sweet, secure berth he perceived as Raymond's, where everybody was responsible for him, and he wasn't responsible for anything. Especially he hated him because their father had left him three million dollars and Charlie nothing. His father had said no to him, had always said no, but in the end he'd said yes to a mental case. He'd given his money to an idiot who didn't even know the meaning of the word money, just to keep it out of Charlie's hands.

Reaching across the table, Charlie grabbed Raymond's arm savagely, squeezing hard, speaking in a low, harsh voice only for Raymond's ears.

'People are watching, okay? Like you're some goddamn retard! Now . . . shut . . . the . . . fuck . . . up!'

Instantly, Raymond stopped speaking. Satisfied, Charlie let go of his brother's arm, and Raymond began to rub at it furiously, glaring at Charlie. He dug into his backpack and pulled out a red notebook, one that Charlie hadn't seen before, and began to scribble, scribble, scribble, his eyes darting angrily from the notebook to Charlie.

'Not getting maple syrup is *not* an ominous event,' Charlie said sarcastically. Sarcasm was lost on Raymond.

'This is . . . Serious Injury List. July 15, 1988. Charlie Babbitt. Squeezed and burned and hurt my arm. . . .'

A stab of guilt passed through Charlie, making him angrier than before, but he fought it back, reaching for the red notebook. 'Lemme see that.'

Over Raymond's dead body. He pulled away, moving the book to the other side of the table, shielding the precious thing from Charlie's grasp and his prying eyes.

'All right, forget it! Ha!' And Charlie took one of Raymond's devices for his own. '*Ha! Ha! Ha!*' he challenged.

Raymond wasn't to be deterred. He had already retreated and shut the world out; he was alone with the Serious Injury List. He kept his head down and his nose in his notebook, continuing to write, holding his arm wrapped around the little book so that Charlie Babbitt couldn't see the magical words.

''Course, you're number eighteen. Serious Injury List. In 1988.'

It was past nine thirty and on the way to ten in the morning. Dr Bruner must be at his desk by now. Charlie went to the wall pay-phone with a heavy handful of change. Behind him, at the table, Raymond sat eating tiny squares of pancakes speared on toothpicks. It was taking him for ever. Charlie was right after all; pancakes *do* slide off toothpicks.

As Charlie punched the phone number of the hospital on the touchtone panel, he kept Raymond in his line of sight. He was feeling a pang of uncharacteristic nervousness. His mouth was dry, and his hands a little sweaty. For ten years, ever since he'd left home at the age of sixteen and gone out on his own, Charlie Babbitt had taken care of himself. And he hadn't done such a bad job of it either. Sure, he might have done a lot of things he wasn't crazy about, but survival was the name of the game. And he'd survived. More than survived.

But Charlie Babbitt had never done anything like this before. Susanna's stinging words kept buzzing around in his head like a swarm of unwelcome bees. *Kidnap. Respect. Using everybody.* He felt distinctly uncomfortable. Kidnapping is a federal offence, punishable by imprisonment for life. Can a person kidnap a brother?

The phone on the other end of the line rang a few times and was picked up. A woman's voice answered, and Charlie asked for Dr Bruner. After a few seconds, he heard a familiar voice.

'Dr Bruner here.'

'Dr Bruner, this is Charlie Babbitt.'

There was a second's pause, and then the voice asked calmly, 'Where are you, son?'

'That's not important,' said Charlie tersely. 'What matters is who I'm with.'

He glanced over at Raymond again. His brother had just dropped his toothpick on the floor, and the greasy little piece of wood rolled under the table. Raymond bent down to look after it longingly.

'You have to bring him back, Mr Babbitt,' said the psychiatrist.

'Yeah. No problem,' Charlie answered agreeably. 'Soon as I get what's coming to me.'

'And what would that be?'

At the table Raymond had made his decision. He climbed slowly off the chair, got to his knees and went searching for the precious toothpick.

'That would be one point five million dollars, sir. I'm not greedy. All I want is my half. Ray can start a collection of solid-gold toothpicks.'

'I can't do that, Mr Babbitt. You know I can't.'

Raymond emerged from under the table clutching his

dusty prize, a toothpick covered in syrup, butter and indescribably mucky fuzz from the diner floor. He looked as happy as Raymond could ever look.

'You can't use that, Ray!' Charlie called urgently. 'It's dirty!'

'Just bring him back, Mr Babbitt.' Dr Bruner's voice went from gentle and patient to authoritative. 'Bring him back now.'

This was going to be harder than Charlie had thought. 'Look, it's not like this is a kidnapping here,' said Charlie, holding his breath.

Raymond looked miserably across to his brother, holding on tightly to the prized toothpick, needing it desperately to keep from starving to death but also needing Charlie's approval. Charlie shook his head. No way.

'I know that,' Dr Bruner responded. 'He's always been a voluntary patient here.' Charlie felt relief surging through him as the threat of life in prison evaporated. 'But that's beside the point,' the psychiatrist continued. 'The fact of the matter is that this is where he can best be cared for. We know what his needs are; you don't.'

This wasn't going as well as Charlie had hoped. He lost his patience, and his voice rose angrily. 'Let's just cut through the bullshit here. I am entitled to part of my father's estate,' he told the psychiatrist coldly. 'If you don't want to cut a decent deal with me, I'll take Raymond back to Los Angeles. I'll stick him in some kind of institution out there, and we'll have a custody battle over him.'

Sadly Raymond let the dirty toothpick droop in his fingers. Charlie had forbidden him to keep it. But he couldn't just let it go or he'd starve. He wandered off in search of more, shuffling over to the waitress station behind the counter. He held out the toothpick hopefully, asking silently for another one, but nobody paid any attention to him, so he began to rummage around, trying to find them for himself.

'I'm his only living relative,' Charlie went on crisply into the telephone, with one anxious eye on Raymond who, he could see, was about to embarrass him in public again. 'Now do you want to fight me in the courts, or can we put an end to this right now?'

Everybody in the diner was staring at Raymond now, but nobody dared to approach him. Sally, the waitress, was holding a hand in front of her face to stifle the giggles. That infuriated Charlie for some reason. Who the hell was she to laugh at Raymond Babbitt?

'It's not your money, Mr Babbitt,' Dr Bruner was saying, but Charlie was distracted by the crisis brewing in the diner. He yelled out, '*Toothpicks!* He needs more toothpicks.'

'I cannot do that, Mr Babbitt,' the psychiatrist went on firmly. 'I cannot do that.'

Now Sally handed Raymond a full box of toothpicks. Clutching them tightly to his chest, he shuffled back to his table to finish the pancakes.

'Then I'll see you in court!' snarled Charlie, slamming down the phone. He was pissed as hell as he marched back to the table, where Raymond was spearing little squares of pancake with toothpicks from the box. 'C'mon, let's go,' he ordered, gesturing for Raymond to stand. The tone of his voice brooked no opposition.

Raymond stood up awkwardly, knocking the box of toothpicks off the table to the floor. The box flew open, and there were toothpicks scattered everywhere.

'Shit!' exploded Charlie.

But Raymond was looking down at the toothpicks on

the floor. 'Eighty-two,' he said quietly. 'Eighty-two, eighty-two, eighty-two.'

'What does *that* mean?' demanded Charlie.

'Toothpicks,' said Raymond.

Charlie shook his head impatiently. 'Ray, there's way more than eighty-two toothpicks down there.'

Raymond's expression didn't change; it remained at nil. 'Eighty-two, eighty-two, eighty-two. 'Course, that's two hundred and forty-six total. Toothpicks.'

Gaping, Charlie looked down at the floor. Two hundred and forty-six. He turned to Sally Dibbs. 'How many toothpicks in a box?'

The girl picked up the toothpick box and read the figure off it. 'Two hundred and fifty.'

Charlie grinned at Raymond. 'Close enough. C'mon, let's go. We've got ground to cover and time's wastin'.'

As they walked to the door, Sally Dibbs called after them.

'Hey! There's four left in the box!'

All the way to the Cincinnati airport Raymond sat beside Charlie in the front seat of the '49 Buick, watching the scenery but muttering his loony litany under his breath. The call letters of the radio station they were listening to on the car radio. Over and over, over and over, the magic incantation to protect him from harm. Charlie was too glum to break the spell. Let the damn autistic savant, or whatever the hell he was, mutter and mumble all he wanted to. Charlie Babbitt had problems of his own.

Back in Los Angeles the Lamborghini deal was still hanging fire. Charlie had lost precious time here; God alone knew what had gone wrong while he was away. As soon as they had left the convertible in the airport parking lot, Charlie parked Raymond too. Throwing quarters into the snack-vending machine, Charlie pulled out packages of Fritos, Cheez Doodles and potato chips. He pushed Raymond into one of the little chairs in the departure lounge, the ones with the mini television sets on the chair arms, and left him to snack and watch closed-circuit programmes and double-length commercials while he put in a call to Babbitt Collectibles.

Using his telephone credit card, Charlie got Lenny Barish on the phone to learn just how bad things had become in only two business days. A lot worse, evidently. Hearing Charlie's voice, Lenny nearly whimpered with gratitude. He'd been holding the fort alone, and the Apaches were getting mighty close. It was hard to circle only one wagon. Right after he heard Charlie Babbitt's voice saying hello, Lenny started pouring out the latest list of misfortunes and miseries.

'Right, mechanics don't work on Sunday,' Charlie put in with rich sarcasm. 'You tell him he *finds* those nozzles. He finds 'em *today*. Or I rip his bladder out through his belly button!'

He listened to fifteen seconds more of Lenny's whining, while his hazel eyes scanned the lounge for Raymond. There he was, still in his chair, watching television and munching on salty, fat-rich snacks.

'Lenny, the loan guy is not the problem. Wyatt can't find the cars to take them. Once we locate the nozzles, everybody cools out, even –' Lenny's voice babbled in his ear again, moaning about the buyers, who were on his back without mercy. 'Lenny, you *can't* let them walk,' argued Charlie. 'If they back out, how do I pay Wyatt? And how can I give these guys back their downs, huh? That money's in *Milan*, Len.'

More complaining from Lenny Barish, and Charlie

rested his forehead against the metal of the phone-booth panel to cool his brow. Silently he pounded the panel with a frustrated fist. Christ! Didn't anybody know how to think any more? To simply use his head?

'You have to *sell*, that's how!' he barked into the phone. 'You think! You talk! You beg!' A pulsing headache moved from the back of his skull to the area around Charlie's eyes, and he winced with the pain as he came to a decision.

'Tell them they each get ten off the back end,' he said at last. 'That's half our profits. Tell them it's *all* our profits, understand?' Charlie looked at his watch. Almost take-off time. 'Listen, I'll be in LAX in three hours. I'll call 'em then. Yeah, from the airport, I promise. Right. Right. Hang in there, kid. Don't lose it.'

He hung up the phone and checked his Rolex again. Less than ten minutes to get to the plane. And Raymond moved slowly. If you hurried him, he stopped moving at all. Loping over to where his brother was sitting, glued to the mini-TV, Charlie asked, 'So, how was Wapner? Who won?'

Raymond didn't look away from the screen. 'The plaintiff. Damages in the amount of three hundred and ninety-seven dollars. And court costs.'

'Great,' said Charlie with false heartiness. 'I liked his face.'

Now Raymond looked up, puzzled and suspicious. '"He" was a girl. He was Ramona Quiggly.'

'We've got six minutes,' said Charlie briskly. 'Let's hustle.' Grabbing up his bag, he led the way down the concourse to the departure gates with Raymond trotting behind him. Raymond's hands dangled awkwardly like paws; his head was tilted to one side like a dog's.

Charlie was beginning to perceive that this head position of his brother's signalled a state of what Dr Bruner called 'not-fear'. It signified that things were okay with Raymond for now, although they could change to panic at any given moment by a sudden threat to Raymond's security.

As they changed right now.

The concourse was glassed in by windows looking out on the tarmac, so that departing passengers could share in the thrill of the jumbo jets and DC-10s taking off and landing. Charlie pointed to a jet standing just beyond the window and called over his shoulder to Raymond.

'That's our plane, the one over there. Beautiful, huh? You've never been on a –'

Something, some growing instinct, told Charlie to turn around. Raymond had stopped cold, staring through the glass at the jetliner. He had already begun that monotonous mumble that Charlie recognized as a sign that extreme fear was taking hold.

'Crash,' muttered Raymond. ''Course, that . . . that . . . plane . . . crash in August. August 16, 1987. One hundred and fifty-six people were . . . They were all . . .'

'That was a different plane, Ray,' Charlie put in hurriedly. 'This is a beautiful plane. This one is safe.'

'Crash,' Raymond said almost inaudibly. 'And burn.'

Christ! Why now? Why me? Charlie looked at his watch again. If they were extremely lucky and moved very quickly, they had four whole minutes before take-off.

'We have to fly home, Ray.' He spoke quickly, urgently, hoping to get his message across. 'It's important. What did you think we were doing here? See, this is an airport. This is where they keep the planes!'

But Raymond stood still, immobilized, staring out the window. He appeared to be paralysed, unable to take a step. Charlie thought fast.

'That crash. Was it the same airline as this one? The same name?'

'Same name,' answered Raymond.

'I never liked them,' agreed Charlie. He scanned the overhead monitor showing departures and arrivals, looking for another flight to Los Angeles. 'How 'bout . . . American at six fifty-thr—'

'Crash,' Raymond answered, fear almost tangible in his voice. He reached around behind him for his backpack, for the Ominous Events List notebook, proof positive, but Charlie held up a decisive hand to stop him.

'Spare me the notebook. I'll take your word on it.' Back to the monitor went Charlie to try for another flight. 'Maybe . . . Continental, huh?'

'Cra –'

'And burn, yeah. See, Ray, every airline has, like, one crash. But all the other planes are perfectly –' Charlie broke off, realizing that this was a futile endeavour, like trying to explain quantum physics to a golden retriever. He changed his tactics.

'Is there maybe one airline that never crashed?'

'Qantas,' said Raymond instantly.

Charlie uttered a frustrated bark of mirthless laughter. 'Out*stand*ing. We just go through fucking Australia!'

He'd had enough. He'd had all that he could stand. He heard that meter ticking on his life again, and he was standing here arguing logically with a lunatic. Beautiful! Raymond was going to get on that plane if Charlie had to lift him bodily and carry him there, kicking and screaming. Once off the ground, his brother would have no choice. With a headset, an in-flight movie, little bags of peanuts and yummy meals in plastic trays, Raymond might settle down for the three hours it would take to LAX.

'That's it! You're getting on the plane!' Charlie grabbed Raymond by the sleeve and began tugging him forward. At once Raymond went rigid, absolutely rigid, as though rigor mortis had set in. His head shook violently from side to side, the eyes rolling in his head, as all the alarm systems of his paranoia were triggered. It was his very existence that was threatened here. Crash and burn, crash and burn . . .

Raymond's appearance was so startling that Charlie let go and took a step backward. He recognized that his brother had already retreated far into his private world, a world where he couldn't be reached. No amount of cajoling or bags of Cheez Doodles would bring Raymond back now. The seconds were ticking away on Charlie's wrist, adding up to minutes. Soon they'd be adding up to hours. The situation called for desperate measures, forceful ones. He reached for Raymond again, taking his arm firmly and pulling at him.

'Ray, you are killing me here,' Charlie whispered harshly, through gritted teeth. 'My fucking life is coming unhinged. Now, *you get on that plane!*'

Raymond still kept shaking his head from side to side. No. No. No, no, nonononononono. His flesh was like stone, and he wouldn't move; he was rooted tightly to the spot. He had already begun the frantic whispering that characterized his panic. In desperation Charlie grabbed hold of his brother, locking him in a bear hug, trying to drag him off. Christ, he was heavy for so small and thin a person. A dead weight.

Twisting his body, Raymond managed to work one

hand free. He brought it up to his mouth and bit down fiercely on the back of it. Hard. Really biting, as though it weren't his own hand but that of a deadly enemy.

'Stop that, goddamn it!' yelled Charlie. 'STOP IT!' Seeing it made him feel sick. He'd never encountered any behaviour like this before in his life.

But Raymond wouldn't, or couldn't, listen. With all his strength he bit at his hand, all the while glaring ferociously at Charlie, as if it was Charlie he was biting, not himself. It was a terrible thing to have to watch. Frustrated beyond control, enraged to the point of violence, Charlie lost his temper completely. He raised his fist and brandished it at Raymond. But Raymond stood his ground, biting, glaring, biting. It was hopeless, an exercise in futility.

Sighing, Charlie lowered his fist. His shoulders slumped in defeat, and the fight went out of him. He was licked, and he knew it.

'Okay, it's okay,' he told his brother quietly. 'We'll drive, okay? We'll take the Buick and we'll drive. Raymond? Okay?'

Raymond didn't answer, but Charlie could sense a slight softening of his rigid body. The hand stayed in Raymond's mouth, but the gnawing appeared to have stopped.

Charlie drew a deep, ragged breath. 'I said it's okay,' he told his brother in a voice so low that only Raymond could hear it. 'No airplanes. I'm ... I'm ...' He hesitated. 'I'm sorry. All right? All right, Raymond?'

Very slowly the hand came down from Raymond's mouth, and the paranoia began to recede from his shoe-button eyes. The two brothers stared at each other for a long moment, then Charlie turned and began walking the other way, away from the departure gates. A second later Raymond came trotting after him, his head cocked at that doggie angle.

CHAPTER SEVEN

'Can I drive, Charlie Babbitt?' Going west on the highway, the sweet Buick convertible eating up the road. Charlie drove easily, one hand on the wheel, his elbow resting on the door, the wind whipping his thick, dark hair around his forehead, music on the car radio, feeling relaxed and not too shabby after all. The engine was in great driving shape; they were making good time; and Raymond had behaved himself pretty well so far. If Charlie didn't know better by now, he might even assume that his brother enjoyed riding in the car. Well, maybe the Buick, with its old memories and associations with Daddy, created a no-fear response in Raymond.

'You know how to drive?' Charlie looked over at Raymond, amused.

'No. Can I drive?' When Charlie didn't answer, Raymond's fingers reached out slowly, slowly, until the tips of them touched the steering wheel.

Charlie sat up straight and turned a scowling face to Raymond. 'Never, *never* touch the wheel!' he commanded. 'Or the gear box. This thing,' and he pointed it out to his brother. He waited for Raymond to start his whispering or his jerking, but Raymond merely subsided in his seat, his face, as usual, unreadable.

Driving to LA with Raymond, Charlie had plenty of

time to think, to formulate a plan. Now that he knew that kidnapping charges weren't hanging over his head, he could go on to the next step. And that was to call his lawyer in L A and outline the situation to him.

The news was good, almost better than he'd expected.

Obviously, Charlie's attorney explained, Raymond Babbitt was in no condition – and never would be – to take possession of three million dollars. Having him officially declared mentally unsound would be the easy part, what with Raymond's hospital record and diagnosis. Becoming his guardian was the next logical step because whoever got custody of Raymond would also get custody of the money. Amd who better to be Raymond Babbitt's official guardian and custodian than his loving brother Charles Babbitt?

So that was the objective of Charlie's scheme, to obtain official control of Raymond Babbitt. And all it required was a custody hearing at which a reputable psychiatrist would testify on Charlie Babbitt's side. Somebody who would document that Charlie was the right custodian for Raymond. That would be the hard part, but Charlie had boundless faith in his own abilities to manipulate.

A few miles outside Tulsa, Oklahoma, Charlie stopped at a gas station with a telephone booth and loaded his pockets with quarters. Not trusting Raymond alone with the Buick, he pulled his brother into the booth with him and shut the door behind them both.

With two bodies in the little glass phone booth it was pretty crowded, and a frightened look came into Raymond's eyes, but Charlie was too busy consulting the telephone directory to notice.

'Too small here,' said Raymond nervously.

Damn! No yellow pages, only white. Out of the corner of his eye Charlie saw Raymond's hand snake out and push the booth door open. Impatiently he slammed the door closed again.

'Too small here,' said Raymond again, and his body began to quiver.

'Just one little second, Ray,' called Charlie, distracted. He punched 555-1212 for Information. 'Hello, Tulsa Information? Do you have a listing of psychiatrists in your area?'

Now Raymond was struggling to get out of his backpack. The booth was such a tight squeeze that he was finding it difficult, and this was a new and terrifying experience for him. The backpack was supposed to go off and on, on and off.

'No, but this is an emergency,' Charlie said urgently into the telephone. 'I need to find the best psychiatrist in Tulsa.'

Now Raymond had the pack off and was rummaging around in it desperately, trying to keep it off the ground by cradling it between his body and the glass wall of the booth. Things kept falling out on to the floor of the booth, while he looked on in horror. Wrong. This was wrong. Not supposed to happen.

'Maybe the streets,' Charlie prompted the operator, unaware of his brother's rising panic. 'Can you look at the listing by streets and find something in the high-rent district?' Mustering all the sincerity he could, he aimed it straight into the phone, both barrels. 'I don't want to frighten you, ma'am, but you could be saving someone's life here.' *Yeah, mine.* 'Thank you so much . . .'

At last Raymond found what he'd been so desperately looking for, the blue notebook. At once he began to write in it.

'Schilling!' cried Charlie happily. 'Great name. Sounds like a doctor. Just a minute. Let me get a pencil.'

There was Raymond, conveniently using the very materials Charlie needed, pencil and paper. Reaching over, Charlie tore them from Raymond's disbelieving hands and used the book to jot down the doctor's phone number. Gasping, Raymond fought with Charlie to get his precious book back. But his brother simply turned his back on him as he wrote.

'Four-one-nine-three, is it? Got it. Thanks a million.'

He hung up the phone and, while Raymond watched in horror, he ripped the piece of paper bearing the doctor's phone number out of the book and stuffed it into his pocket, handing the wounded notebook back to his brother as though nothing had happened. Raymond's face looked as though pieces of his flesh were being ripped off, but Charlie took no notice.

Snatching the precious thing back, Raymond immediately began writing in it, glaring at Charlie. Scribble, glare, scribble, glare.

Charlie shook his head. 'Y'know, taking your notebook is not a Serious Injury.'

'That's the red book. This is *blue*.'

'Forgive me. I lost my secret decoder ring.' Charlie laughed. With the phone number safely in his pocket, he was feeling pretty chipper.

' 'Course, you're already number –' began Raymond balefully.

'Eighteen. I know.'

'In 1988,' Raymond finished.

Charlie turned back to the phone, pulling the doctor's number out of his pocket and throwing quarters down the slot.

'Too small here,' protested Raymond.

'Small and safe,' Charlie answered cheerfully, not picking up on the rising note of panic in his brother's voice. 'You could get hurt out there. And you don't want to miss the party . . .' He glanced over at Raymond, who was squinting at him with suspicion.

'That's right, there's a little party in your honour. Little custody hearing coming up. Our lawyer's getting it ready right now.' He put the receiver to his ear. Good: the line was ringing. 'You know why this party's for you?'

Raymond shook his head.

'Because you are the three-million-dollar man. And that –' The phone was picked up at the other end, and suddenly all of Charlie's concentration was on the call.

'Yes. Is Dr Schilling in, please? I'm calling long-distance. From Bummer, Missouri. It's an emergency.' Behind him Raymond's voice, suddenly filled with genuine panic.

'Oh! It's . . . it's . . .!'

Charlie turned. Raymond was staring at his watch, his eyes practically popping out of his head. He was so upset he couldn't speak, only gasp out strangled syllables that had no meaning. But now the voice on the other end of the phone claimed Charlie's attention. Whatever it was, Raymond would have to wait.

'Ma'am, we'll be in town at the end of the day.' Charlie spoke quickly, urgently. 'And we need a consultation. Desperately.'

Raymond's world had begun to fall apart. Here he was, trapped in a telephone booth with his brother who wouldn't listen to him. 'It's . . . it's *eleven*!' he moaned at last. 'It's eleven minutes to Judge Wapner's *People's Court*.' Raymond couldn't believe it. His watch told him eleven, and there was no television set in sight. Nothing but a few gas pumps, a vending machine for drinks and snacks, and this monstrous glass phone booth into which Charlie had locked him.

He began to bounce off the glass in his desperation. Moving in small circles, Raymond was like a little animal seeking a way out of a trap. Everywhere he looked, glass walls hemmed him in. Like a fox or a weasel, he'd chew his leg off if he had to.

Oh, Christ! Raymond was fucking losing his grip, and Charlie couldn't even get the fucking doctor on the phone! He was still dealing with the fucking receptionist, who held the power of fucking life and death over him. 'Well, couldn't he stay late for *one* extra appointment? Just today?' He put as much honey as he possessed into that wheedle.

Raymond was now babbling, his eyes wide in terror and only one thing on his mind. Wapner. He had to have Wapner. If he didn't, the whole thing would come tumbling down and he'd be lost. Wapner was one of the linchpins in the elaborate protective structure he'd constructed carefully over so many years. Wapner meant no-fear.

'*Eleven* minutes to Wapner and we have *no* television and it's gonna be . . . it's gonna be . . .' He didn't dare even give voice to the words 'too late'. Those two words might kill him.

'I know. I understand.' Charlie practically wept into the phone, watching Raymond going to pieces right in front of him, 'But he's a *doctor*! You can't imagine how needy this –'

'We're *locked* in this box. *Locked* in here for *good*. With *no* television . . . and it's . . . it's . . . it's . . .' Raymond's eyes rolled around in his head, and Charlie was afraid he'd pass out. Raymond was like a bird beating against the bars of its cage until its heart bursts in its little feathered chest.

'I'm begging you, okay?' implored Charlie. 'A man is *begging* you.'

'Oooh . . . Oooh . . .,' Raymond had begun to shriek.

'Okay,' Charlie decided in despair. '*You* talk to the patient.' He shoved the receiver into Raymond's face.

'OOOOOH!' screamed Raymond. 'It's gonna be a . . . It's gonna be a . . . OOOOHH!'

Charlie pulled the receiver back. 'Ma'am? Yes, I'll hold.' *Good job, Raymond.*

'And . . . they're not *actors* . . . They're real . . . real *litigants* . . . with cases filed in the . . .'

'Yes, ma'am, six o'clock. We won't be late. No, I promise, we won't be late. Not one minute. And God bless you.' Charlie hung up the phone, every muscle in his body trembling with relief. For the first time he looked fully at his brother. Raymond was skewered to the walls, entirely unhinged. He'd freaked out totally. He couldn't breathe.

'Ray,' said Charlie casually. 'Whattya say we . . . oh, go find a television set?'

Air exploded in Raymond's chest. He could only nod. Charlie reached over and slammed the door of the telephone booth open, grabbed Raymond by the arm and hustled him out of there, racing for the convertible.

' 'Course, now it's *ten* minites to Wapner.'

They were, needless to say, somewhere at the ass-end of nowhere on a really deserted stretch of nothing. This was farm country, and the houses stood acres apart, separated by fields of crops. Tall stands of alfalfa waved on either side of the road. Not a house in sight, not a motel or even a bar. Charlie kept his eyes open for telltale TV antennae on rooftops, but there weren't even any rooftops.

Raymond had begun his usual jittering, his eyes glued to the face of his watch, calling out the minutes as they ticked ominously by. Nine minutes to Wapner. Eight minutes to Wapner. His anxiety was contagious; Charlie was beginning to feel nervous himself as his eyes scanned both sides of the road.

At last a farmhouse. A real, live house, with lights on and everything. Better yet, a satellite dish in the side yard, which meant that this house picked up a lot of channels.

Saved. They were saved . . . almost. Charlie gunned the Buick through the gate of the picket fence and slammed on the brakes. They came to a stop right in front of the porch. But how to get into the house? By now Raymond appeared just about ready to self-destruct. Charlie could imagine him going up in a puff of lunatic smoke, all because he'd missed an episode of *People's Court*.

Thinking fast and furiously, Charlie led Raymond up to the front door.

' 'Course, now it's *four* minutes,' announced Raymond direly.

Charlie grabbed him by the shoulders, forcing his brother to look directly at him. 'You want to get in there to see the show?' he demanded.

It was a rhetorical question, and Raymond was too spooked to articulate an answer. Only his nodding head said yes; the rest of him twitched and ticked like a bomb ready to go off.

'Then you listen up,' Charlie told him urgently. 'There's not another farm in sight, okay? This is your only chance. If you play this weird, you don't get in. Are you listening?'

Raymond was listening. He had grasped enough of the concept to be more terrified than ever. 'You don't get in', 'Only chance' – these were perilous words.

'You stand there,' Charlie commanded, 'and you look *normal*! You know what normal is?'

Looking Raymond over swiftly with a sharp eye, Charlie unbuckled his brother's belt and pulled his trousers down from Raymond's armpits to his waist, like normal people's. He re-buckled the belt.

'And don't wear your pants up there!' he scolded. 'You're gonna nerd everybody out. Stand still! And keep your trap *shut*!' Opening his own mouth, Charlie snapped it shut to demonstrate. Raymond imitated him perfectly. Open. Shut. Got it.

It wasn't much, but it would have to do. Charlie Babbitt drew in his breath, plastered his Number Five Smile (sincere, friendly) all over his face and knocked on the door. Behind him he could hear Raymond bouncing up and down like a kid who has to go to the bathroom, and he gestured sharply for his brother to quit it.

The young housewife, with a runny-nosed baby riding on her hip and two more children hanging on to her legs, opened the door. She saw an incredibly handsome young man with a sincere smile and, behind him, an ordinary-looking man of about forty, normally dressed, wearing his trousers buckled normally around his normal waist.

'Good afternoon,' Charlie said politely, all business. 'I'm Donald Clemens, ma'am, with the A. C. Nielsen Company. You're familiar with our work?'

'Nielsen,' repeated the young woman. 'You mean the TV ratings people?'

'That's right.' Charlie nodded approvingly, awarding a gold star to a prize pupil. 'You've been selected as a preliminary candidate to become our next Nielsen Family in the tri-county area.'

The woman's eyes widened, but then her face fell. 'Well, my husband's not home,' she began doubtfully.

But Charlie was on a roll here. 'If selected,' he went on rapidly, 'you would share the responsibility for shaping the television programming viewed by the entire nation. In return for which your family would receive a cheque in the amount of two hundred and eighty-six dollars each month.'

Two hundred and eighty-six dollars? Charlie could see the struggle taking place in the woman's mind. However, he was running out of time. How long could Raymond possibly hold it together when the minutes to Wapner were dwindling to a precious few?

'Maybe when my husband –'

Charlie shook his head, cutting her off. 'This is our only swing through the area, ma'am,' he told her with crisp finality. 'If you're too busy to see us, we'll move on to other candidates.'

The woman bit her lip, torn. Two hundred and eighty-six dollars was a mighty tempting piece of money, especially with crops being so thin because of the drought. Still, when Dwayne came home, he'd be madder than hell that she let strangers into his house.

'All this visit requires,' Charlie said briskly, 'is that we examine your television receiver. And watch one designated programme for a brief period of time.'

'How brief?'

Behind him Charlie could hear ominous sounds coming from where Raymond was standing. 'Brief,' he said quickly.

'How brief?' she asked again.

The noises behind Charlie became louder. 'Thirty minutes. That's the requir –' The woman was looking over Charlie's shoulder now, trying to see what was going on behind him. Nimbly he moved to one side, blocking her view. He himself didn't know what the hell was going on back there, but he did know that, whatever it was, it wouldn't be normal.

'Who's he?' the housewife demanded.

Charlie didn't turn around; he didn't dare. He felt himself beginning to sweat. 'Uh, that would be my partner, Mr Bainbridge. He does the actual sample viewing.'

The expression on the woman's face was now curiosity mixed with a kind of horror, informing Charlie that something major was taking place behind his back.

'He's been doing this for, oh, I guess . . .' He broke off lamely, realizing that he'd lost it. The woman's eyes were glued to Raymond, following his every move with fascinated disbelief. Sighing, Charlie reluctantly turned around.

Star pitcher Raymond Babbitt was on the mound again, lost in some imaginary World Series that would shield him from the terrible reality of ninety seconds to Wapner and no TV. He was winding up with those jerky, uncoordinated movements of his, and his eyes were darting from base to base, checking the runners. It was three and two on the batter again.

'Full count,' he uttered.

Charlie watched helplessly as Raymond went through his awful wind-up and delivered the pitch with a little skip and a clumsy hop. Shit! He turned back to the door, only to find that it had closed in his face. And he certainly couldn't blame her. He'd do the same thing himself, faced with a lunatic like Raymond Babbitt pitching baseball on his front porch. Oddly enough, he felt disappointment along with his impatience – disappointment for Raymond's incalculable loss. And the unfamiliar and uncomfortable stab of disappointment made him madder yet.

'That's it! Game's over! Rain-out!' Charlie yelled at Raymond angrily. 'You don't get to see the programme.'

Raymond's dull eyes began to roll in their sockets as he danced from foot to foot. He couldn't believe what Charlie was telling him. No Wapner? It was the end of the world! No, impossible. He pointed to his wristwatch.

' 'Course, it's . . . it's . . .'

'One minute to Wapner,' Charlie confirmed. 'And you blew it. You did it to yourself, pal! I had you in there. You were in there. You were eating popcorn on her rug. Defendants, plaintiffs, you had it all. They're making legal history in there, but you're on the outside looking in. Just a putz with his nose pressed up against the glass because –'

But Raymond couldn't hear him. All he understood was that Wapner wasn't happening, wasn't going to happen, and he went totally out of control, a terrified animal scurrying into a hiding place so far inside his head that nothing could reach him. He continued to babble, but the words made no sense, not even to Raymond himself.

'It's . . . gonna . . . be . . . It's gonna . . . be . . . It's . . . *gonna be a* . . .'

Stammering to break through, with no way to express the horror of it all, no words to tell Charlie his world was being destroyed and himself along with it, Raymond held out his arms stiffly and clapped his hands. Once, twice, like a demented seal. He clapped and clapped, unable to stop.

Charlie knew he had to do something, and fast. His brother was going to pieces right in front of his eyes, fragmenting into jagged shards of frenzy. He turned to the door and knocked on it. It opened right away; the woman had obviously stayed pressed to the other side of it, watching Raymond through the glass panes.

'I lied to you, ma'am,' Charlie said quickly. 'And I'm sorry about that. That man . . . That man, uh, he's my brother.'

The woman looked from the insane seal to the handsome boy in front of her. 'Your brother,' she echoed dubiously.

Charlie nodded. 'And if he doesn't get to watch *People's Court* in about thirty seconds, he's going to throw . . . well, a fit. Right here on your porch. Now you can help me, or you can stand there and let it happen.'

The woman thought it over a second. 'We like *Wheel of Fortune*,' she said finally. 'Think he'd settle for that?'

And in fifteen seconds Raymond Babbitt was sitting, as promised, on the rug in front of the television set, and there was Judge Wapner presiding, dispensing justice impartially to real litigants, and the world was coming back together again. And the hell with *Wheel of Fortune*.

Charlie breathed a deep and audible sigh of relief; the disaster had been averted, and he'd learned, first-hand, a mighty valuable lesson. Never, *never*, NEVER let Raymond Babbitt get further away than a sixty-second walk from a working television set during the fifteen minutes before *People's Court* went on the air. Not unless Charlie wanted to see his brother go off again like a hydrogen bomb.

While Raymond Babbitt sat cosily in front of the TV, munching on pretzel sticks (the family had no popcorn) and raptly watching Wapner, and while the mother – whose name, it turned out, was Eve – and her three children sat on the sofa and chairs, just as raptly watching Raymond watching Wapner and jotting down careful notes in his little green notebook, Charlie Babbitt went into the kitchen to take care of business.

He'd been expected in Los Angeles within three hours of his last phone call, but that was two days ago, and he was still only in Oklahoma. Alone Charlie could have made much better time. But Raymond needed more pit stops than a four-year-old, what with potty, snacks, meals and frequent TV. Now Charlie was out of touch with LA. The most important man to reach was Eldorf, his mechanic. The creditors could wait. Lenny Barish would simply have to stall them off a little longer. As for Susanna – well, that still hurt too much. Charlie tabled her in his mind, filing her away for when he could better deal with her.

Using the housewife's kitchen phone, Charlie dialled Eldorf's number and gnawed nervously at his thumbnail while waiting for the mechanic to answer. When Eldorf picked up the phone, the news was bad. No fuel adaptors for the Lamborghinis; they hadn't located any yet.

'Look, it's a stinking nozzle!' yelled Charlie into the phone, pacing the kitchen floor. 'It's a hundred-dollar part! I've got more money than you've ever seen tied up in a . . .'

Eldorf's aggrieved excuses came chattering through the receiver.

Charlie sighed. This was getting him nowhere. He glanced at his Rolex. He and Raymond had only a little under thirty minutes before their appointment with Dr Schilling and a good half-hour drive ahead of them into Tulsa. If they were late, the psychiatrist might not wait for them. And it was vital that Charlie consult this doctor because right now his own lawyer in LA was taking steps to set up a custody hearing for Raymond Babbitt.

'So, you call Information, okay? Every goddamn mechanic in the US and Canada if you have to. Offer them whatever it takes. *Somebody* has to have a part.' Shit! He should have shipped those cars to Oregon for registration weeks ago, when he had the chance. Now he was cooked.

But not as cooked as he was going to be if he was late for this appointment with Schilling. From the TV set in the living room Charlie could hear Judge Wapner presenting his decision on the last of the three cases on today's docket.

'. . . and, accordingly, find for the plaintiff in the full amount claimed, four hundred and fifty-nine dollars.' The sound of the gavel was music to Charlie's ears.

Great. The damn show was finally over, and not a minute too soon. Now they could go. Charlie uttered one last threat into the telephone. 'Do it. Or I'll kill you.' Then he hung up hurriedly and almost ran into the living room.

'I used my phone card, okay?' he lied to Eve. By the time she got her telephone bill, Charlie Babbitt would be not only far away and long gone but living happily ever after on Daddy's millions.

'Great decision,' he told Raymond heartily. 'Thanks, Eve. Thanks, kids. Come on, Ray, let's hit the –'

' 'Course,' said Raymond instantly, 'after a word of interest to all, we'll be interviewing today's litigants.'

Charlie shook his head, no. 'It's over, Ray. She won. Her bunnies died. The guy was scum. He's paying for it. It's over.'

Raymond just looked up at Charlie with cold blankness, but Charlie knew that look by now. It was pregnant with sinister meaning.

'We're late for Tulsa, Ray,' Charlie said hurriedly. 'The doctor won't wait. And it's real import –'

'We're gonna . . . gonna ask the litigants . . . to . . . comment –'

Charlie heard the dim rumble of an underground volcano, and he shut his eyes at the awful memory of the burning, molten lava. 'Ray,' he begged desperately, 'I got you here. You saw the show. I'm asking one little favour. One . . . compromise. Skip the tag and . . .'

'Comment on . . . today's proceedings,' Raymond finished, with a sharp squint from his shoe-button eyes. Charlie heard the volcanic rumblings getting louder, closer. He could feel the heat beginning to rise from underground.

'Sure,' he said coldly, hating Raymond at that moment as much as he'd ever hated anybody. He was helpless and he knew it. And right then Charlie believed that somehow Raymond knew it too. 'Take your time.'

Raymond sat back to give all his attention to the commercials. He put another pretzel stick into his mouth and bit down on it with a satisfied crunch.

It took Charlie twenty-two pedal-to-the-metal minutes to do the thirty-five-mile drive; thank God the highway patrol was cooping somewhere else tonight or the Buick would have had Smokey on her sky-blue tail all the way into Tulsa. Drawing up in front of the medical block in which Dr Schilling had his office, Charlie slammed on the brakes and leaped out of the car. Running around to the passenger's side, he yanked the door open and pulled Raymond out.

'Doc's across the street. Now move it!'

Raymond began to shuffle across the street with his usual slow gait when Charlie halted him.

'Stop, Ray. Come here.' Going up to Raymond, Charlie unbuckled his brother's belt and pulled his trousers way up, buckling them high in the way Raymond always wore them.

'That's much better. Now, let's get going.'

CHAPTER EIGHT

Dr Schilling was still waiting for them; it was only three minutes after six – nobody could call that really late. Charlie and the doctor introduced themselves and shook hands, while Raymond toddled around the office, examining everything with his customary blankness. God alone knew what he was registering, filing away in that unfathomable mind. When he got to the large glass tank of Siamese fighting fish, Raymond stopped, pulled a notebook from his backpack, a black-covered one this time, and settled himself down next to the tank to watch the fish and record their movements.

'He's my brother,' said Charlie. 'He's autistic.' He almost said 'an autistic savant', but something – he wasn't sure what – made him withdraw the word 'savant' before it was uttered. He didn't really know much about that side of his brother, about his abilities, apart from what he'd seen of Raymond's total recall, but he sensed that his brother's savantism would interest Dr Schilling more than Charlie wanted him to be interested. All he had was a couple of questions he wanted answered, and then they would be out of there. Charlie didn't have time to stick around Tulsa while Raymond went through some weird scientific tests with electrodes on his head.

But he told the psychiatrist what he knew of Raymond

– his freak-outs, when he pitched baseball, the notes he was always scribbling into different notebooks, the way he ate cut-up little pieces of food with toothpicks, the rigor mortis and the panicked whispering, and how Raymond couldn't deal with the possibility of missing *People's Court*.

Distinguished, neatly barbered and very well dressed, Dr Schilling had the look of a professional man. And yet there was something about his eyes that Charlie didn't trust, and his voice was too smooth.

'Raymond. You like the fish?' the doctor called over.

'Pitiful,' said Raymond, still scribbling.

'Ray –'

But the psychiatrist cut Charlie off with a rapid gesture. Let Raymond say whatever he wanted to. Whatever came into his head. What else were they there for?

'And how can I help you?' Dr Schilling's words were addressed to Charlie, but his gaze was directed at Raymond.

Charlie's eyes narrowed as he thought a moment. How much did he have to tell this man? More than he wanted to, he decided.

'My lawyer says that the whole custody thing – conservatorship, he called it – it ... well, it all comes down to what some psychiatrist ... recommends to the court.' Charlie tried to sound like a Babe in the Woods, young and charming, innocent and harmless.

Understanding at once, Schilling nodded. This was hardly a case of brotherly love. Money was involved here, possibly a great deal of money. 'So?'

'So I'm paying you. For a consultation.'

'Consultation,' repeated the psychiatrist with a deliberately blank stare.

'Yeah,' nodded Charlie, determined to get through to the man if it killed him. 'Just tell me what the shrink, uh, doctor will ask him.'

Dr Schilling smiled and shrugged his shoulders. 'How the hell would I know?'

'What would *you* ask him?' persisted Charlie.

'Does he like the fish?'

'And what did that tell you?' demanded Charlie.

'They're pitiful. Look, there are no answers here, Mr Babbitt. What do you want me to tell you?'

Charlie drew a deep breath and let it out. He put his cards flatly on the table. 'How to win.'

'You believe in miracles, son?' the psychiatrist asked softly. It was not what Charlie Babbitt wanted to hear.

'Look, this hour's expensive. And it's going by.'

Dr Schilling nodded and smiled, neither a friendly smile nor a warm one. 'Well, your brother has all these . . . anxious behaviours. Like that thing you're doing to your nail.'

Instantly Charlie pulled his thumb out of his mouth; he'd been gnawing at this thumbnail again. He felt really stupid about having been caught at it. It completely destroyed the cool image he always wanted to project.

'The note-taking, the baseball pitching, all the rituals, They protect him from his fears.'

'I know that,' Charlie said impatiently. 'What's your point?'

'Only that if he did less of this ritual behaviour, then the doctor might find him less fearful. And decide that –'

'I was a good influence on him,' interrupted Charlie thoughtfully, his eyes narrowing as he considered Schilling's point.

Dr Schilling nodded again. 'You'd like to establish that he's healthier, happier, out of the institution. And with you.'

'So, just get him to quit some of this stuff, huh?' It sounded simple enough to Charlie.

The psychiatrist's smile widened caustically. 'And if you can do that,' he said, 'with even one of Raymond's behaviours in only a couple of days, I'll back you for a Nobel Prize.'

Charlie bristled but decided to let the doctor's sarcasm roll off him; he didn't have time for it. 'Well. I'm gonna have a try.'

'You might start,' said Dr Schilling mildly, 'by putting some lead in his pencil.'

The sexual metaphor took Charlie Babbitt completely by surprise. Get Raymond laid? *Raymond?* Shocked, he looked over at Raymond. His brother was still concentrating totally on the tank of Siamese fighting fish, still scribbling away. But there were no marks on the page. His automatic pencil had run out of lead.

'You'll never guess what I thought you meant.' Charlie grinned at the psychiatrist.

But Dr Schilling did know. 'You mean sex?' he asked with a small, tight smile. 'That would be the neatest trick of all.'

On the long, weary drive between downtown Tulsa and the Texas motel at which they finally stopped – Highway 44 to Oklahoma City and then Highway 40 into Amarillo – Charlie's shrewd brain turned the problem over and over. Assignment: autistic Raymond – change a deeply ingrained behaviour pattern. Sounded easy on the surface, but how do you change something you don't understand? Although he'd had some graphic glimpses of *how* his brother reacted in certain situations and was beginning to recognize some of the situations that triggered Raymond's psychotic behaviour – the *when* of it – Charlie hadn't the foggiest notion of *why* Raymond functioned the way he did.

He went over in his head what Dr Bruner had told him back at Wallbrook. No connection. You couldn't get through to Raymond because there was no reaching him. The mechanism for forging connections, let alone relationships, was just not there in Raymond Babbitt's case. Charlie was just beginning to comprehend what Bruner had meant. And if you couldn't even connect with the guy, how in hell were you supposed to change him?

It had been a long, wearying day, even for Raymond, who took frequent little catnaps during the drive and who never seemed to be tired. Even Raymond was willing to turn off the T V set before the late movie and get ready for bed. He was in the motel bathroom brushing his teeth when Charlie came in to take his bath in the big, old metal tub, the motel being too cheap to provide a shower.

Raymond had used almost half a tube of toothpaste and was foaming at the mouth like a rabid dog. He was brushing, brushing, brushing away, while toothpaste was everywhere – his face, his ears, even his eyebrows, wore a white film of paste. The handle of the toothbrush was covered in toothpaste, as was the basin; there were disgusting gobbets of paste on the bathroom floor near Raymond's feet. Raymond was staring into the mirror over the basin, evidently enjoying the sight of all that bubbling dentifrice foam.

'Ray,' protested Charlie, his stomach turning.

But Raymond paid no attention. He squeezed even

more toothpaste on to his brush and began to brush harder than ever, creating more foam.

'You like to brush your teeth,' Charlie remarked, shaking his head.

No answer. Raymond went on brushing compulsively, obsessively. The sight unnerved Charlie; it was more than he could stand after a long, rough day, On top of that greasy hamburger he'd eaten an hour ago at a diner, the sight of all that goop was making him physically sick.

'Stop that, will ya?' he demanded, running out of patience. 'You look like a nutball. If the shrink in California saw that, he'd lock you up and throw away the key.'

Raymond only brushed harder.

'I said stop it, Ray!' yelled Charlie angrily. 'And I mean it!'

Raymond didn't stop, but he mumbled through the foam, and Charlie caught the words. 'You like it, Charlie Babbitt.'

'The hell I do!'

'You say, "Funny Rain Man . . . funny teeth."'

Charlie froze. Had he heard his brother right? *Funny Rain Man . . . funny teeth.* Rain Man? 'What'd you say?' he demanded, looking hard at Raymond.

'Funny,' mumbled Raymond through a mass of tooth-paste.

'Yeah, funny what?'

'Funny teeth.'

'No,' Charlie said firmly. 'The other thing. Before that.'

But Raymond's attention was now focused on his own teeth; he was watching himself in the mirror again, brushing and making foam, making foam and brushing,

Charlie went over to the basin and unwrapped one of the two 'sanitary' glasses provided by the motel. He filled it with water and held it out to Raymond.

'Here.'

Raymond stared at it blankly, as though he'd never seen a glass of water in his life.

'Rinse!' commanded Charlie. 'And spit.' Thrusting the glass into Raymond's hand, he took away the ghastly paste-covered toothbrush. Raymond stood holding the alien glass as though it might go off in his hand.

'*Now!*' Charlie barked.

Taking a hurried sip of the water, Raymond swallowed hard, then looked at Charlie for approval. Not knowing whether to laugh or cry, Charlie merely shrugged. It was better than nothing. Raymond sipped and swallowed again. His mouth was now fairly clear of toothpaste, although it was still smeared all over his face.

His hazel eyes serious, Charlie took the glass away and set it down gently on the basin. He didn't want to spook Raymond, not now.

'I like it . . . when you brush your teeth,' he prompted. 'I say . . .'

But Raymond didn't pick up the cue. He said nothing.

'"Funny Raymond,"' said Charlie in a near-whisper, his eyes intent on his brother's face.

'You can't say Raymond,' his brother said matter-of-factly. 'You're a baby. You say Rain Man. "Funny Rain Man."'

A rush of memory flooded through Charlie Babbitt's veins, the memory not of events but of feelings, long-ago lost feelings. Feelings of love and comfort such as he hadn't felt in more than twenty years. He just stood there in the bathroom, stunned. Stunned as though he'd been poleaxed.

'You . . . you're the Rain Man?' he managed to gasp at last. Charlie didn't know what to think. The Rain Man wasn't real. He was little Charlie Babbitt's imaginary friend.

Reaching into his pocket, Raymond pulled out his wallet. It was the handmade kind that is often manufactured in long hours of occupational therapy. Two pieces of pressed plastic, the outer one embossed to look like leather, both pieces pre-punched with little holes for the vinyl lacing to be woven through by clumsy hands. With careful, careful fingers, Raymond drew out of this wallet his most prized possession and handed it reverently to Charlie.

Charlie took the photograph and stared at it. It was creased and worn at the edges, as though it had been handled over and over again for years. As it had. The photograph showed a young man of about eighteen, dark-eyed and solemn-faced, his hair brushed neatly. He was staring at the camera, unblinking. Charlie recognized him.

In the boy's lap was a pouting toddler clutching a blanket. The baby was cuddled close to the young man. There was no doubt about it. The baby was Charlie Babbitt; the young man, Raymond Babbitt. Brothers.

'Daddy took the picture. By himself,' Raymond said proudly.

Charlie couldn't take his eyes off the photo; he was amazed almost beyond words. He and Raymond. Charlie and Raymond. Charlie and Rain Man.

'And you . . . lived with us? Then?'

'You lived with us then,' said Raymond. Was he only parroting Charlie, or did he know that he was the elder brother, with a rightful seniority? Sinking down on to the edge of the bathtub, Charlie continued to stare at the photograph, trying to put all this together in his head.

'When . . . when did you leave?' he asked at last in a low voice.

'It was Thursday,' Raymond said promptly.

Thursday? Charlie could only stare.

'It was snowing outside. I had cream of wheat for breakfast. You spat yours out. So Maria gave you bananas and milk. And she stayed with you when Daddy took me to my home. January twenty-first. Nineteen sixty-five. On a Thursday.'

'Jesus,' breathed Charlie softly. 'That's when Mom died. Just after New Year.'

'And you had the blanket. And you waved to me from the window. Bye-bye, Rain Man. Bye-bye, Rain Man. Bye-bye, Rain Man. Like that. Thursday.'

Somewhere deep in Charlie's memory an echo reverberated. He saw . . . he remembered . . . snow. And the necessary and comforting smell of the tattered old blanket. And waving. And, later, crying. Crying for Rain Man. He wanted Rain Man, only Rain Man didn't come. He never came again, so Charlie grew up imagining him imaginary.

Now Charlie looked at Raymond as if for the first time. And it *was* the first time. And he saw in his brother's face the ghost of an eighteen-year-old face, once precious and beloved, now absurdly smeared with toothpaste and devoid of expression.

'You used to wrap me,' Charlie whispered, remembering. 'In that blanket. And you sang to me.'

For a moment Raymond stared at Charlie as though he didn't know what his brother was talking about.

Blank. Then, very softly, he began to sing. Almost tune-fully.

'She was just seven-teen.
You know what I mean.
And the way she looked was way be-yond compare . . .'

'So how could I dance with another,' Charlie chimed in.

'Oooh,' sang Raymond in a shaky imitation of John Lennon's falsetto.

'When I saw her stand-ing there?' they finished, almost together.

The song was over. Charlie fell silent, still wrapped in astonishment. He looked at his brother, his autistic brother who'd been locked away for twenty-four years, his brother whom once he'd loved and needed with a baby's dependence and then forgotten and transformed into something imaginary.

'I used to like it. When you sang to me,' he told Raymond with quiet sincerity.

Raymond looked back, and for an instant Charlie believed that he'd broken through to him, that there was going to be a moment of genuine connection, but Raymond turned back to the basin, picked up his foamy toothbrush and squeezed some more toothpaste on it. If there had been a connection, it was broken now.

Charlie set the photograph down very gently on the edge of the bathtub and turned on the taps. He put the plug into the drainage hole, and the tub began to fill.

'No, no, no, no, no!' Raymond's voice was filled with fear, cracking with some unknown, unspeakable horror. Charlie looked up quickly. Raymond was staring down into the rising water of the bathtub, and his eyes were terrified. 'No! No!' he continued to cry out.

'Take it easy, Ray,' Charlie commanded. 'No what?'

'No because.' Raymond was wringing his hands together, and his body was jerking; Charlie recognized all the panic signals. He had to defuse Raymond before he went off.

'Because what?' Charlie demanded. 'Ray, tell me, because *what*?'

'Because ... because ... because ...,' babbled Raymond. Then in a different voice, with a harsher tone, he screamed out, '*What do you WANT?*'

And Raymond let out a loud shriek, a bone-chilling yell of anguish, and ran stumbling towards the bathtub, trying to stem the flow of water with his hands, in his panic ignoring the taps. Water squirted everywhere, splashing walls and ceiling, splashing Charlie, drenching Raymond.

For a moment Charlie stood paralysed, then he grabbed at Raymond and tried to drag him back bodily from the bathtub.

But Raymond was too strong for him. He pulled away and snatched Charlie by the shirt, holding him tightly. In his eyes was a fury that Charlie had never before seen there. And from Raymond's lips came a torrent of words in a voice that Charlie had never heard.

'No! No! It's scalding! It's burning him!'

Now Raymond's grip on Charlie was so ferocious that Charlie's shirt began to rip. He shook Charlie hard, again and again, until Charlie's head snapped back and forth. And all the while Raymond shouted in that different voice, that voice filled with loathing.

'I told you *never*! I told you *never*! What do you want? You want to kill your brother? I *told* you! I *told* you. I told you ... I told you ...'

The voice died away; the shaking stopped. Staring at Charlie, Raymond let go of his shirt very slowly. He was shivering all over, and the fury had drained out of him completely, leaving him a terrified child.

For a minute Raymond had been not himself but his father. It was Sanford Babbitt's voice that had come roaring in accusative fury from his mouth. And Charlie, turning on the water, had been not Charlie but Raymond, Raymond on that awful day twenty-four years ago when 'it' had happened. And, in the bathtub, unseen but nevertheless very real, there sat a little baby, Charlie, only two years old. And the water was hot, too hot.

Charlie saw it all now. Remembered it all. An eighteen-year-old boy who just wanted to give his baby brother a bath but who didn't know how to regulate the taps. Who was incapable of testing the water first. An autistic who meant no harm, who wanted only to emulate the behaviour of his mother Eleanor who had just gone to live with the angels. Eleanor putting baby Charlie into the tub. Running the water. But the water was hot, too hot, not hot enough to burn or scald but hot enough to make baby Charlie cry.

And the father, rushing in, distracted, shrieking in fury. The father who had recently lost his wife, whose first son was an autistic with a mind locked away from the real world, whose other son was only a baby, a baby crying because Rain Man had run the bathwater too hot for a baby's delicate skin.

And Raymond, who was blessed and cursed with total recall, unable to forget a single syllable of the terrible words that his father had screamed at him that day, carrying them around in the depths of his poor damaged brain for twenty-four years, only to have them wrenched out of his mouth in Sanford Babbitt's very voice at the horrid sight of Charlie Babbitt and a bathtub filling with running water.

And Charlie, who had always felt contempt for losers and lame ducks, never pity, saw it all and was torn with pity for his brother. Gently he reached his hands out to Raymond, cradling the back of his brother's head.

'It's okay, man,' he said softly. 'It's okay, man. I didn't burn. I'm fine.'

At Charlie's touch Raymond stiffened. Don't touch. Never touch him. Charlie took his hands away.

'You burned,' said Raymond in a small, strangled voice. 'And you were . . . a little baby. Burned. And I have to go . . . to my home.' He kept his face turned away from Charlie's, looking instead over Charlie's shoulder.

'No, Ray,' Charlie said earnestly, his eyes searching for Raymond's, trying to establish contact, 'I didn't burn. He was just an asshole. Look at me. Look at me. Please. That's when Mom died. That's why he put you away, the bastard.'

But Raymond's gaze was still directed over Charlie's shoulder and, on his face, a stricken look. Charlie turned around to see the taps still running. The terrifying flow of water filling the tub. Quickly, he made a dart at the taps and turned off the water.

When he turned back, Charlie found Raymond on his knees on the wet bathroom tiles. He knelt there, frozen, his hands clasped close to his chest, his eyes staring blankly at the taps, now stilled.

'Ray? Ray? They're off. It's okay.'

But Raymond was past hearing any words of comfort. The trauma of reliving the twenty-four-year-old night-mare had been too much for him, and he had turned himself off, just like the water, retreating into a place of ice and bitter cold. He was shivering, and his teeth were chattering, and he rocked himself back and forth, back and forth, as though trying to keep warm. Rocking and staring at the taps.

'Jesus!' exclaimed Charlie, alarmed. 'Are you cold, Ray? Just a second.' He ran into the bedroom and looked around for something to use, then he grabbed a blanket from the bed and carried it back into the bathroom with him. Kneeling down on the floor beside his brother, Charlie wrapped Raymond gently in the blanket.

When he felt the warmth and the rough, woolly texture of the scratchy blanket around him Raymond allowed his body to ease just a little. The shivering stopped. Then, moments later, the rocking ceased. But his staring eyes never left the bathtub taps, as though they possessed some malevolent, mysterious power to hypnotize him. And in a few seconds the whispering began. Whisper. Whisper. Whisper. Whisperwhisperwhisper. A mantra of madness.

'What is it, Ray?' asked Charlie softly. 'Secret thoughts?' He leaned closer to his brother to hear better.

'C-h-a-r ... l-i-e ...,' Raymond was spelling in a whisper. 'C-h-a-r ... l-i-e ... C-h-a-r ... l-i-e ...' Over and over. A protective litany, a magic name.

Charlie sat back on his heels, stunned, while the ache of pity spread from his heart throughout his entire body. He wanted to reach over and take his brother into his arms for comfort, but he knew that any such gesture would freak Raymond out. Don't touch. Never touch him. But he had to do something, had to bring him back somehow. Charlie began to sing.

'She was just seven-teen.
You know what I mean.
And the way she looked was way be-yond com-pare.
So how could I dance with another . . .'

Raymond's whispering tailed off, and his eyes stopped staring at the taps.

'Oooooh, when I saw her stand-ing there?' finished Charlie. He looked sharply at his brother, and it seemed to him that Raymond's tensions had eased, although he was still locked away in his private world, out of Charlie's reach.

Christ, flashed through Charlie's brain. *What an irony! Who's the Rain Man now? Who's doing the singing, and who's the baby in the blanket? Rain Man, Rain Man, I love you.* Only Raymond couldn't love. Could never love. The piece was missing.

It was late, very late. Raymond was sleeping soundly on one of the twin beds in the room, but Charlie was lying wide awake in the other, smoking and thinking. No, not thinking so much as trying *not* to think. Charlie had never been so tired in his life. He was worn to the bone, and every muscle in his body was sore. He felt as though he'd taken a beating, inside and out, and all his internal organs were bruised from being punched. This had been the heaviest night of his life so far, even worse than the nights right after he'd left home and was on the run, scared as only a kid who has no home and no mother and father can be scared.

He hurt; he was lonely; and he needed human comfort. Charlie Babbitt, who never needed anything from anybody, who strolled through relationships keeping one eye on the nearest exit, who manipulated everyone he came into contact with, who called the tune and named the dance without paying the piper – this same Charlie Babbitt admitted to himself now that he needed someone to love, someone who would love him back. He needed Susanna.

It was late, yes, but it was an hour earlier in Santa Monica. Charlie pulled the phone towards him and dialled Susanna's number.

At the other end of the line he could hear ringing, and with his heart in his mouth Charlie waited for his girl to pick up the receiver.

'Hello?'

'Hi, it's me,' he said softly.

No answer. Nothing.

'Well, you didn't hang up. Does that mean we're engaged?'

Susanna didn't rise to the bait. 'How's your brother?' she asked finally.

'Well, you know Ray. Party, party, party.'

To this Susanna made no answer. If he couldn't be serious . . .

'I . . . I just want to hear . . . it's not over,' said Charlie into the phone. If only he could see her face to face instead of having to depend on goddamn telephone wires. If only he could hold her in his arms, he'd be able to convince her to come back to him. When Susanna didn't speak, he added, 'I mean, I'm scared. I'm scared it's over.' Holding his breath, Charlie pressed the receiver hard against his ear, so as not to miss a sound.

Susanna sighed. 'Don't ask me today, Charlie. You won't like the answer. Let it sit.'

Charlie chuckled bitterly. 'Something I'm not good at, letting things sit.'

'There're a lot of things you're not good at,' Susanna replied with equal bitterness. She'd been hurt, and hurt bad, and she wasn't eager to jump back in the ring for another bone-shattering round with the champion. Not when the scars hadn't healed yet.

'Yeah, well,' answered Charlie with difficulty, 'I'll get one of Ray's notebooks. Start keeping a list.' He waited for Susanna to react to his pitiful little joke, to say something, and when she didn't, he blurted out his plan.

'I'm . . . going to get custody of Ray. From the court. It starts with a shrink interview as soon as I get back.'

Was he out of his mind? 'Charlie, there's no way you could win that. Not a chance in a billion.'

'I'll win it. I have to.'

'Dr Bruner took care of him for more than twenty years. You've known him four days. Can you hear how crazy you sound?' She paused, not sure whether to feel sorrier for Raymond or for Charlie. But Susanna's loyalties ran deep. 'Can you hear it, hon?' she added earnestly.

She didn't understand. Nobody understood. 'Look, I'll call you when I get in. Okay?'

Susanna didn't say yes, but she didn't say no either. Charlie took what comfort he could from that fact.

'Well, I'll see you,' he whispered into the receiver, and, when Susanna didn't answer, he hung up the phone and put it back on the nightstand. Turning over on to his back, Charlie took the ashtray and set it on his chest. Smoking quietly, he stared into the darkness.

In the motel bathroom at the bottom of the water in the bathtub, floated a photograph. It was creased and somewhat faded, but it showed clearly a solemn-faced eighteen-year-old boy and a baby wrapped in a blanket. Brothers.

CHAPTER NINE

It really was about time to buy Raymond something new to wear. His only shirt and trousers were getting pretty filthy, and his underwear was turning an unattractive shade of grey. Money was the problem.

Charlie was running low on cash; the Buick chug-a-lugged gasoline in the thirsty way that 1949 automobiles guzzled pre-OPEC fuel. Motel bills for two weren't cheap, but especially expensive were their meals and the continual procession of Raymond's snacks. Raymond was at his happiest, if you could call it that, when he was ripping open the sealed top of a bag of Fritos or Cheez Doodles. Charlie's bank account was way down low, and the last time he'd used his cash-machine card, the machine had refused to hand over any money. If he tried to use it again, the machine would probably chew it up, spit it out in his face and place Charlie under arrest.

They were now living on Charlie's gold American Express card, but as Charlie hadn't paid his bill for two months, they were on the thin edge with credit too. Any minute now the card might be refused, and then where would they be? Naturally, Charlie didn't share any of this with his brother; even if Raymond didn't understand, and he was unlikely to understand, he might just catch the drift and freak out.

On the outskirts of Albuquerque Charlie pulled into a shopping mall that had a K-Mart, and Raymond was treated to everything new, head to foot, courtesy AmEx. New underwear and socks, brand-new cotton trousers and shirt. His new outfit seemed to tickle him; at least, when he was trying things on he didn't withdraw and didn't make a scene.

Partly to reward him and partly so they wouldn't have to face any dangerous repetitions of the scene on the farmhouse porch, Charlie threw in a Watchman, a little Sony TV on a leather wrist strap that Raymond could carry around with him easily. That way, said Charlie, he'd always have Wapner 'on hand'. Even though Raymond didn't get the joke, the Watchman was received with the closest thing to enthusiasm that Charlie had ever seen his brother show, and it made him feel good to be able to give Raymond a little pleasure.

Raymond wore his new clothes out of the store. Charlie went next door to the laundromat, threw into the wash Raymond's old clothes and a few things of his own and left his brother sitting on the bench in front of the machines with a bag of tortilla chips while he gassed up the convertible. When Charlie came back to the laundromat, Raymond was sitting exactly where he'd left him, watching the clothes go around and around in the drier. Around and around. Around and around.

Charlie walked over and sat down beside his brother on the bench. Raymond didn't look up; his eyes were fixed on the drier, around and around.

'See, this is the stuff you gotta watch out for when you meet the shrink,' Charlie scolded. 'Just staring like this, at nothing. I mean, he takes one look at that and locks you back up in the zoo.'

But Raymond wasn't listening; his thoughts were elsewhere.

'See the red one,' he said tonelessly. 'It always falls the same.'

Charlie looked at the tumbling laundry, and he noticed his own red shirt in there with the rest, but he couldn't see what Raymond saw so clearly. To Charlie laundry was laundry. No more, no less. He shook his head when he noticed the little Sony Watchman sitting next to Raymond on the bench. It was on, picture but no sound, just sitting there flickering silently. Picking it up, Charlie snapped it off.

'You ought to turn this thing off when you're not using it,' he admonished Raymond. 'If you run down the batteries, where'll we be when Wapner's on, huh?'

Clearly Raymond wasn't listening. 'Mommy washed my laundry. And we watched it. Like this.' His voice was very soft, recalling a good memory for a change. A no-fear memory.

Mommy. 'I can't remember her,' Charlie said quietly. 'I try. And sometimes I almost, kind of . . . but I think it's just from pictures.'

'I read to her. Out loud. Every story,' said Raymond. His eyes were still on the tumbling laundry, watching the red shirt fall.

'And I bet you sang to her, huh?'

'No. She sang to me. I sang to you.' Around and around, with Raymond's eyes fixed on every revolution.

'Oooooh!' sang Charlie in his best Beatles falsetto, trying to get Raymond's mind off the laundry, to encourage him to join in the song. If he didn't start changing some of this bizarre behaviour of his brother's now, he wouldn't have a prayer when the shrink examined him at the custody hearing.

But Raymond wasn't interested in the song. He was concentrating only on the red shirt, which always fell in the same place in the tumbler of the drier.

Charlie stuck his face up close to Raymond's. 'Gimme the smile. The Dazzler,' he commanded, showing his own.

Raymond hesitated, then mimicked a big smile, lots of teeth.

'Aw *right*!' Charlie applauded. 'Now a laugh. Your best laugh.'

This time the hesitation was longer, but at last Raymond uttered his version of a laugh. 'Heh. Heh. Heh.'

'Po-tential, Ray. You got po-tential.' Charlie grinned widely at his brother. Raymond actually seemed to be making progress, and Charlie was mighty pleased with himself. *Keep it up, just keep it up.*

'You got potential, Charlie Babbitt. Daddy said.'

Charlie's grin faded as the unwelcome memory of his father and his father's harsh authority intruded. Potential. How he hated that word when his father spoke it in his autocratic voice.

'Yeah,' he answered flatly. 'One little thing. Call me Charlie, okay? Without the Babbitt.'

Raymond said nothing. His eyes flicked back to the drier, and he became engrossed in the laundry again. Around and around.

'The red one, huh?' Charlie rested his cheek on his left hand and watched the drier tumble the clothes. Raymond raised his left hand to his cheek in an identical gesture, and for a few peaceful minutes they sat side by side on the laundromat bench, watching the red shirt going around and around, around and around, and always falling in the same place.

But Charlie didn't have the leisure at his disposal that Raymond had; he was a businessman with business to take care of. Leaving Raymond on his own to watch the shirt, Charlie headed for the phone booth outside the laundromat and dialled the Babbitt Collectibles number.

'Lenny, it's me.'

'I've been sitting here by this phone three *hours*, man,' came the accusing whine.

'Yeah, I'm sorry. I've had ... things to do.' How could he explain Raymond to Lenny? 'I had to buy ... some clothes and stuff.'

'Charlie, it's all over,' Lenny cut in. 'All over.'

'Take it easy, kid. I'm in Albuquerque. I'll be there in –'

'Wyatt found the cars. He found 'em. He got 'em. They're gone.'

Charlie opened his mouth and shut it again silently. What can you say to the end of the world? He could feel the blood turning to ice in his veins as his heart became a giant frozen stone lying heavy in his chest. It was all, as Lenny had just said, over. He closed his eyes, unable to think of anything. The worst had happened, and Charlie Babbitt's mind was pulling a total blank.

'Bateman wants his down payment back. They all do.' Lenny went on announcing the details of the disaster of the day. 'That's ninety thou, Charlie.'

As though he needed reminding. Fifteen thousand times six was ninety thousand. Ninety thousand dollars. It might as well be ninety million for all the meaning the number held. Ninety billion. So what? He didn't have it. He didn't have ninety cents. He was ruined, finished, washed up, buried. Charlie Babbitt was a dead man.

'He says you won't get a gig *washing* Lamborghinis when he's through with you,' continued Lenny, rather savouring this part. Charlie had put him through hell these last few days, running out of town, staying out of touch, leaving him alone to take the heat. Now it was Charlie's turn to get scorched, and Lenny couldn't really say he was sorry. 'By Friday, he says. What do I tell him?'

Inside his head Charlie heard a great thunderous shout of hollow laughter. What the hell did it matter what Lenny told Wyatt now? Wyatt had pulled the plug on Charlie's life, and it was swirling right down the drain.

'Tell him the cheque's in the mail,' he said and hung up the phone. In his imagination he could see his future, and it wasn't pretty.

Charlie just sat there, staring at the congealing food on his plate. He moved it around a little with his fork, but nothing could induce him to take a bite. He wasn't hungry, would never be hungry again. Dead men don't eat. He stubbed his Lucky out right in the middle of his plate of chopped steak and sighed again.

In contrast to Charlie, Raymond had eaten very well. The little cut-up squares of hamburger had vanished more quickly than usual down his throat, one by one. Raymond had had a good day. New clothes and a Sony Watchman for Wapner. A nice long drive in Daddy's car down a desert highway from Albuquerque to Joseph City, Arizona. And now they were in this comfortable truck stop with a big, modern diner, and he'd had a well-done hamburger that even came with French fries. Charlie had cut up the food and put ketchup on it. Raymond enjoyed the taste of ketchup, especially on French fries.

And there was this little jukebox, right on the wall over their booth. With lots of songs. One hundred and forty of them. The songs were all listed on fourteen plastic cards, and if you found the one you wanted to hear, you put in a quarter and punched in a letter and a number and out came the music. Raymond, fascinated, turned the plastic cards rapidly, click, click, click, click.

Somebody must have put a quarter in because Raymond could hear singing. A woman's voice. Patsy Cline singing 'Sweet Dreams'.

'E–19,' said Raymond.

Listlessly, Charlie looked across the table at his brother. Patsy Cline. So what? Then a question occurred to him. 'That number. B–19.'

'*E*–19,' corrected Raymond.

How was it possible? Raymond had turned the card catalogue so fast that he couldn't possibly have read the selections, let alone memorize one or two. Nobody could do that.

'That's the song we're hearing?'

'That's the song. We're hearing.'

Charlie stared at Raymond, gnawing on his thumbnail, while an idea dawned in his mind and hope dawned in his heart. 'Put your hands over your eyes.' He demonstrated.

Raymond, who could imitate any simple gesture, put his hands over his eyes. Charlie began flipping through the plastic cards.

'"The Gambler". Kenny Rogers,' he called out at random.

'J–12,' Raymond answered promptly and correctly.

'"Cheating Heart". Hank Williams.'

'"*Your* Cheating Heart",' corrected Raymond seriously. 'Hank Williams, *Junior*.'

'Okay, show-off. What's the number?'

'L–4.'

This was fucking unbelievable! Charlie's bad mood evaporated like an ice cube on a stove. A huge grin shone all over his face. '"Blue Moon of Kentucky". Bill Monroe.'

'And the Bluegrass Boys. P–11,' Raymond answered promptly.

Sonofabitch! And with his hands over his eyes too! He was a genius! Raymond Babbitt was a fucking genius! 'Remarkable abilities,' Dr Bruner had said. 'Autistic savant'. *I'll drink to that!* thought Charlie happily. Those remarkable abilities might just save Charlie Babbitt's ass!

'Ray, bro, we're gonna have some fun,' he promised his brother. 'Have you ever played cards?'

Charlie bought three decks of poker cards and threw the jokers away. Using the hood of the Buick as a card table, he spread out the cards and showed the decks to Raymond to familiarize him with the ace-to-king sequence. Then he shuffled all three decks together at once, making a huge pile of cards with a shuffled-in dozen of everything – twelve aces, twelve twos, twelve threes and so on – while Raymond watched him with a rapt face, very seriously.

'You paying attention?' he demanded.

Raymond nodded. He was paying attention.

'You ready?'

Another nod. Raymond was ready.

Now Charlie grabbed up the fat triple deck and began to deal cards at a furious rate, face up, on the hood of the car. Each card was visible for only a split second and was covered immediately by the next card dealt.

Flip, flip, flip, flip. The pile got higher. When he had a little more than half the triple pack left, Charlie looked over at Raymond, then laid the remainder of the pack, face down, on the hood of the car.

'Okay. What's left in here?'

Raymond didn't hesitate for a second. 'Nine aces, seven kings, ten queens, eight jacks, seven tens –'

Charlie held up his hand, and the flow of words stopped. A natural. A goddamn natural card-counter, terror of the blackjack tables! Gambling casinos would be brought to their knees. Casino pit bosses would tremble if they knew what Raymond Babbitt's abilities were. Tremble, bar him for life from the tables and post his photograph prominently in the office of every gambling house in America: 'Do You Know This Man?' And here he was, Charlie Babbitt, sitting on a goldmine and not even knowing it.

'Po-tential,' murmured Charlie happily, as he considered the possibilities. 'The man has po-tential. Are you ready to go for it?' he asked Raymond.

'Ready to go. For it.'

'Let's do it! Hop in.'

When Raymond was safely in the Buick, Charlie floored the gas pedal and they took off like a big-ass bird. The cards on the hood of the car went flying out into the road, leaving a trail of hearts, clubs, spades and, best of all, diamonds.

They were on their way to LA but, first, a short detour. A visit to Las Vegas, gambling capital of the US of A, to let Raymond Babbitt be the guy who put the 'savant' in 'autistic savant'.

Joseph City, Arizona, was no further than a hundred miles from Las Vegas, less than a two-hour desert drive. The convertible left Highway 40 and picked up Highway 93, straight into Vegas. As they rode along, Charlie gave Raymond a run-down on the rules of the game, going over them only once, knowing now that Raymond was unable to forget anything he heard or read.

'Twenty-one: remember it. That's the name of the game. They deal the cards out of a shoe, but it's only *called* a shoe – it's not the kind that goes on your feet, so don't expect it to look like what you're wearing. The most important thing to bear in mind is that the house has to stand on seventeen. The dealer can't draw a card if he's showing seventeen. If the dealer has seventeen, and you get more than seventeen but under twenty-one, you win. Got that?'

'Got that.'

'If you draw too high a card and you go over twenty-one, you go bust. You lose. Money. Got that?'

'Got that.'

'If you draw a ten of any kind – ten, jack, queen, king – plus an ace, you've got the big win. Blackjack. Got that?'

'Got that.'

'If you want the dealer to give you another card, you scratch the table, like this, or you say, "Hit," but if you don't want another card, then you shake your head, no, or say, "Stick." If you're showing eighteen, you stick. Don't ever draw on eighteen or over. Got that?'

'Got that.'

'So if you can count what's already been played, and you know what's left in the shoe, and you know the shoe is fat with tens or with little cards, you know whether to hit or stick. But it's better to hit and get big numbers than to stick with little numbers, so it's better if there are a lot of tens in the shoe. Got that?'

'Got that.'

'There'll be at least three decks in the shoe at one time, maybe more. Maybe four or even five decks. You've got to count them all, no matter how many decks they use. Got that?'

'Got that. Can I drive, Charlie Babbitt?'

'No. Now listen to me. So when there's lots of tens left, tens and picture cards, then it's good. For us.'

Because Charlie didn't say, 'Got that?' Raymond didn't have an answer.

'C'mon, say it!' Charlie prompted impatiently.

'Tens are good, tens are good, tens are good, tens are *good*!' Raymond seemed pretty pleased with himself, possibly because Charlie was so pleased with him.

'Okay. And you're gonna bet –'

'One if it's bad, two if it's good.'

'And,' prompted Charlie, waiting to hear the most important lesson of all, the one he'd drilled into Raymond for the last ten miles.

'Keep my trap shut.' Raymond opened his mouth and shut it with a snap, looking to Charlie for his brother's approval.

Charlie nodded. 'Casinos have house rules. The first one is they don't like to lose. So never, *never*, show you're counting.'

Raymond turned to his brother and said, 'I'm counting, I'm counting, I'm counting, I'm counting, so *ha*!'

'If you say that in Vegas where anybody can hear you, then I wouldn't be able to see you. Ever again.'

Raymond subsided in his seat, thinking that one over. Elation oozed out of him, like air from a pricked balloon. He looked so hangdog that Charlie gave him an encouraging smile, and Raymond, as though on cue, returned the imitation grin.

'C-H-A-R . . . L-I-E,' he called out cheerfully. 'C-H-A-R . . . L-I-E.' This time it was very different from his manic whisper.

Anybody can play keno or the slots. You can be dressed in rags with feathers in your hair, you can be mad as the Hatter and the March Hare put together, and you could still play keno or the slots. But if you cross that casino floor and sit down at a table, at blackjack or baccarat or some other high-ante gentleman's game, then you'd better be looking good, looking like a winner who can afford to lose. Because the casino has its eye on you, and bizarre behaviour isn't tolerated, even among high rollers. So Raymond started out in the batter's box with two strikes on him. He not only acted like someone off the funny farm; he dressed the part.

Okay, clothes maketh the man, and as long as Charlie's AmEx held out, he could do something about Raymond's appearance. A decent haircut and a manicure for starters. A new suit, one that fitted instead of those ballooning K-Mart work clothes, and sharp shoes with a high shine, and Raymond could be transformed from the ugly duckling into the glorious swan.

But the swan was no less psychotic than the duckling, and the future was just one big, worrisome question mark. Once you got past the suit to the eyes – blank and staring or, worse, rolling around – what then? What if Raymond got crazy right there at the blackjack table? Good old unpredictable Ray. Never a dull moment with that guy.

But Charlie had to chance it. A couple of decent wins, and they were out of there. He had to win at least enough to pay off Wyatt's loan and give the customers back their down payments. Otherwise he could never do business in Los Angeles again. Maybe he could salvage the car deal. Maybe he could even go back to LA with a fortune in his pocket. Why not? Plenty of other gamblers had. It all depended on Raymond.

They reached Vegas just as night was beginning to fall and the Strip was lighting up with miles and miles of neon – tumbling dice, wagon wheels, flamingos, neon signs for the MGM Grand, the Sahara, the Desert Inn. Raymond had never seen anything like it, and his eyes were popping out of his head as he twisted his neck back and forth to see all the garish gaiety.

Tonight a cheap motel. Tomorrow they'd put the finishing touches on Raymond, getting him dolled-up enough to look good in a big casino. Then tomorrow night, that was the big night. They'd hit the casino at Caesar's Palace and let Ray strut his stuff.

Charlie sighed and shook his head. Too bad he wasn't a praying man: this would be a really good time for it.

CHAPTER TEN

Miracles can happen. It was a true miracle that Charlie's AmEx Gold Card didn't go 'tilt' at the tailor's the following morning. Instead the credit card took a major beating and came up smiling. Both Charlie and Raymond were fitted for the latest Italian cut in a pair of nearly matching suits – snugly tapered, double-breasted with high narrow lapels, the finest English woollen cloth. Murderously expensive, of course, but who was worth it more than they?

Along with the suits went a couple of cream-coloured linen shirts and a pair of matching green neckties, one for Raymond, one for Charlie. Raymond seemed to like the neckties best, especially the fact that his was identical to his brother's. While Raymond struggled to get his trousers belted up around his chest again, Charlie extracted a promise from the tailor that both suits would be altered and ready to wear out of the store by not a minute later than five p.m. *today*.

When the gold card was put through the little machine that passes judgement, Charlie felt butterflies like eagles churning around in his gut; all the cash he had left was what he needed to buy into the game tonight. If his credit card should be rejected – or, worse yet, seized – this could be the end of the line for Charlie Babbitt and his dreams.

But miracles do happen, and the card was still percolating. Aw *right*! The next stop was a classy men's grooming salon to put the finishing touches on Raymond. Expensive haircut, facial, manicure, shoeshine – the works. Raymond sat fascinated, watching the entire make-over process silently, his shoe-button eyes taking everything in without undue alarm. Only the hot towel threw him into a near-panic. When he saw it coming, steaming and wet, Raymond stiffened in his seat and God alone knows what would have happened if Charlie hadn't intervened so hastily.

'No hot towel.'

'But, sir, to open the pores it is necessary –'

'Read my lips. *No hot towel.*'

So Raymond could tolerate it again, as the barber snipped and the manicurist buffed and the shoes were polished to a high shine.

What emerged from all this costly service surprised even Charlie, who'd engineered the whole thing. Raymond looked . . . normal. Better than normal – almost splendid. If he could hold it together like this, especially in his expensive new Italian threads, there wasn't a casino in the country that would turn him away.

They had the day to kill, so Charlie drove Raymond around Vegas to show him the sights. Las Vegas by day is tawdry, like a whore who has slept in her make-up. The buildings, lit up by coloured neon and many thousands of watts of electricity, look garish in the strong sunlight of the Nevada desert. But Raymond didn't seem to mind. He gawked at everything: the long Strip, with its huge, high-rise hotels and their Arabian or ancient Roman themes, their prominent marquees featuring star acts; the cheap little marriage chapels; the motels with slot machines in every room and all the bathrooms.

Decades ago Las Vegas was little more than a pit stop on the way to California, a 'last-chance' place to gas up and have a meal before the long drive across the western desert. Then somebody had done the smart thing and legalized gambling in Nevada. Almost overnight, here on the fringe of the desert, had arisen a city dedicated to only one thing – gambling. A recreation devoted to taking your money away and keeping it. Everywhere you went in Las Vegas you could lose a few bucks or more.

In the tacky little luncheonette where they stopped for a midday meal the decorative motif was a pair of 'lucky seven' dice – up on the wall, printed on the paper placemats and on the spotted greasy menus. On every table there were keno cards; a row of slot machines stood along the far wall. When the waitress came to take your order, she could pick up your keno card and your gambling dollars at the same time. The sound of the keno numbers being called out overrode the Country and Western music on the jukebox.

The keno fascinated Raymond. He could easily have spent the day and the evening just watching the little numbered ping-pong balls bouncing around merrily in the vacuum and popping up to deliver winning numbers. It was like counting and watching the clothes in the drier all put together. Watching him, Charlie thought that if anybody could learn to win at keno, Raymond could. No doubt his cunning savant mind had already perceived a repetitive pattern in the seemingly random winning numbers and was working out the probabilities. But keno was a penny-ante game for little blue-haired ladies who sat around all day working a couple of cards at two bucks a pop, like nursing a drink. Little fish.

What Charlie was after were big fish, a high-stakes

game at a high-stakes casino. Blackjack at Caesar's Palace. To win big would take a miracle even bigger than obtaining two expensive suits on an unpaid credit card. But Charlie was counting on that miracle, although flashes of anxiety still gnawed at him intermittently. Everything was hanging on the turn of a few cards and on Raymond's freakish ability to predict those cards without getting caught and without staging one of those self-abusive episodes that Charlie had come to know so well.

The '49 Buick stopped for the light at an intersection. Raymond was staring in fascination at one of the big Strip hotels, its marquee lit up by many bulbs.

'Lots of light bulbs, huh?' Charlie smiled.

'Lots of bulbs, huh,' answered Raymond.

'How many bulbs, Ray?'

'Two hundred and seventy-eight.'

'The Rain Man has spoken.' Charlie laughed.

They had a fighting chance.

Another miracle. The suits were ready on time and, wonder of wonders, tailored to perfection. That is, Charlie's was perfection; Raymond's would be perfection if he didn't yank his belt up all the way to his chin, as Charlie could see he was itching to do. But they looked like a million bucks in small bills. Just like two eastern potentates, they drove up to the majestic Caesar's Palace, handed the keys over for valet parking and entered the hotel.

Raymond had never seen such splendour. He followed Charlie at a short distance, turning his head to gaze at the coloured waters of the marble fountain, at the large statues of the ancient Roman emperors and at the avenue of elegant boutiques at the far side of the lobby.

There were slot machines, and there was keno, and he was fascinated by both. For a moment Charlie almost lost him when Raymond shuffled over to try his hand at the slot machines Nothing happened because he hadn't grasped the basic principle behind the one-arm bandits: money first, *then* you pull the lever. He was still tugging at the lever without success when Charlie located him and threw a quarter into the slot.

The tumblers spun around. Raymond's head spun too as he watched. At last they came to rest. Two bars and a lemon, a loser. Even so, between the excitement of the keno and the excitement of the slot machines Raymond was reluctant to leave, but Charlie promised him, 'The sooner we play cards, the faster we get back here.'

As they made their way across the lobby to the casino, they heard a loud commotion behind them. They turned to look. One of the slots had paid off a big jackpot; bells were ringing loudly, and silver dollars were pouring down into the basket. The winner, a plump, pretty, grey-haired woman named Mitzi, was jumping up and down and screaming for joy. Everyone around her was crowding in to hug her for luck.

'See? Winning is *great!*' Charlie punched home the moral. 'She won. She's happy. Everybody's hugging her.' Raymond turned from the victory scene to look straight at Charlie. A beat too late Charlie remembered that Raymond couldn't stand to be touched by anybody. Even the possibility of being touched was already making him stiffen up.

'Uh, when you win at cards, nobody hugs.'

None the less Raymond's feet, attracted by the sounds of happiness, began carrying him back to the slot machines. He wanted to see the tumblers go around again, see the pictures come up, hear the bells ringing for *him*. Charlie had to stop him, and fast.

'If we don't play cards, and win money, they'll take you back to the house for the strange,' he told his brother in a low voice. 'And you know how they'll take you?'

Raymond didn't reply but kept his eyes fixed on Charlie, waiting for the answer. Sticking his arms straight out at right angles to his body, Charlie made himself into an airplane. He began making jet-engine noises while pretending to fly through the air. 'Rrrrrrrrrrrrrrrrrrrrrr.'

The message was cruel, but it was loud and clear, and it got through to Raymond. Turning away from the slot machines, he followed Charlie in the direction of the casino. Walking tall and looking good, the Babbitt Boys stepped down, side by side, into the large, dark, circular room where the real action was. Their attitudes – Charlie's real, Raymond's an exact copy of Charlie's – said, 'The players have arrived. Let the games begin. Make way for the man who broke the bank at Monte Carlo – and the other guy is his brother.'

There is no day or night in a gambling casino. The action is round-the-clock, all day, every day. Casinos are kept dark, but each gambling table is illuminated by low-hanging lights, so that it is something of an island, isolated from the others and complete unto itself. That way the gamblers are less distracted, and the casino owners can keep better track of the action. Most of the action in the vast ocean around the islands is the trotting of beautiful waitresses bearing drinks. Thirsty gamblers never have to leave their tables.

Charlie had worked out a simple system for their betting. Raymond would bet one chip if he thought the cards were not in their favour, two chips if the shoe was loaded with tens and he was pretty sure they'd win. Charlie would do the actual big betting: small amounts to stay in the game when Raymond bet one chip, large amounts when Raymond bet two.

Charlie had just enough money in his secret stash to buy a handful of chips. Not the five-dollar red chips or the hundred-dollar black chips but a solid handful of green ones, worth twenty-five dollars each. With luck he and Raymond would be turning green into black and white – the white chips were worth five hundred dollars apiece. With phenomenal luck they'd be cashing in yellow chips, a grand apiece, or maybe even the best of them all, the purple, worth five thousand beautiful smackeroonies each.

The casino was crowded and busy. Gauging the action, Charlie led Raymond past the dice tables and the roulette wheel – Raymond had to be led almost forcibly past the spinning roulette wheel – to the blackjack tables at the back.

'What are we playing?' he whispered to Raymond. Just checking.

'Cards. Twenty-one.'

'That's the name of the game, Ray.'

The blackjack tables were so crowded that it took them a few minutes to find two seats side by side. Charlie put a small pile of green chips in front of him and a small pile in front of Raymond. Then he closed his eyes, drew a deep breath and crossed his fingers.

An hour later the two were still sitting there, and the two little stacks of chips had grown into two very large ones, and not all green either. There were black chips mixed in with them and even a couple of yellow chips. Raymond's savant talents were indeed awesome; Charlie's dream of bliss was coming true right before his eyes.

What Charlie hadn't realized about his brother, and certainly couldn't know about autistic savants in general, was the length and depth of the concentrated attention that somebody like Raymond could bring to bear on something that involved him totally. In the last few days that they'd been on the road together Charlie had seen only the downside of this concentration. For example, Wapner. When Raymond was getting ready to watch *People's Court* an earthquake couldn't have attracted his attention. If there was something he had his mind set on, even something as trivial as a snack, nothing could deter him from it.

It was integral to Raymond's autistic personality, native to his damaged brain, that everything was of equal value to him. Life and death were of no greater significance to Raymond Babbitt than Cheez Doodles and Wapner. This single-mindedness Charlie had always interpreted as Raymond's stubbornness, and it had caused him no end of pain in his butt, but now he was reaping its rich rewards because Raymond's concentration was something rare and wonderful to behold.

Another plus: Raymond was concentrating too hard to act bizarre. He was unconscious of his surroundings, so nothing threatened his survival. All his attention was focused on the three decks of cards in the shoe. He was working his counting mojo on the shoe, and he was *hot*.

Not everything worked, though.

On this latest deal Raymond was showing eighteen. Charlie drew a six and a four. Perfect. No way he could go bust on the next card. But it had to be a ten for him to make twenty, a sure win.

Raymond scratched the table, the signal for another

card. Charlie opened his mouth to protest. You don't draw to eighteen. Prime rule. Hadn't he told Raymond never to draw to eighteen? At eighteen you stick.

'You want a card?' the dealer asked, surprised.

'He doesn't want a card. Ray, you've got eighteen,' Charlie interposed quickly.

'I want a card,' insisted Raymond.

Shrugging a little, the dealer dealt a card from the shoe. It was a ten of clubs. Raymond went bust. What's more, the card should have been Charlie's rightful ten. Raymond should have stuck, and Charlie would have had his twenty. Almost certainly good enough to beat the house, which was showing fifteen. Both of them would have won. But something in Raymond had gone awry, and now both of them had lost this one.

'See, you took my card,' said Charlie with a scowl, unable to conceal his irritation.

Mistake. Taking him literally at his word, Raymond lifted the ten of clubs off his little pile and put it neatly on Charlie's, even smoothing it down to make it look better.

'I can't take yours,' Charlie said, returning Raymond's card. 'I need my own.'

Mistake number two. 'There's lots of them,' said Raymond confidently.

At that the dealer's eyes flickered. Only a little, but Charlie saw it and began to worry. Even so he doubled down, separating his six and four and doubling his bet for two hands instead of one. The dealer just glanced at him, the shoe stopping for a moment.

'Lots and lots of them,' said Raymond.

The shoe moved around the table, dealing out cards. A queen to the guy at the head of the table, ten to the woman sitting next to him. Charlie got a jack. And for himself the dealer turned up another queen. The house went bust, and Charlie pulled in a large stack of chips.

'Lots and lots,' Raymond said again. That flicker in the dealer's eyes again, a little stronger this time. Lots and lots of tens. Was this guy card-counting? Better add another deck to the shoe.

The next card from the shoe was the white marker, calling for a new shuffle. It was Raymond's turn, among the players, to put it back in the shoe for the next shuffle, so the dealer laid it politely on the green-felt table in front of him.

That threw Raymond off completely; Charlie hadn't told him anything about this. As the dealer looked at him expectantly, he turned blankly to his brother.

'Put the marker in the cards, Ray.'

'Where?'

'Anywhere you like, sir,' said the dealer.

With hesitant fingers Raymond picked up the white marker and looked over at Charlie for moral support. Charlie gave him an encouraging nod, but Raymond held the card in his hand, unable to act. He kept staring at the marker in his hands and at the large shoeful of cards in front of him. Back and forth, back and forth, with everybody watching him and wondering what the hell was going on. Charlie nodded again, more urgently. He was terrified that the table would be catching on to Raymond, on to the fact that he wasn't wrapped too tight.

'Today,' said Charlie.

Raymond looked up, his face a question mark.

'Do it today,' Charlie told him impatiently.

'Thursday,' said Raymond, and went back to his work, the unresolvable dilemma of the marker and the shoe. Holding the white card over the shoe, drawing it back, holding it out, drawing it back . . .

'Will you just put it in there?' snapped Charlie, blowing his cool, slapping Raymond on the shoulder.

Raymond flinched. His hands moved, and the white marker was buried in the cards. The little cliff-hanger was resolved but not without everybody at the table watching the drama unfold – watching and maybe wondering.

'Does this get me on the list?' Charlie asked lightly, but only half-joking. He was genuinely sorry he hit Raymond, even if it was only a tap.

Raymond gave the question thought. 'Wasn't a Serious Injury,' he decided. ''Course, you *are* number eighteen . . .'

'In 1988, yeah,' Charlie said with a smile. 'So, tell me. How does someone, y'know, get off the list?' He looked earnestly at his brother.

'People go *on* the list. They don't go *off*.' Raymond sounded pretty definite.

Charlie nodded a little sadly and was surprised by the feeling. He wished that his name wasn't on his brother's Serious Injury List.

'Bets, guys?' prompted the dealer.

Charlie looked up, startled. For a minute he'd almost forgotten where he was and what he was there for. For a minute he'd been alone with his brother; he and Raymond had shut everybody else out. Four pairs of eyes, belonging to three other players and the dealer, were staring at him with puzzled speculation.

Raymond put one chip into his betting box, a sign to Charlie that the odds weren't in their favour. So Charlie bet one chip too.

'Ooops,' said Raymond suddenly. Wrong signal. He put in a second chip. Hurriedly Charlie pushed a big stack of chips into his box.

'You boys all set?' asked the dealer, amused. He dealt from the shoe. Raymond pulled a nineteen, and Charlie . . .

'Blackjack,' called the dealer. 'The house pays double.' The other players went bust, but the dealer drew a five of hearts to the sixteen he was showing. 'Twenty-one. Name of the game,' he announced, pulling in all the chips except Charlie's.

Charlie grinned ecstatically as he raked in his winnings. The player next to Raymond, a greying executive in an expensive suit, leaned over and spoke to him. 'Like your tie.'

'It's green.'

'I noticed.'

'At my home,' confided Raymond, 'if you don't . . . don't wear green on St Patty's Day, you get . . . you get a *pinch*, a big pinch, and a *hit*!'

The greying man's eyes widened in surprise. 'Well, uh, St Paddy's Day is eight months off.'

Now play stopped. Calloway, the pit boss, accompanied by a uniformed guard, came to the table on his rounds. It was time to remove the cashbox, full of money, to the casino safe and to count the dealer's remaining chips to make certain they tallied with the pay-out. The pit boss was carrying a clipboard on which was attached a yellow notepad, the sight of which made Raymond's eyes snap open. A clipboard. He could use one of those.

'Keep it up,' the player said, gesturing enviously at Charlie's stack of chips. 'You boys can wear money on St Pat's. Gonna give us the secret? How do you boys do so well?'

'We cheat,' Charlie answered lightly.

The pit boss was toting the rack now, marking down

amounts on his yellow pad. Raymond didn't take his eyes off him and was making complementary marks in an imaginary notebook of his own. The dealer grinned at him.

'He's just counting the chips in my rack,' he told Raymond.

Raymond's expression didn't change. 'There's one hundred and eighty-two white ones, and one hundred and fifty-nine green ones, and ninety-four red ones, and seventy-three black ones,' he said without taking a breath.

This made Calloway look up, startled. He finished his count and tallied his figures against Raymond's, and his face was more astonished than before. 'Uh, thanks,' he said, staring at Raymond, who returned his look with a blank stare of his own.

The dealer's eyebrows shot up in surprise. 'What? You been counting all along?'

Raymond looked alarmed. This was the question that Charlie had warned him about, and if he messed up, Charlie would never see him again. Never, never, *never*! He opened his mouth wide and closed it again with a snap. Trap shut.

'He means the chips, Ray,' Charlie put in hastily before Raymond could say anything incriminating. 'Yeah,' he said to the dealer, 'he likes to do that.' Charlie was getting just a little bit uncomfortable. There was too much conversation going on around Raymond; too much unwelcome attention was being paid to his brother.

The pit boss left with the cashbox filled with money, and now the shoe was going around the table again. Raymond had two chips in, signalling lots and lots of tens left in the shoe. Charlie, following his lead, had bet a major bundle. One thousand dollars, his biggest bet yet. This was make-or-break time.

Good old Raymond. He had drawn a twenty. As for Charlie, a good eleven. Any ten would give him blackjack. The odds for a win were excellent. Charlie doubled his bet. There were two thousand dollars of his winnings sitting in his box now, riding on the turn of a card.

Raymond nodded to the dealer, signalling for another card. An audible gasp went up around the table. He was asking to draw to a twenty. It was bad enough that Raymond had drawn to an eighteen against all of Charlie's instructions. But a twenty! The odds against his going bust on the next card were astronomical, especially when the shoe was filled with lots and lots of tens. Besides, twenty was an almost certain win. The dealer was showing sixteen.

'You don't want a card, Ray,' Charlie said very firmly. 'You've got twenty.'

But Raymond kept nodding to the dealer; yes, hit me again.

'Not a good idea, Ray,' said the grey-haired player sitting next to him.

'Ray, I'm doubling down on an eleven here,' Charlie growled desperately through clenched teeth. 'This is *two thousand dollars*!' Raymond didn't glance in his direction. Charlie leaned over to his brother. Panic time. 'Ray, if you take my ten, I'll . . . I'll pull your trousers up another six inches. That'll put him right around your ears!'

'I want a card,' said Raymond again to the dealer. His expression was a total blank.

The dealer looked around the table and shrugged. No skin off his ass if the players were loony. He moved the shoe towards Raymond and dealt him a card.

It was an ace. An ace! Raymond had twenty-one.

And now the card to Charlie. A queen. Charlie had twenty-one.

Charlie could hardly believe his eyes. He swallowed hard, and his palms were wet with perspiration. As for Raymond, all he said was, 'Name of the game.'

Not a lot goes on in a gambling casino that the casino doesn't know about. At every casino there's an 'eye in the sky', a kind of mezzanine where casino executives can look down upon the action through one-way mirrored glass. If they see anything different, anything . . . original, they can keep an eye on it, check out its development and decide what action they should take.

And the casino had had its 'eye in the sky' looking at Charlie and Raymond Babbitt for the past hour. Donahue, a guard with a pair of binoculars, had been watching Charlie's chips piling up. The shift boss, a burly man named Rosielli, came up behind him and looked over his shoulder.

'The same two guys?' he asked.

'Yeah. The kid's way up and climbing,' answered Donahue.

'What do you see?'

The guard lowered his binoculars thoughtfully. 'Well, he's not front-loading. Don't see any capping or dragging. And we keep changing decks, so he can't be marking anything.'

'So that leaves counting.' Rosielli's eyes narrowed. 'So he's counting. Throw him a bigger shoe.'

Donahue shrugged. 'We did. We're up to six. There's no one in the world who can count into a six-deck shoe.'

'So. He's just on a roll.' But Rosielli didn't believe it

himself. There had to be something, something vital, they were missing.

Donohue turned his glasses back on to the floor, seeking the blackjack tables. 'A roll that's very long and very steady. Like a machine.'

Rosielli thought a minute. His eyebrows met over his nose and his face took on a hard look.

'Run a videotape on him,' he decided.

'Kelso's already ordered one,' said Donahue.

CHAPTER ELEVEN

When they got up from the blackjack table at last Charlie was exhausted, drained of energy. His brain felt deep-fried. Raymond, on the other hand, didn't appear tired at all. He was still revved up and ready to go for another couple of hours. Counting the cards had exhilarated him; even he had caught some of the excitement of winning. Raymond was conscious of having done well and aware that Charlie Babbitt was pleased with him.

It was still early, not even eight o'clock. Even so, all Charlie's instincts told him to quit now, while they were still well ahead. They'd won big, very big. Tomorrow was another day. One more day in Vegas, and they could leave like a pair of conquering emperors, carried out on the shoulders of slaves. This table had become just a little uncomfortable for Charlie. He and Raymond had already attracted too much attention from the dealer and from the other players. That handsome, grey-haired man seemed to be positively fascinated by him.

Tomorrow, with another table, another dealer, another group of players, they could do it again. That is, *Raymond* could do it again. Charlie was only along for the ride, or so it seemed to him.

Also Charlie needed tomorrow to go over a few things with Raymond, a few of those crucial little details he'd forgotten about, like those that Raymond had messed up today, calling attention to himself. Tomorrow night Ray would be letter-perfect, and the next day, their Vegas detour over, they'd be on their way again to Los Angeles in triumph.

But first Charlie needed a hot bath and a good night's sleep . . . and to talk to Susanna once more. There had been an empty spot inside him ever since she'd high-tailed it out of Cincinnati. He missed her a lot, although it didn't occur to him to admit as much to himself or her. He missed her partly for her earthy humour, partly for the sex, but a big part of him missed her because she was so together, so centred, so *sane*.

Try travelling around with an autistic person for the better part of a week; by the end of a few days you almost begin to share those hallucinations. Another few days with Raymond and Charlie too might be planning his day around Wapner. Also he was getting anxious about the upcoming custody hearing for Raymond. He needed Susanna's moral support, needed to know that she was out there pulling for him while he was in there battling it out with some psychiatrist. Besides, Charlie wanted to prove to Susanna, as well as to the psychiatrist, that he really had been good for his brother. It had become a challenge, a matter of pride for Charlie. Maybe more than that. Maybe it was to himself that he had something to prove.

Having parked Raymond at a small table in the bar with a ginger ale in a tall glass and a bucket of fresh potato chips, Charlie went to the lobby and phoned Susanna. Instead of her peppery Italian accent, he got her bland answering machine and hung up. Frustrated, he gave in to a whim.

Swaggering up to the front desk, he registered himself

and Raymond for a duplex suite. They'd earned it, especially Raymond, and winners deserve the cream that floats to the top of the bottle. Losers stay in motel rooms; winners sleep in duplex suites at Caesar's Palace. Coming back with the room key in his hand, he slumped down next to Raymond and ordered a scotch on the rocks. A double.

Raymond's eyes were almost sparkling as he looked around him. All of this was new, all of it wonderful and memorable. He was so excited he could barely sit still and kept fidgeting around in his chair.

'You have to go to the bathroom?' Charlie asked, misinterpreting Raymond's body language. Raymond gave him the silent stare that Charlie recognized as no. When Raymond actually said no, he usually meant yes. When he was silent, that was probably no.

'Well, I do,' said Charlie wearily. 'Come on.'

But Raymond was looking over Charlie's shoulder now, obviously fascinated by what he saw. Charlie turned and followed his brother's gaze. Sitting on a tall stool at the bar was a gorgeous girl in her early twenties. Pretty face, lovely hair, great body. Obviously a pro. The hookers of Las Vegas are some of the most beautiful girls in the world – at least, the ones who work the top hotels. The girl was half turned away from them, visible mostly in profile, and she didn't see Raymond staring at her.

Raymond watched the girl, and Charlie, touched and amused, watched Raymond watching the girl. 'I'll be back in a minute,' he said, smiling. 'You stay put. Promise?'

Without taking his eyes off the girl, Raymond nodded. Charlie reached over and rumpled his brother's hair just a little, pulling his hand away before Raymond could stiffen at his touch. 'You be good.'

As Charlie disappeared into the men's room, the girl turned around and caught Raymond's gaze. Immediately a bright, professional smile flashed across her perfect face. But there was no hardness in the smile because she was still too young and too pretty and too successful to have been battered by life into callousness.

Imitating her, Raymond gave her his best Charlie smile, the Dazzler. From a distance, and with that grin on his face, he appeared to be a well-dressed man looking for a little action. That brought her to her feet, and, carrying her drink with her, the girl walked over to Raymond's table and sat down next to him, gazing into his eyes.

''Evening,' she said in a soft voice.

Raymond hesitated while he scanned his memory for the right thing to say. What he came up with was Charlie's conversation with the young waitress in that diner back in Cincinnati. The one who'd given him a whole box of toothpicks.

'Actually, it's a beautiful morning,' he answered, mimicking perfectly, thanks to his total recall, Charlie's carefree come-on tone. 'So, uh, what's fresh today?'

'Well, sugar, I guess . . . me,' was the predictable response, but now the girl eyed Raymond oddly. This guy appeared normal enough. He was neat and clean, and his suit was obviously expensive, but there was something . . . something a little *off* about him. That smile, for instance. It was beautiful, dazzling even, but it didn't . . . *change*. It sat on his face as though it had been pasted there. And his words . . .

'In fact,' Raymond continued his uncanny recall of Charlie's conversation, 'we were wondering –'

'We?' The girl's eyes opened wide, startled, and she looked around the table in case she'd missed something or somebody.

'. . . what's exciting around here? After dark?'

'Well, darlin', I guess that's me again,' the girl answered flirtatiously, snuggling an inch or two closer to Raymond.

But now, like a wind-up toy whose battery has run down, Raymond fell silent. He was out of conversation because that was as far as Charlie had got with the waitress before Raymond had freaked her out, sending her scampering away. There was nothing else in his memory. As for communicating on his own, that was not a Raymond thing to do. Yet there was something about her that was attractive to Raymond, something that he couldn't define but that gave him the feeling of no-fear. In actual fact, although he didn't make the connection in his head, it was her passing resemblance to Vanna White in the TV programme *Wheel of Fortune*. When Raymond sat watching *Wheel of Fortune*, looking at Vanna turning the letters, he was almost always munching on something tasty and feeling un-threatened. This girl even dressed a little like Vanna, bare-shouldered and glittery.

Now she was sitting close to Raymond and looking at him seductively. Obviously she expected him to go on making conversation. The smile vanished from his face, leaving the usual blank, slightly disoriented expression in its place. With an effort Raymond said slowly, 'I'm Raymond. You're sparkly.'

Oh, god. The girl, who had been edging closer, sat up straight and looked at him sharply. What was he, a feeb? A tard? There was no way that she could understand what somebody like Raymond was about and nothing in her experience to equip her to deal with what he was. But her perceptions were acute enough to tell her that here was somebody different, somebody lost, somebody who didn't have both oars in the water. And her little girl's heart went out to him, as it would to a stray dog or cat. Besides, he interested her; she'd never sat this close to anybody like Raymond before, and she found herself curious to know more. But she was a working girl, so she had to keep moving right along.

'Thank you, Raymond,' she said softly. 'My name is Iris.' At his timid nod, she continued. 'Raymond, do you like me?' This time his nod was less timid, stronger. 'Why did you say those things?' she asked him curiously. 'Before . . . About after dark and all that.'

'This is just stuff you say,' answered Raymond gravely. 'To a pretty girl. Like Sally Dibbs. I know her telephone number. Four-six-one-oh-one-nine-two.'

Iris reached over and touched Raymond's hand, very lightly. Instantly he stiffened, not as much as he usually did, yet enough to make her pull her hand away. She wasn't hurt or angry, just more curious. Questions kept running through her mind. Was this guy as harmless as he appeared? Was he a simple retard? Why, if he was retarded, was he sitting in the Caesar's Palace bar wearing such an expensive suit? And for Iris the all-important question: was there money in it for her? Could this guy be a potential john?

'He doesn't have any money,' said a man's voice behind her, almost as though somebody had been reading her mind. Iris turned. A really gorgeous young man was regarding her with a hostile look, the corners of his full lips turning down, a scowl furrowing his brow.

'That's all right, sugar,' Iris answered with her best professional smile. 'We're just talking.'

Charlie leaned over the table. 'Time to get some sleep. Say good night,' he told his brother shortly.

Raymond shook his head from side to side stubbornly. He wasn't ready to leave. Besides, it was too early to go to bed yet.

'Ray, c'mon upstairs,' ordered Charlie.

'You go to sleep. We're just talking.' Raymond's lips set in a stubborn, even defiant, line.

'What room?' Iris put in swiftly. 'I'll bring him right up.'

Charlie thought it over. On the one hand, he didn't trust this little floozy alone with his brother for a single minute. Who knows what information she might worm out of him? Besides, a wrong move could send Raymond into one of his fits. On the other hand, he recognized Raymond's stubbornness as something that could also lead to major trouble right here in this bar. At any moment Raymond might decide to pitch one of his weird anxiety fits; he'd done it before with a lot less provocation. This young hooker was obviously something he thought he wanted in the bizarre way that he wanted things like Judge Wapner.

And, on the third hand, didn't that psychiatrist in Tulsa, Dr Schilling, say that sex for Raymond was impossible? A miracle? And wasn't Charlie out to prove to a custody hearing that he'd made changes for the better in Raymond Babbitt? What if something could happen between Raymond and this girl? Even if that something wasn't the act itself, wouldn't it prove that, under his brother's care, Raymond had learned to reach out to another person?

And, on the fourth hand, wasn't Raymond entitled to a little something for his big win at the tables?

Charlie decided. 'That's all right,' he told Iris. 'I'll wait over there.' He gave the girl a don't-fuck-around glare and walked over to stand at the bar, where he could keep an eye on both of them. He was feeling a little jealous, although that wasn't the sensation he acknowledged.

Iris turned back to Raymond. 'I don't think he likes me.' It didn't take a rocket scientist to figure that one out.

'He's my brother. I live in his room.'

'He seems young to be your brother. How old are you, Raymond?'

It was a question that Raymond had no answer for, and his face began to crumple a little around the edges, as it did whenever he felt himself cornered.

'What's wrong?' Iris asked, puzzled.

'How old am I, Iris?'

The girl smiled and reached over, smoothing down the hair that Charlie had rumpled. Feeling her touch, for a split-second Raymond's body tensed. But there was something in her soft, womanly hand on his hair that brought him a no-fear memory of Mommy, and he relaxed again.

'You're forty, sugar,' Iris murmured, not missing by more than a couple of years. 'And . . . very attractive. Raymond, I'm sort of . . . working . . . now, so I have to go. But it was very good meeting you.' She stood up, but something in Raymond's face, a kind of silent pleading she thought she read in his eyes, reached out to her and she sat down again.

Obviously, Raymond wasn't . . . normal. He had no experience with women; anybody could tell that. He had no money; of that Iris was pretty certain. And business was, after all, business. A girl had to make use of her assets while she still had them. The working life of a successful Las Vegas hooker was perhaps seven years, tops. That's when the management of the best hotels allowed you to hang out and mingle with the customers. But then, sometimes even before you hit thirty, you were forced down the ladder to work the cheaper bars and hotels. These were Iris's prime years, the years when her face was still unlined and her body taut and firm, no sagging anywhere. Time was passing, though, and time was money.

And yet there was something so lost and lonely about this small man who lived in the room of his younger brother, who never took his angry eyes off him. And he really seemed to like her. Iris hesitated for a couple of heartbeats, then she made her mind up.

'Would you like to have a date with me?'

Raymond nodded seriously. 'What is that?'

'It's where we . . . talk. And maybe dance. Just for a little while. Would you like that?'

The look on Raymond's face told her that he would.

'Okay, later tonight. Right here. At ten o'clock. Before I start my work.' Iris stood up, smiling down at Raymond. 'Tell your brother. Ten o'clock. Right here.'

Walking off, she turned and waved at Raymond, who sent her back an exact replica of the wave. When Charlie returned to the table, he saw a look on Raymond's face he hadn't seen since he gave Raymond the Sony Watchman. It was the Raymond Babbitt limited version of feeling pleased with himself.

Depending on your point of view, Charlie's duplex suite was either glamorous and luxurious or tinsel-tacky and overdone. No expense had been spared to give the high-rollers a set of plush surroundings. The thick carpeting underfoot, the glittering chandeliers overhead, the soft, comfortable furniture, the sleeping quarters upstairs with rich velvet bedspreads on king-size beds – all had been designed to impress.

Raymond was obviously impressed. He stared around him, drinking everything in, tucking it into his memory bank. This place had every modern convenience. He recalled the words from television commercials. Now he saw their meaning.

'You like this room?' asked Charlie with a frown. 'I don't. There's nothing here that ... feels good.' He threw the room key down carelessly and went to the bar to pour himself a drink. Charlie Babbitt was running on empty, feeling strangely low. Here he was a big winner, with all this money in his pockets; he ought to be high as St Peter's gate, and yet he was depressed. 'Winning. Winning feels good, but you're the guy doing the winning.' Charlie's voice dropped. 'I'm just watching.'

Watching. Raymond struggled to understand. 'Like ... the laundry, Charlie Babbitt?'

Charlie shook his head. 'No. Watching the laundry doesn't make me feel like a loser.' He looked up at his brother, who had climbed the stairs to his own bedroom balcony – Charlie's bedroom was on the floor below – and was checking out the 36-inch TV set.

'Watching you save my ass shakes me up a little, I guess.' He followed Raymond upstairs. It was suddenly important to him to make his brother understand.

Raymond was sitting on the edge of the vast bed, experimenting with the remote control. Throwing himself across the bed on the other side, Charlie sighed.

'We won a lot of money tonight, Ray. Enough to pay off just about everybody. And put my life back to where it was.'

Charlie began to whisper to himself, whisperwhisperwhisper, just as Raymond always did when he was frightened. Raymond couldn't hear what he was saying, so he crawled over the huge bed on his hands and knees and put his ear up close to Charlie's lips.

'And that's the bad news,' whispered Charlie.

Raymond had never seen Charlie feeling low. Angry, laughing, teasing, pouting, wheeling and dealing, yes, but despondent never. He didn't comprehend despondent; he had no word for it. Raymond was never depressed. He was either in a state of fear or of no-fear or coming out of one state to go into the other. He looked at his brother, saying nothing, puzzled and a little alarmed. Charlie Babbitt had taken the place of Vernon as the person Raymond was dependent on for his needs. Charlie's low spirits made Raymond anxious. He liked it when Charlie smiled; it induced no-fear in him. But Charlie wasn't smiling now.

'Secret thoughts,' muttered Charlie, sitting up and stretching. He had nobody to confide in except Raymond, and he was never exactly sure how much Raymond did or didn't understand. Seeing the look on his brother's face, he gave Raymond a crooked little smile. 'It means I have my life back, Ray. And I don't want it. And I don't know –' The smile faded and disappeared, and a strange new look crept into Charlie's hazel eyes. 'I don't know why I ever did,' he finished softly.

Exhaustion took hold of him suddenly, and Charlie felt that he was crashing. He yawned widely until tears squeezed out of the corners of his eyes. Even though it was still early on the clock, it was time for bed; they'd had a long, full afternoon, and tomorrow was bound to be another big day. He was tempted simply to close his eyes and go to sleep, just the way he was now, curled up on the bed, fully dressed and with his shoes still on. But that didn't make any sense. He'd only wake up in a few hours feeling sticky and horrible, his new suit and shirt a mess, and with a headache and a terrible taste in his mouth. Better do it right.

Pulling himself off the bed, Charlie headed for the bathroom to brush his teeth. On his way he began to discard his clothing – first the jacket and then the shirt and tie, leaving a trail of rumpled clothing on the carpet behind him.

Shit! If he wanted to wear these again tomorrow night, he'd better keep his clothes in decent shape. Sighing, Charlie backtracked and picked up his clothes, putting them neatly on hangers for the hotel valet to clean and press.

Raymond followed Charlie into the bathroom, still trying to understand what his brother had told him. He caught the expression in Charlie's eyes and the different tone in Charlie's voice, but he had no idea what they meant.

Taking the cap off the toothpaste, Charlie picked up the genuine bristle toothbrush that the hotel supplied. Squeezing the paste on to the brush, he took a good, long, hard look at himself in the mirror, seeing himself for the first time.

For ten years now Charlie Babbitt had been on his own, taking care of himself with a ferocity that ensured his survival. But in the process he had lost a lot – not only a home and what was left of his family but also his boyhood. He had been forced to become a man almost overnight. He'd grown up too damn fast. Now, at twenty-six, he felt old. And, worse, he felt alone. Damn it, he *was* alone. Charlie Babbitt was trapped inside a prison of his own making. While saving his own ass, he'd forgotten about other people. Building his own defences, he had stepped on a lot of feet; he'd made enemies with his hustling; he'd pushed everybody away from him and become paranoid. Now nobody but Susanna even dared to come close. And he might just have lost Susanna. He'd been phoning her and getting only her answering machine and no call-back.

In many ways Charlie was exactly like Raymond. Raymond too had to fight to survive. Raymond too had built an elaborate set of defence mechanisms that walled him off from others. Deep down Charlie, just like Raymond, was afraid to be touched. Charlie and Raymond had each created a world which he alone inhabited; both Raymond and Charlie were the sole centres of their existence, interested in nothing except what affected their personal comfort or safety.

The difference was that Raymond had been born deficient, while Charlie had attained his deficiency through hard work and constant practice. Raymond couldn't connect with another human being because he'd been damaged and a vital piece of his brain was missing, the piece that communicated. Charlie couldn't connect with anybody because he'd forced himself to forget how. Feelings slowed him down and got in his way. For the first time Charlie Babbitt realized what he'd been doing to himself all these years, how he'd cut himself off, insulated himself from uncomfortable human emotions. And he realized something else too, something even more important. Raymond had never been close to another human being because *he could not*; Charlie had never been close to another human being because *he would not*.

Charlie Babbitt was as slick as a weasel; he could manipulate with ease and skill everything and everyone in his environment. Raymond Babbitt couldn't eat with a fork, but inside, where it counted, Raymond was the better man because he'd never done anybody any harm.

What a pisser! Charlie Babbitt had set out on this zany cross-country marathon in order to hold his autistic brother to ransom, to imprint on his puzzled brain new behaviour patterns, no matter how false, useless or temporary, and all to get his hands on a great big chunk of money. What a great plan, and it even appeared to be working!

And now, suddenly, the fucking money didn't matter. Dragging Raymond out of a protective environment in which he'd survived for over twenty years, Charlie had never given his brother a second thought. Why should he, Charlie Babbitt, Mr Gorgeous, Mr Clever, consider a mental patient's rights or comforts? Remembering the thoughtless acts, the careless cruelties, inflicted on Raymond in the last few days, Charlie shuddered. He wanted to tell his brother how sorry he was. But he knew that Raymond couldn't understand. Even so, Charlie felt he owed Raymond a lot, more than merely the winnings from the blackjack table.

Raymond's brown eyes met Charlie's hazel eyes in the mirror over the basin. The question – unanswerable – was still in them. Charlie gave him a big, reassuring smile.

'So tell me about your hooker. Pretty lady, huh?'

Hooker?

'The girl. In the bar.'

'Iris,' said Raymond. 'We have a date. Later. Tonight. Ten o'clock. Right here. Tell your brother.'

A date? Charlie's grin widened around the toothbrush in his mouth.

'I have to . . . dance. In my date,' Raymond said, sounding scared.

Charlie took the toothbrush out. 'Hey, dancing's easy,' he reassured his brother. 'I'll show you how later. Just gimme an hour to rest up.'

But Raymond wasn't reassured. 'Now,' he insisted. 'Now is when . . . I don't know how.'

This obviously meant a lot to him, and the new Charlie, the one with the good resolutions, nodded. Rinsing the paste out of his mouth, he set the toothbrush down and gestured for Raymond to follow him. The two went back to the bedroom, where Charlie snapped the radio on, twisting the dial until he found some mellow music, easy listening, a romantic melody heavy on the strings.

'Okay. Now come over here and face me. Put your hands out. No, don't pull back. You want to learn to dance, don't you? Well, this is dancing. You have to hold your partner. No, don't look at your feet,' Charlie instructed. 'Just walk where I push you. Try to follow the music.'

Off they shuffled, slowly and awkwardly, Charlie leading and Raymond taking the girl's part. Although he was clumsy and not well coordinated, Raymond didn't do all that badly. His posture was rigid, and his arms stuck out stiffly, but his feet somehow almost managed to keep time.

'You're doing well,' Charlie said after a few minutes of moving around on a dime. 'Pretty soon you can push me.'

After a few minutes more Charlie tried a turn. Raymond stumbled a little but righted himself. They tried another turn, and this time Raymond negotiated it successfully. They switched positions. Now Raymond had the lead, and he was coping with it surprisingly well. His face was serious, lips set, and it took enormous energy just to remember to keep his eyes off his feet.

'Sonofabitch!' Charlie marvelled. 'You can do this, can't you?' Raymond didn't answer, but he pushed Charlie into a turn. And then another.

'Take it on home, Ray. You can dance with a goddamn girl!' Charlie laughed, proud of his brother and proud of himself too. 'C'mon, say it!'

'Dance ... with a ... goddamn girl!' echoed Raymond.

A sudden wave of unexpected affection washed over Charlie, and for a moment he forgot himself. For the space of a handful of heartbeats Charlie forgot who and what Raymond was, remembering only that this was his brother. His brother Rain Man. Grabbing Raymond tightly, he hugged him hard.

Raymond stiffened, terrified. Nobody had ever grabbed him like this before; nobody had ever held on, squeezing the life out of him. He felt as though he couldn't breathe, and all his alarms were instantly triggered.

Just as quickly as he'd forgotten, Charlie remembered. This was Raymond, and Raymond freaked out if he was touched. Letting go of his brother, he backed off. But Raymond's panic didn't lessen. He began to breathe hard, almost panting, while his eyes rolled back and forth in his head.

'C'mon, man!' exclaimed Charlie, dancing round like a prize fighter to make Raymond feel better. 'Brothers do this stuff all the time! It's not faggy. It's *brothers*! Are you my brother?'

But it was too late; Raymond was already deeply into his withdrawal. His hands were twisting each other nervously, his fingers entangling.

Now Charlie found himself getting inexplicably angry. He was too tired to think clearly. Also he was hurt, although he didn't yet acknowledge it even to himself. And he didn't recognize that he wanted, *needed*, to break through to Raymond, to force some recognition from his brother of the blood-bond between them. Wasn't this Rain Man, who used to sing to him when he was only a baby wrapped in a blanket? Charlie refused to believe that somewhere in Raymond an emotional recognition of that bond wasn't lurking, just waiting for Charlie to pull it out into the open. By force, if necessary.

'Are you, or are you not, my goddamn *brother*?' he demanded hotly.

Raymond couldn't understand why Charlie was suddenly so angry, but he understood that question. Brothers. He was. Charlie Babbitt's brother. He nodded fearfully, keeping his eyes fixed on his brother Charlie Babbitt. He knew the word; it was the relationship he couldn't comprehend.

'Then give us a goddamn *squeeze*!'

Charlie lunged at Raymond and threw his arms around his brother again in a tight bear hug. Desperate with fear, Raymond pushed hard at Charlie, using all his strength, and for a few minutes they grappled silently together, stumbling around the room in an awkward embrace.

But Charlie wouldn't let go. He had the crazy idea in his head that if he held on long enough, hugged strong enough, he could *force* Raymond to respond. His affection and the urgent need he felt to communicate with Rain Man could reach right down into the depths of Raymond, his Ray, his brother, and bring up the lost person, the *real* person, the *normal* person, buried inside him.

Summoning up a strength he never knew he possessed, a strength born only of extreme terror, Raymond pushed hard and violently, breaking Charlie's hold. By now, fear had taken him over completely, and his withdrawal into his secret self had triggered all his rituals – the whisperwhisperwhisper, fast and crazed, the wringing of the hands, the rigid limbs, the staring eyes.

But Charlie wouldn't yield. He was determined not to give up, not to let Rain Man slip away from him. The doctors were wrong; they *had* to be wrong. They were full of shit; what did *they* know? Were they Ray's brother? Raymond was all the family he had in the world, and he wasn't going to let him live and die alone in autistic withdrawal. He, Charlie Babbitt, would save him, would succeed where the shrinks had all failed.

'Shit, Ray,' he breathed, dancing around his brother. 'You really hurt my feelings! And feelings are the most important hurt.'

The rapid whispering continued as Charlie stalked Raymond, forcing him back into a corner. These were shock tactics; Charlie had got a tight hold on the stubborn theory that if he scared his brother deeply enough, he could frighten him all the way into normality.

'I'm gonna start a Serious Injury List,' threatened Charlie. 'And you'll be number one, man. Number *one*. In 1988.' He flung himself on his brother again, hugging him, holding him so tightly that Raymond couldn't break free.

'C'mon, man, hug me back!' he urged. 'Hug me back. Hug me back, Ray. Just one time. *One* time. C'mon! Just see how good it can feel!' Tears started in his eyes, stinging his eyelids; he'd never wanted anything so much in his life as he wanted Rain Man to return his hug. He hadn't felt such a strong emotion since the day, twenty-four years ago, that Rain Man had gone away and never come back. He'd cried then; he was crying now. He wanted Rain Man back.

Possessed entirely by fear and frustrated fury at his own helplessness, Raymond put the back of his hand into his mouth and began to bite it, very hard. It was the most extreme demonstration of his autistic behaviour, this unconscious act of self-destruction.

And it snapped Charlie out of his delusion, brought him up cold. He understood in a flash, now and for ever, that Rain Man no longer existed, had never actually existed except in his own baby memory. There *was* no normal person trapped inside this small body. Raymond Babbitt was a high-functioning autistic. Period. End of quote. He was capable of enjoying some minor pleasures to a minor degree, perhaps. And he possessed some remarkable savant abilities, certainly. He might, with love and care, even appear to make a little progress. But Raymond Babbitt would never be normal. Never. Be. Normal.

It was as if a pail of icy water had been thrown over Charlie. He let go of Raymond at once, backing away with his palms out in that universal gesture of submission. 'Hey, look, it's *over*! Ray, stop that, *please*!'

But Raymond was tracking through a desert waste somewhere within his brain, searching for his redoubt, trying to stay alive, unable to keep from biting his hand. He didn't feel the pain, or, if he did, he associated the pain with the mysterious protective magic he practised for his survival. Grabbing his arm, Charlie forced the hand out from between his brother's teeth, prying Raymond's jaws apart.

The back of Raymond's hand was covered with bite marks, making Charlie want to weep with guilt.

'Forget it, forget it,' he pleaded. 'I'll never do that again. I promise. Never, never again.'

Slowly, very slowly, Raymond began to come back a

little. His gasping abated, became breathing again. But the fear still remained in his eyes, in the rigid stance of his small body.

'I was stupid, okay?' said Charlie softly and with infinite sadness. 'Brothers hug. We're not brothers.'

Like a summer storm, in which the lightning flashes and the thunder roars and the down-rushing waters flood the streets, the fight was furious but soon over and, by Raymond at least, apparently forgotten.

While Charlie showered and put his rumpled clothing back on again, getting ready to escort Raymond to the bar for his ten o'clock date, Raymond sat on the bed and watched game shows on TV, calmly waiting for the hour to arrive when he'd dance with Iris.

Charlie had just emerged from his bedroom and was knotting his tie when a knock sounded at the door. Before he could answer it, the suite door opened. Susanna stood in the doorway, cheeks flushed, dark hair tangled, as though she'd thrown on anything to make the plane on time and fly all the way across the desert at night. Which she had. She looked wonderful.

Charlie ran to hug her, holding her close and laughing.

'Hey, you look terrific,' he said with his face buried in her thick, curly hair. 'Ray, Susanna's here!'

Raymond turned and regarded her solemnly. Susanna waved, and he waved back in imitation.

'How did you know we were here at Caesar's?' Charlie's hazel eyes were puzzled but happy.

'I was talking to Lenny.' The girl's bright black eyes dropped, then looked frankly into his. 'I'm sorry about your business,' she said softly.

Charlie shrugged lightly. 'Oh, don't worry. There

have been some startling developments. Ray, tell her what we've been doing.'

'We played cards. We played blackjack and I counted cards,' Raymond said promptly.

'What?' gasped Susanna.

'It's a long story,' Charlie put in hastily, eager to get Susanna alone. 'We'll talk about that after we have a nap.' He grabbed her arm possessively, and led her towards his bedroom.

'How are you, Ray?' she called over her shoulder.

'I don't know.'

Their lovemaking was better than Charlie or Susanna ever remembered it being. But whether that was because Charlie was too tired to be anything but low-key and tender, or because they'd been apart for days, or because he was expressing some new-found feeling, who can say? At any rate, after their passion was spent they lay side by side, naked, on the rumpled sheets, wiped out but feeling close and very mellow.

Susanna ran her fingernail lightly along Charlie's bare shoulder and down his arm. 'Are you really happy to see me?' she asked in a soft voice.

Charlie leaned over and nuzzled her small, perfect breast. 'Of course. What do you think? Haven't I just been acting happy?'

'Well, I ask because you never tell me these things. Like whether or not you really missed me. Not this,' and she swept her arm out in a gesture meaning the sex they'd both enjoyed, 'but *me*. Susanna.'

'You know I do –' Charlie began, but Susanna cut him off.

'Then why can't you tell me that?' she demanded, her eyes flashing. ' "Susanna, I missed you. I want to see you." You know those words. There are millions of those English words. It would be nice –'

At that moment there was a knock on the bedroom door, and Charlie leaped off the bed.

'Saved by the bell,' Susanna muttered.

'C'mon in,' Charlie called, wrapping a towel around his waist and throwing the door open. Raymond was standing there, holding his Watchman in his hand.

'It's six minutes to my date.'

'He has a date?' Susanna asked, surprised.

Charlie was hopping on one leg, pulling his trousers on. 'Well, sort of, yeah. C'mon, Susanna, get dressed fast. We gotta be downstairs in six minutes.'

'Five,' said Raymond.

The three of them arrived downstairs at the bar with a minute to spare. Raymond was still clinging to his Watchman, his eyes glued to the little screen. Safe in his jacket pocket was hidden the something that Charlie Babbitt had given to him to give to Iris.

'Ray, you know, you could have left your TV in the room. You don't need to take that thing on your date.'

'They're dancing,' said Raymond. He held out the Watchman. On the three-inch screen Fred Astaire and Ginger Rogers were stepping out beautifully; Ginger's gown swept out around her like a cloud, while Fred's feet moved over the stage like stardust made flesh.

'What does she look like?' Susanna whispered to Charlie.

Raymond heard her. 'She looks like cafeteria food,' he told her. 'She has the skin for cafeteria food.'

Charlie threw his head back and uttered a loud laugh. 'I don't think I've heard that one before.'

'Is that good?' Susanna asked with one eyebrow up-lifted.

As they were looking around the bar for Iris, an official of the casino approached them.

'Mr Babbitt?'

'Yeah, right,' said Charlie.

'Mr Kelso would like a word with you.'

Uh-oh. Charlie felt a sudden pang of anxiety. This didn't sound too good. He'd won too much damn money and these bozos were not happy. Take it slow. It was unlikely that the casino was going to shake his hand and congratulate him; on the other hand, it was unlikely they'd shoot him. Play it cool, he told himself. Keep it together. They've got nothing on you. You're clean. Even so, he was less than comfortable.

'Susanna, you want to watch after him for a few min-utes?'

Raymond didn't look up from his Watchman when Charlie left, except to glance at his wristwatch.

'She's not here. It's ten-oh-one. She's not here,' Raymond announced. Susanna eyed him anxiously. But Raymond didn't seem unduly disturbed; he was still completely absorbed in the Fred and Ginger movie on his Sony Watchman.

Charlie followed the casino official through a door marked 'Private: Entry Forbidden', which led to a long corridor off which a number of doors opened. Each door led to an office or a suite of offices for casino personnel. At the end of the corridor the lettering on one door said 'Mr J. Eugene Kelso' and, in smaller letters underneath, 'Director of Security'. The casino official pushed the door open and beckoned Charlie inside.

They were in an outer office, well furnished and

bright with modern paintings and a sleek ebony-wood desk at which sat a secretary beautiful enough to be a model. At her nod the official led Charlie to the broad oak door of the inner office, knocked quietly once, then opened the door for Charlie, saw him inside and left, closing the door very softly after him.

The office of the security director was large and luxuriously furnished; it spelled m-o-n-e-y to Charlie, who was impressed despite himself. Behind a wide antique desk sat a distinguished man with a handsome face and greying hair. Charlie's startled eyes snapped open. The smiling man who'd been sitting next to Raymond at the blackjack table all afternoon, the man who'd asked Raymond all those questions, was a top casino official, director of security, Mr J. Eugene Kelso! Only now he wasn't smiling.

Charlie felt the back of his knees giving way. With a gigantic effort he managed to stroll coolly to a chair and sit, not fall, down. For a long minute the two men were silent, looking at each other, then Mr Kelso spoke quietly.

'Congratulations, Mr Babbitt. You've won . . . let me see – He consulted a payout slip. 'Eighty-six thousand three hundred dollars. That's a great deal of money.'

'Not so much,' Charlie said with outward composure, while his heart hammered in his chest. 'Not when you consider the really high rollers.'

'Well, it isn't the amount. It's the potential . . . for disruption.' Mr Kelso leaned back in his high leather chair and put the tips of his fingers together. 'Counting into a six-deck shoe is quite a feat. In fact, it's one worthy of special attention. My own attention. I don't play cards with everyone, Mr Babbitt. I don't like cards.'

Charlie put on his best air of boyish innocence. 'I'm afraid I really don't know what –'

'We have videotapes,' Mr Kelso cut in abruptly, and a new coldness entered his voice. 'We analyse those. And we share them with other casinos. The tapes suggest, Mr Babbitt, that you should take your winnings and leave the state.'

Charlie opened his mouth to speak, but the security director cut him short. 'All you have to do is close your mouth and go home. And that's the best odds you're gonna see for a while.' He looked sharply at Charlie. 'I'd take them.'

The menace in Kelso's voice was faint but unmistakable, a dagger sheathed in velvet. Suddenly Charlie Babbitt felt an urgent need to see LA again. He wanted to go home.

Iris didn't show up for the date. By ten past ten Raymond was quite ready to give up and go home. Since he had no expectations, he suffered no disappointment, and he seemed content enough to follow Susanna's suggestion that they go back upstairs to watch TV in the suite. In fact, so caught up was he in the Rogers–Astaire film on the tiny screen he carried that he wasn't thinking about Iris at all.

With Susanna he walked slowly to the elevator bank, his eyes on his little Sony. Susanna looked over his shoulder. On the screen Fred and Ginger were dancing magically to 'They Can't Take That Away From Me'.

'Probably Iris dances like that,' Susanna said brightly. 'That was too bad. But there'll be other chances. Lots of pretty girls would . . . love . . . to dance with you, Raymond.'

Raymond didn't react; all his attention was focused on Ginger.

'Iris was real pretty, huh?'

'I don't know.'

The elevator arrived, and the doors opened silently. Susanna stepped inside and waited for Raymond. He shuffled in slowly, still watching his movie with rapt attention. They had the elevator all to themselves.

'Was she the prettiest girl you ever saw?' she persisted.

'I don't know,' he said again.

The music from the dancing scene filled the elevator. It was melodic, romantic – irresistible. Impulsively, Susanna reached out and touched the red 'Stop' button on the control panel. The elevator shuddered a little, then stopped with a small jolt. Startled, Raymond looked up from his Sony.

'I like this music,' Susanna told him gently. 'Do you think you could show me? How you'd dance with Iris?'

This was too new a development for Raymond; he drew a total blank. But there was such a sweet familiarity about Susanna that he wasn't alarmed. Gently, the girl took the Watchman out of his hand and laid it down on the floor of the elevator. The music flowed upward, wreathing them in its sweetness.

Susanna stepped closer to Raymond, holding her arms out in the dance position. 'Is it like this?' she asked.

Raymond simply stood there, looking blankly at her, his head tilted sideways in his characteristic way.

Susanna smiled reassuringly at him and gently lifted Raymond's arms, placing them around her neck. Very slowly, she began to dance and ... after a few beats, Raymond began to dance with her. Their bodies pressed together, they turned around in that confined space, following the music, Raymond remembering what

Charlie had taught him and doing it . . . with a certain style. Raymond style.

The song came to an end, and the two of them parted.

'Iris missed a beautiful dance,' Susanna said quietly.

'And a kiss.'

A kiss? Susanna took a step back, startled.

'Charlie Babbitt said. If she was nice to me. To give her. A little kiss.'

Susanna thought it over a second or two and then nodded. She stepped up to Raymond and said softly, 'Show me how.'

Raymond pursed his lips like a little kid forced to kiss a maiden aunt. Shaking her head, smiling, Susanna said, 'Open your mouth. And kiss . . . like you're eating something very soft. Something that tastes very good.' She parted her red lips, showing Raymond how.

Opening his mouth in imitation of Susanna, Raymond received his first kiss. Susanna kissed him gently and tenderly. They kissed for a few seconds and then, finally, Susanna pulled away.

'How did it taste?' she asked him.

'It tasted wet,' said Raymond.

'Then we did it right.' The girl laughed.

Reaching into his jacket pocket, Raymond brought out the secret something he was keeping for Iris and held it out to Susanna. Astonished, Susanna looked from his face to the two hundred dollars he was offering her, then back to his face again.

'Charlie Babbitt said,' said Raymond.

CHAPTER TWELVE

The drive back to Los Angeles passed quickly. The air streaming past the Buick convertible was hot and dry but not unpleasant. Susanna sat next to Charlie in the front seat; Raymond sat in the back, alternately looking out at the desert scenery and watching a western on his little hand-held Sony TV. The hand he'd bitten so badly was now neatly bandaged up by Susanna. From time to time Raymond leaned forward into the front seat, reminding Charlie that he had promised to take him to a Dodger game. In Los Angeles. Wasn't that why they were all going to Los Angeles? To see the Dodgers play? Charlie Babbitt said. Charlie had almost forgotten that promise, made a week ago, but now he reassured Raymond that a visit to Dodger Stadium was a certainty. In the cards, he said. It was in the cards for sure.

Every muscle in Charlie's body was screaming out for rest. He hadn't slept in what seemed like days because he and Susanna had passed the night in making love. After all, how many times would they have the opportunity to bed down in a duplex suite at a class hotel? Tired as he was, though, Charlie felt good. He had his bail-out money in his pocket, his girl by his side again, his brother in the back seat; the casino hadn't fed him to the sharks one leg at a time. Life was not so shabby after all.

Once he even let Raymond drive the Buick. For five minutes. The road was empty of traffic; the car was doing no more than twenty miles an hour. It was Charlie's foot on the gas pedal, but Raymond's hands were on the wheel, and Susanna was laughing hysterically in the back seat.

'You're driving, man. Watch the road,' cautioned Charlie.

'I'm an . . . excellent . . . driver,' said Raymond.

At Santa Monica they let Susanna off at her apartment and headed for Charlie's place. Charlie lived in a modest apartment in one of the million Spanish-style apartment complexes that are sprinkled throughout Los Angeles's side streets. They all look alike. A tall avocado tree drops mushy, inedible fruit on the terracotta tiles of the roof. A central courtyard with a swimming pool surrounded by strap-shaped agapanthus leaves and the round blue heads of the flowers when they blossom. Sometimes it isn't blue agapanthus; it's orange clivia. Same difference.

Every apartment on the ground floor opens on to the courtyard. Every apartment on the second and third floors opens on to a balcony overlooking the swimming pool. There is no fourth floor. Their design inspired by the Spanish Mission theme, the apartments feature stucco walls, phoney brick fireplaces and minuscule kitchens. The only difference among them is the rent, and that's based on geography; what you pay for is the location of the neighbourhood. Charlie's little place was on the outer fringe of Brentwood, just close enough to share the same post code, so the rent was astronomical.

Charlie pushed open the door for Raymond and, carrying the bags, struggled past him, bumping into Raymond's backpack. Raymond stood fixed in the doorway, looking around.

'Do we live here?' he asked finally. ''Course, they moved the *bed*.'

'Ray, *I* live here,' Charlie answered quietly.

'Where do *I* live?'

'Your room's there.' Charlie pointed to the little spare room he used sometimes as a guest room and sometimes as a home office. It held a desk and some files, a chair or two, but the bed was folded up inside a sofa. Raymond shuffled over to have a look. Instant anxiety.

''Course, somebody *stole* the bed. My room ... is ... without any ... any ... it's bedless. I'm gonna be ... *bed*less ... in –'

'In 1988.' Charlie finished with a smile, which seemed to calm Raymond somewhat. 'You get the magic room. Where the sofa *turns into* a bed. Then we push it under the window. You like it under the window. Just ... right.'

Raymond thought that over and found it acceptable. But another problem presented itself at once. ''Course, my books –'

'Right.' Charlie nodded firmly. 'We'll get books. Go in and make a list. Of what we need.'

This went down well. Raymond entered his room eagerly, slipping off his backpack and digging for the correct notebook. He enjoyed making lists; lists were comforting, except for the Serious Injury List and the Ominous Events List.

Charlie headed straight for his answering machine to check his phone messages. The digital read-out said three. He pressed the rewind and then the play buttons.

'This is to confirm Mr Raymond Babbitt's interview with Dr Marston,' said a voice with clipped British accent. Evidently an expensive secretary. 'Ten o'clock tomorrow morning. Four-five-oh Roxbury Drive. We'll see you then.' Click. Good. He'd been expecting this call.

'Hi, it's me.' Susanna's sweet accent came softly over the phone. 'I just . . . I was hoping you guys got home okay. So. Hope you're all right.' Click. Just hearing her voice made him feel good.

'Can I see the TV now?' called Raymond from the next room.

'Mr Babbitt, this is Walter Bruner.' The last message took Charlie totally by surprise. 'I'm at the Bonadventure. I think we should talk.' Click.

Oh, shit! Bruner! Charlie wasn't ready for Bruner. A sinking feeling crept into Charlie's gut. He hadn't expected the psychiatrist to come all this way to track him down. But, on second thoughts, why wouldn't he? Over three million dollars were at stake here. For that kind of money Charlie would push a peanut with his nose all the way to New Zealand. Wearing a ballet tutu.

It was just that Wallbrook seemed so far away now, as though it were long ago in the distant past. Charlie didn't associate Raymond with Wallbrook any more. They were brothers.

After talking to Dr Bruner at his hotel and arranging to see him, Charlie had time only to shower, grab a quick shave and put on a sport shirt and jeans. Raymond was in his room, sitting happily on his sofabed, watching morning game-show repeats and snacking on tortilla chips.

When Dr Bruner rang the apartment bell, Charlie let him in grudgingly, looking over the doctor's shoulder to make certain Bruner hadn't brought any security guards with him to snatch Raymond back by force. But the doctor was quite alone, and he didn't even appear to be angry. He entered the apartment with a pleasant smile and one question.

'Raymond?'

'In there.'

Dr Bruner went to the doorway of Raymond's room and took a look. He looked healthy, unharmed and very Raymond. Although Bruner took mental note of the fact that Raymond's hand was bandaged, he said nothing.

'Is there somewhere we can talk privately?' asked the psychiatrist.

'Outside.'

The two men stepped out into the courtyard, leaving the door ajar so Charlie could hear Raymond if his brother needed anything.

'I'll come right to it,' the psychiatrist said crisply. 'As we speak, my lawyer is meeting with your lawyer. And explaining to him . . . the facts of life.'

'Facts of life,' repeated Charlie, keeping his voice level.

Bruner nodded and reached into his pocket. He pulled out an official-looking document and held it out to Charlie, who looked at it but didn't touch it. 'This is a temporary restraining order preventing you, under criminal penalties, from removing Raymond. Until the hearing is concluded.'

The doctor looked keenly at the young man, but Charlie's expression didn't change. He was damned if he was going to let this shrink shake him up.

'You see, Charlie,' continued Dr Bruner, 'when the hearing is over, Raymond will be *committed* into Wallbrook. For the first time in his life. And he has you to thank for that.'

Charlie's chin went up defiantly. 'That's up to the judge, isn't it?'

'The judge will listen to the psychiatric investigator. His name is Dr Marston. You'll meet him tomorrow morning.'

'Great. Maybe *this* guy has an open mind.' But Charlie had that sinking feeling again, deep in the pit of his belly. They were ganging up on him here; all those shrinks stick together.

'I gave him boxes of files on Raymond,' Dr Bruner said with the ghost of a smile. '*Boxes.* This isn't a close call, son. It's a formality. Your brother is a very . . . disabled individual. Haven't you noticed?'

'Well, you should see him now,' Charlie barked hotly. 'What he can do. He . . . he *smiles*, for chrissakes!'

'I know,' replied Bruner. 'Susanna told me.'

Susanna? What the hell was going on here?

'I saw her today,' the psychiatrist explained. 'She thinks Raymond's made progress.' He smiled. 'She even thinks *you*'ve made progress. I hope she's right. About you. As for your brother, well, I know it's easy to be swept away by enthusiasm. A change of scenery, new adventures, and they can seem to blossom. Temporarily.'

Charlie felt anger welling up in him. What did this guy know about the days he'd spent with Raymond? Zero! He wasn't even there! He never saw a thing!

'They plateau,' the doctor continued. 'And then regress. A lifetime of autism isn't cured by a vacation, Charlie.' He shook his head.

'Then again,' retorted Charlie, 'it isn't over till it's over.'

Dr Bruner's smile faded, and a new, stern expression took its place. 'It was always a lost cause, Charlie. Your father made my powers as trustee totally discretionary. That means whether or not you win custody of Raymond, I won't have to pay you a dime.'

That was a body blow, and Charlie's face showed it had caught him by surprise and hit him hard. But he said nothing, determined at all costs to hold on to his cool.

'Now here's my chance to surprise you,' continued Dr Bruner. 'I came here with a chequebook. It belongs to Raymond. And I'm prepared to write you a cheque. A very, very big one.'

'And why is that?'

'I don't think you have a chance in hell, Charlie. But that's a chance I'm not prepared to take. Your brother's life and happiness and well-being are on the line here. Those are very precious to me. I don't choose to gamble with them, however safe the odds.'

'You're buying me off.' A cynical grin crossed Charlie's lips. *He's scared I've got a real chance here.*

'I'm responsible for spending Raymond's money for his benefit. And this is the best money he'll ever spend.'

'How much?'

'Two hundred and fifty thousand dollars. And no strings. Just . . . walk away.' Dr Bruner took out the chequebook and a Mont Blanc pen with a solid gold nib, wrote the cheque and handed it politely to Charlie.

Charlie accepted the cheque gravely and read it carefully. It was beautifully written; Dr Bruner's handwriting was almost calligraphy. 'Charles Babbitt,' it read, 'the sum of two hundred and fifty thousand dollars and no cents.' Gorgeous. A shame to cash a beauty like this. For a moment Charlie mused over all the good living a quarter of a million dollars could buy. Then, without a word, he tore the cheque slowly into four meticulously matching pieces and handed them politely back to Dr Bruner.

The interview was over.

★

Of course, Raymond had it firmly in mind that today was the day they were going to Dodger Stadium to see the ballgame. And, of course, when Charlie was forced to tell him that there was no baseball game in the *very* immediate future, it upset Raymond so much that he went deep inside himself and began pitching one of his imaginary big-league games.

This was a worst-case scenario come to life. In a couple of hours they were due at Dr Marston's office to prove to an investigating psychiatrist that Raymond Babbitt was better off with his brother Charlie Babbitt, that Charlie Babbitt had worked wonders – almost miracles – with his autistic brother. And here was that very same autistic brother firmly locked into one of his grotesque fantasies.

'Frank Robinson, strike three!' called Raymond from the pitching mound. He was very angry with Charlie Babbitt. Charlie Babbitt had *promised*. 'Harmon Kille-brew, strike three!'

'Look' Charlie explained for the sixth time, 'we can't go to the Dodger game today. We have the hearing, the big hearing!'

'Henry Aaron, strike three!' Raymond was on a winning streak, striking out the big ones, one by one, as they came into the batter's box. His fast ball was unhittable, his curve ball the terror of the bullpen.

'Ray, stop a minute, please!' Charlie begged.

Raymond paused in mid-pitch, one foot in the air, the imaginary ball clutched tightly in his imaginary glove.

'I'm sorry about the game. And when one guy says he's sorry, the other guy says –'

'Pete Rose, strike three!'

'Fine.' Charlie shrugged bitterly. 'Get your rocks off.'

'Babe Ruth, strike three!'

'All right,' Charlie growled, his patience at an end. 'That's enough of that!'

But Raymond was pitching harder and faster than ever. 'Mickey Mantle, strike three!' He was striking out the superstars; the legendary hitters held no terror for him.

'Ray, I said stop it!' Charlie took a step or two towards Raymond, desperate to bring him back out of his fantasy.

'Charlie Babbitt, strike thr –'

'Foul ball!' called Charlie, and that stopped Raymond cold. Foul ball? Not a strike-out? For a long moment the two brothers stood eye to eye, then Raymond picked up one foot and went into one of his long wind-ups.

'You want to strike me out?' demanded Charlie. 'Then let's do it for real.'

And he led the astonished Raymond out of the house, around the corner and down two streets to the playgrounds in the nearby park. On the way they made one stop, to pick up a six-pack of Coors for Charlie.

A hot July day, the kind that makes dogs pant with long, dry tongues and cats curl up in patches of shade to sleep for hours. Kids come out to play sports, but their enthusiasm soon wanes, and they wind up lying around on the grass with their cans of soft drinks, talking about ballgames instead of playing.

A couple of boys, aged maybe ten, maybe eleven, were lying around just like that. They'd come out to the park to shag a few flies, but the heat had overcome them. Now they reclined on the grass, drinking Coke, watching some neighbourhood all-stars playing basketball. Their baseball and bat lay neglected on the ground near by.

'Hey, fellas,' called Charlie. 'Use your bat and ball for a minute? For ten bucks?'

For ten bucks? Was he serious? Sure, mister! The shorter of the two boys picked up the ball and tossed it to Raymond. Catching it awkwardly in both hands, the bandage getting in his way, Raymond managed somehow to hold on to it and clutched the precious object to his chest. He'd pitched many a major-league game in his time, but never had he held a real baseball in his hands. He examined it with awe.

Charlie picked up the bat and pointed to a near-by empty diamond. 'We'll be just there, guys.' With the bat and the six-pack he ran over to the diamond, Raymond trotting behind him, eyes filled with wonder.

Charlie knelt to dust off home plate. Raymond came in through the chain link fence and started towards the infield.

'Hold on, ace. The mound's over there! You're the pitcher, aren't you?'

The pitcher? Raymond Babbitt the pitcher? The concept of reality floored him, and he stood rooted to the spot, totally bewildered.

'Let's get loose, baby! Umpire's not gonna wait all day.' Squatting down behind the plate, Charlie became the catcher on Raymond's team. With hesitant steps, Raymond approached the mound. Charlie pounded into his bare hand as if it were a glove, and yelled his version of the confidence-building words that pitchers expect to hear from their catchers.

'Don't stare at it like it's a goddamn hand grenade. You know what to do with it. Burn it in here!'

Raymond stared around the empty diamond, not knowing what move to make. Or how to make it.

'Bottom of the ninth,' called Charlie, becoming the

sports announcer, setting the scene for him. 'The fall classic is knotted at three and three. The Cincinnati Reds, one out away from ending forty years of humiliation.'

Raymond caught Charlie's eye and held it.

'And they've gone to their ace,' announced Charlie. 'The man who's brought them all this way. Raymond Babbitt. The legendary Rain Man. Asked to do it just one more time.'

In answer to the question in his brother's eye Charlie nodded. *You can do it, Ray. You can do it, Rain Man.*

'First warm-up throw, now. Into the wind-up –'

Raymond's hands were at his waist. His leg kicked out in that funny little way it did whenever he pitched. He brought his arm up and pitched the baseball hard. The ball sailed up high, at least eight feet over Charlie's head, rattling into the backstop and dropping to the ground.

'Aw*right*!' yelled Charlie. 'Smoke! The man is throwing smoke!'

Raymond showed his teeth in his frozen smile. The inning was moving along, only one out to go. Score tied, the potential winning run on third; two other potential runs on second and first. Could he do it? Could Rain Man strike out the heavy hitter, Charlie Babbitt?

Now Charlie, in his other identity as Raymond's catcher, retrieved the ball and walked out to the mound, a serious look on his face. This was a big out for the Reds, three men on and two down. Only this last Yankee batter stood between them and the World Series championship they'd fought so hard to gain.

The sports world and the fans held their collective breath as pitcher and catcher put their heads together for a strategy conference.

'Way to show 'em the dark one, ace,' muttered Charlie, as though everybody was trying to overhear them. 'Now, on the next one, no wind-up.'

'No wind-up?' Raymond looked startled.

'Bases loaded,' Charlie reminded him.

Raymond nodded, his eyes checking the bases. Taking him by the arm, Charlie led Raymond off the pitcher's mound and brought him forward, halfway to home plate.

'Now we're moving the rubber . . . right . . . up . . . here.' And Charlie created a new mound by heaping dirt together with the side of his shoe. Raymond had no idea what was going on; he looked over his shoulder at the real pitcher's mound yards away.

Charlie explained the strategy. 'This way, you don't have to throw so hard. The catcher can't handle your heat, see? Nobody could.'

Raymond nodded. Made sense. Charlie returned to the catcher's position and squatted down.

'Okay,' he called. 'The old change-up now. Lay it in there, nice and easy. Remember, no wind-up.'

Raymond lobbed a blooper pitch that landed in the vicinity of the plate. Charlie gave him the high sign; you've got 'em scared, Ray. Got 'em on the run. The Yankees are shittin' their britches.

'Control!' he yelled. 'Name of the game.'

Rolling the ball back to Raymond, Charlie picked up the bat and hefted it, checking out its size and weight, cutting through the air with practice swings. Now he was both announcer and batter. He stepped fiercely up to the plate.

'Pinch-hitter now for the Yankees. And it will be . . . yes! The Hammer! Charlie Babbitt. And with one swing, the Hammer could turn all this around. The crowd is going wild.' Charlie made some crowd noises and then broke into a chant. 'HAM-MER! HAM-MER!'

On the mound the pitcher checked the runners, making sure they weren't taking long leads off their bases. Now he faced the hitter, his face set in determination. This had to be the last out. The Series hung in the balance.

'So it's down to this. Strength against strength. The Brothers Babbitt to settle it all, and what more could you ask for? Here's the stretch –'

Raymond stretched, pitched and lobbed the ball about three feet outside the plate. Nevertheless the Hammer took a mighty swing . . . and a miss.

'Stee-rike one!'

Raymond did a little dance of excitement as Charlie went after the ball.

'The Rain Man nibbling on that outside corner,' intoned Charlie in his best sports announcer's voice. 'He's got *all* his stuff today. Charlie is going to have to bear down here . . .'

Charlie stepped back into the batter's box and got ready to swing, choking up a little on his bat, shifting his stance an inch or so. The stretch. The wind-up. Here comes the pitch. The ball lobbed straight through the air, heading for the plate. The Hammer swung hard, missing by a mile, as the ball dropped a few inches in front of the plate.

'Stee-rike two!'

By now Raymond was vibrating with excitement. When Charlie swung for the second time and missed, he jumped up and down in place. This was the most astounding thing that had ever happened to him, greater even than the dance with Susanna in the elevator. Even better than the card-counting. This was the big league, the World Series with Rain Man Babbitt on the mound. Striking out the big ones, the stars.

'The Hammer *way* out in front on that one. Raymond Babbitt in *complete* command this afternoon.' Charlie rolled the ball back to Raymond. 'The count is two strikes on the batter . . .'

Raymond picked up the ball, but he didn't go into his wind-up. Instead he stood there shaking his head.

'What's up?' asked his catcher, coming out to the mound for a conference.

'Wrong sign,' said Raymond. 'Can I give him the hard high one?' The catcher thought it over, then shrugged. 'What the hell? Why not?'

Charlie back in the batter's box, ready to swing. This could be the big one. Two strikes on him already, and the Reds stood to win the Series here. It was down to him, to the Rain Man.

The Rain Man took a long wind-up and brought his arm around to pitch a long, hard one. It was nowhere near the plate, nowhere near Charlie's head, nevertheless the batter took a frantic dive and rolled in the dirt to avoid getting beaned by the horsehide.

Ball one.

'Well, it's brother on brother,' announced Charlie, retrieving the ball. 'But no love lost with the world title at stake. Count is one and two on the batter.' He rolled the ball down to Raymond and took up his bat again. In his stance he called across to Raymond, and now the voice he spoke in was his own. No more Rain Man and the Hammer. This was Charlie Babbitt and Raymond Babbitt, one on one.

'This is it, Ray. This is my pitch. I'm gonna hit the goddamn thing to Kansas!'

Charlie's words, the tone of his voice, made Raymond hesitate. He looked over at his brother, standing there waving a mighty bat, and the edges of fear came nibbling in. Raymond took a step or two off the mound.

'Stand in there like a man, goddamn it! Let's see that rainbow. I'm gonna drive it, Ray! Take you downtown, sucker!'

Nervously Raymond stepped back on to the mound and took a long wind-up. Putting everything that he had into it, he threw the ball to Charlie.

It was a long, slow ball. Miraculously, it floated straight across the strike zone, where a blind hitter could catch hold of it. Even more miraculously, Charlie swung at it with everything *he* had – and missed completely. Completely! You could hear the bat cutting the air, and then . . . nothing. Charlie's swing carried him around and dumped him unceremoniously on his ass, down in the dirt right on top of the plate. The Hammer, the pride of the Yankees, had missed the nail. Charlie had struck out, and Raymond had done it. Charlie couldn't believe it; he fucking couldn't believe it. He'd *missed*!

Strike three. And out. The final out. The game was over. The Series was over. And Raymond Babbitt, Rain Man Babbitt, had come through, had won the Series for the Reds. Rain Man had struck the Hammer out! With a yell of jubilation, Raymond leaped into the air, the victor. He did a little victory dance on the makeshift mound.

But when he saw Charlie sitting in the dirt, looking as though he'd lost his best friend, Raymond's elation vanished. He shuffled slowly over to him, a question in his dark eyes. Charlie looked up, stunned, to find Raymond standing over him. Then Raymond sat down next to him on the plate. Brother sitting next to brother, each in his own world . . .

Suddenly Charlie felt a hand touch his face. Raymond's hand. Raymond's hand actually reaching out for him, touching him. And Raymond's voice, low, 'C-h-a-r-l-i-eeeeee.' Only a moment passed, and then the hand came away. Had he imagined it? The feeling in his chest was very real.

'Buy you a beer?' Charlie grinned crookedly at Raymond, reaching for his six-pack, detaching a couple of ice-cold brews, popping the aluminium tabs on the cans, handing a Coors to his brother.

Raymond stared down at the can in his hand. ''Course, they lost the *cup*.'

'Yeah, well.' Charlie smiled fondly at his brother. 'Cups are for girls, Ray. Men drink their beer like this.' Tilting his head back, he took a long swig from the can. Raymond watched him closely, then followed his example. When he lowered the can, there was a look of distaste on his face.

'Y'know, Ray, I really tried to hit the ball,' Charlie said sadly. 'But . . .'

'I made a good pitch,' said Raymond.

Tears sprang to Charlie's eyes, and he blinked them back. 'One fucking *hell* of a pitch!' he agreed. He took another long pull on his beer and wiped his mouth on his sleeve. 'Boy, it's too bad he wasn't here to see it,' he told Raymond softly. 'You striking me out.'

He and Raymond exchanged glances, but it was obvious that Raymond didn't understand.

'I'm talking about Dad, Ray.'

Raymond thought a minute. 'Daddy held you. He kissed you.'

Kissed me? Nah! But . . . 'Did he really?'

'Did he really,' Raymond confirmed.

'Yeah, well ... when I was little, maybe. He just didn't know what a ... winner ... I'd turn out to be. It's a real shame he wasn't here today. So I could show him,' said Charlie bitterly.

'Daddy knew. About showing.'

Now it was Charlie's turn to not understand, and Raymond could see that.

'I said, where's my brother Charlie Babbitt? And Daddy said, he's in California. And some day –' Raymond broke off. Charlie brought the icy can of beer to his lips, a long, hard pull.

'Some day. He'll show 'em all.'

The sky turned dark, light, dark and light again, and the world turned upside down. Charlie's tightly held ten-year grudge slipped out of his heart and drained away into the dirt, along with the spilled beer from the can in his nerveless fingers. His father had loved him.

He'll show 'em all. Sanford Babbitt had said that. He'd loved his son after all, and Charlie never knew it, and now it was too late. Too late. For the first time in his life Charlie considered not the pain his father had caused him but the pain he must have caused his father. So much pain for so many years. First from Raymond, then from the death of his wife, then from Charlie, on whom all his frustrated hopes and expectations had been pinned. And all for nothing. Because there had been no real connection between father and son.

Charlie's lips trembled, and he looked away. When he looked back Raymond was regarding him with large, troubled eyes. Raymond. His brother. His Rain Man. Charlie brought his face close to Raymond's, looked deeply into his eyes. His forehead nearly touched his brother's forehead.

that their foreheads did touch. Twice in one day Raymond had touched him. The two brothers looked into each other's eyes. And, no matter what the doctors said or ever would say, they connected. A real connection.

'Secret hug,' whispered Charlie.

'Actually, I'm an excellent driver,' said Raymond.

CHAPTER THIRTEEN

Charlie Babbitt was ready to kick ass, to bring out all the street smarts, the wily offences and defences he'd picked up in his ten years on his own. He and Rain Man were going to ace this meeting – that is, if Raymond had memorized his part and knew how to play it. Those goddamn headshrinkers would soon find out they'd bitten off more than they could chew when they'd taken on the Brothers Babbitt. After all, who had a more righteous claim to Raymond – some home for the disabled or his own blood brother?

Even so, as he rang for the elevator in the underground garage of the Roxbury Drive building, Charlie had to psych himself up one more time. Who's number one? *We*'re number one. The brothers from hell.

They were looking sharp in their Italian Vegas suits with the matching neckties. Impressive, two heavy dudes. Charlie forced a smile on to his face and hefted his briefcase as the elevator arrived.

The office door had a simple brass plate reading 'Philip Marston, MD'. Charlie pushed the door open and held it for Raymond to go in first. As usual, Raymond paused in the doorway, blocking traffic. Impeded by Raymond, Charlie couldn't follow him through the door; he could only peer over his brother's shoulder.

'Ah, Mr Babbitt?' That clipped British voice again, the one on Charlie's answering-machine tape. Marston's fancy secretary, a willowy looker with 'Efficiency' written all over her in Olde English letters. Matching her perfectly, the outer office also wore an air of quiet, well-bred luxury. Faded chintz on the chairs, but important drawings hanging on the walls. Inevitably, a tank of tropical fish. Did every psychiatrist in America have a fish tank in his office, Charlie wondered.

Raymond nodded. He was Mr Babbitt.

'Fancy a coffee?' the young woman asked politely. She was carrying a tray in her hand, and on it were two cups, a little china pot, cream and sugar. Raymond shook his head. No coffee.

'Please have a seat. We'll be just a minute.' And she was gone, into the inner office of Philip Marston, MD. Charlie followed Raymond into the office, and they both sat down. Now Charlie grabbed this opportunity for a between-the-halves pep talk with his brother.

'Okay. You remember everything?'

' 'Course you do.'

'No, no "'course". We don't say "'course".'

''*Course* we don't.'

'So. Everything stays quiet. The hands are quiet. Voice is quiet. No looking around.' And here Charlie imitated Raymond's anxious little head-turns. 'No notes. No fast talking. And, of course, no what?'

'No whispering,' Raymond recited. 'No spelling. No pitching. No hitting.'

Charlie gave his brother a nod of approval. 'And when they ask about the hand?' He looked significantly at Raymond's bandaged hand.

Raymond put his two hands on an imaginary wheel

and pantomimed driving an imaginary car. Perfect. They had it made in the shade. Smiling, Charlie reached over and smoothed down his brother's suit lapels and neatened his tie, straightening the Windsor knot. 'You're gonna do it,' he told him in a low voice. 'You're gonna make me proud.'

Now he unbuckled Raymond's belt and pulled the waistband of his trousers down from his chest to his waist. He re-buckled the belt. Taking out a comb, he parted Raymond's hair neatly and combed the expensive haircut into place. There! Looking like a million.

Raymond took the comb from his brother's hand and ran it through Charlie's hair, messing up the haircut in the process. Then he unbuckled Charlie's belt and pulled the waistband of his trousers up as high as it would go. There! Looking like a million dollars.

'Po-tential,' said Raymond.

Charlie grinned and opened his briefcase. In it was all of Raymond's stuff, everything he always carried with him in his backpack. 'Okay, it's all here. If you start missing something, or thinking about it, you just look at my briefcase. Then you'll know it's all right here with us. See? The socks, the Watchman, *all* the notebooks.' He reached in and pulled out the red one, showing it to Raymond. 'Like here's the Serious Injury List.'

Charlie riffled through the pages, coming at last to his own name. 'Charlie Babbitt is number eighteen. In 1988.' Next to Charlie's name Raymond had neatly drawn a little star, an asterisk, meaning 'see note below'. Charlie looked down at the bottom of the page. There was the little star again and next to it the words 'Charlie Babbitt is forgiven. July 18, 1988.'

Forgiven. Charlie stared at the words until they became a blur. Forgiven. Christ, that meant a lot! He wanted to share the moment with his brother. But when Charlie looked up again Raymond was busy watching the tank of fish.

'Pitiful,' murmured Raymond contentedly. 'Pitiful fish.'

'How . . . how much do you hear?' Charlie asked softly. But Raymond, absorbed in the fish, didn't answer.

'Ray, look at me.'

Something in the urgency of Charlie's tone must have reached Raymond because he looked up from the fish to meet his brother's gaze. Charlie's words came out slowly and with great difficulty, very different from his usual brash and confident manner.

'If I needed . . . to talk to someone. About something important . . . just for today . . .' He stared into Raymond's eyes. How much could his brother understand of what Charlie was trying to say. 'Can you listen to me? Will you try to . . . really listen? Just for this once?'

Raymond cocked his head to one side, thinking the question over. Then he began to nod his head, and nodded for almost a minute while Charlie waited patiently for him to stop. When at last he did stop, Charlie spoke very softly, but the anguish in his face was evident. This was crucially important to him.

'Ray, I don't know what I want. Guess that runs in the family, huh?'

Raymond didn't get the bitter little joke, but then Charlie never expected that he would. 'There isn't anything in the world that I want,' continued Charlie, his voice cracking a little. He felt so confused, so lost, so desperate. All the things he'd trained himself never to feel. Charlie Babbitt had always known not only what he wanted but also how to go about getting it. Now his entire value system was in ruins at his feet.

'So . . . where do I go?' he asked Raymond.

There were questions to which Raymond Babbitt had the correct answer. How many toothpicks on the floor? What time does Wapner come on the air in the Central Time Zone? Eastern? Pacific Time? How much money had a certain contestant won on *Wheel of Fortune*, and when, and by spelling out what? But he had no answer to Charlie Babbitt's question.

And Charlie Babbitt knew it. Still, he clung desperately to what he had of Raymond's that was uniquely his. Forgiveness. Nobody had ever come off the Serious Injury List except Charlie Babbitt. That had to count for something. And it was there, in black and white, in the red notebook. Charlie read the blessed word again.

Dr Marston's secretary came back into the room. She saw the two brothers sitting side by side. The older of them was impeccable, his hair combed neatly, his eyes intelligent. But the younger, that autistic boy, hair rumpled, dressed in a parody of a suit like Mr Babbitt's, dull eyes staring at a little red notebook. Poor thing.

'If you're ready, Mr Babbitt, the doctor will see your brother now,' she said crisply. To Raymond.

Nodding, Raymond stood up, tugging his jacket into place as he'd seen Charlie do so often. He turned to his brother and made a beckoning gesture with his head.

To Charlie the secretary said in a patronizingly sweet mommy voice, 'Can we get you something? Apple juice? Seven-Up?'

For an instant Charlie could only stare back at her, while a groundswell of ironic laughter spread through him, laughter he choked back so it wouldn't gush from his lips. He stood up, patted his hair down, adjusted his trousers to their usual waist level and picked up his briefcase.

'Bourbon and soda,' he told the stupefied secretary as he marched past her into Dr Marston's inner sanctum. But inside the laughter was mingled with a sense of triumph. *He* had brought Raymond to this; he alone had brought him to the place in his life where he could fool a sophisticated British secretary. Three ironic cheers for Charlie Babbitt! He felt encouraged, ready for anything.

Dr Bruner was in the office with Dr Marston. Both of them waiting, the experts.

''Morning, Raymond,' said Dr Bruner. 'What a handsome suit. Very distinguished.'

To this compliment Raymond answered nothing, but his eyes went skittering around Marston's office – the Degas on the wall, the tall bookcases crammed with volumes. Hundreds and hundreds of books.

'Raymond, this is Dr Marston.' In contrast to his elegant surroundings, Dr Marston appeared to be an ordinary joe. Instead of a suit he wore just a sport shirt and trousers, no tie, no jacket, and his sleeves were rolled up. He was younger than Dr Bruner and better-looking.

'Are they . . . are they all yours?' Raymond asked.

'He means the books,' offered Charlie. 'He was admiring all the books.'

'You enjoy books, do you?' Marston's voice was low-pitched and comforting.

'Oh, Raymond loves to read,' Dr Bruner said. 'And he remembers every word. It's quite remarkable.'

Raymond said nothing, and Charlie thought it best to keep his own trap. Shut.

'That's quite a bandage, Raymond,' said Dr Bruner; Charlie's heart sank. Here we go. 'How did you hurt your hand?'

There was a pause, during which Charlie held his breath. If Raymond didn't tell the cover story exactly as they'd rehearsed it . . .

'In my daddy's car,' Raymond said, just as they'd rehearsed it. 'I shut the door on me. Here.' And he pointed to the back of his hand.

'I see.' Marston sat back in his chair and regarded them both appraisingly. Then he spoke directly to Charlie. 'Mr Babbitt, this is, as you know, not a legal proceeding this morning. No lawyers, no judge, just the people who . . . care . . . about Raymond.'

Uh-oh. Something in Dr Marston's voice set Charlie's motor running and triggered all his suspicions.

'There's no easy way to say this, Mr Babbitt,' the doctor continued, 'but –'

'You've made up your mind,' Charlie interrupted angrily. His mouth was a tight line, and his hazel eyes flashed fury. He glared at Marston, then Bruner; they'd ganged up on him just as he'd always thought they would. They thought he wouldn't stand a chance against them. Well, they were fucking wrong! They weren't going to bully him.

Dr Marston shook his head, but even so Charlie could read the writing on the wall, plain and clear. You lose, asshole, it said. They weren't even going to give him a chance. They weren't interested in how far Raymond had come, or how he could handle himself and the world now. You lose. Well, he'd be damned if he was giving in that easily. There was still a few rounds to go before Charlie Babbitt was counted out.

'I'm not judge and jury,' Marston said softly. 'I'm a doctor. Making a recommendation to a court. Wallbrook is an outstanding facility,' Marston continued. 'Dr Bruner is a respected professional. *Very* respected, I must tell you. Your brother's condition is lifelong. And meticulously documented, I may add.'

Charlie stood up, his expression unreadable, his voice dripping ice. 'Fine. C'mon, Ray, these guys are wasting our time. Let's go hit some baseballs. See you fellas in court.'

'Hold on, son,' Dr Bruner said. 'This man is trying to help you understand something. No one's your enemy here.'

'Yeah, that's right.' Charlie bit off his words contemptuously. 'Nobody wants to lock *me* away for the rest of my life.' Now the anger spilled out of him unchecked. 'But if they were, there's only one person in this room, in this world, who'd stand by me! That man there!'

All eyes turned to Raymond, who'd fished the little Sony out of Charlie's briefcase and was absorbed in changing the channels. He hardly looked the part of a hero.

'And if you think you're gonna take him away from me, you're in a knife fight!'

'Stop selling, Charlie,' said Dr Bruner quietly but with great authority. 'You know, son, your father, for all his faults, didn't let his ego get in the way of the truth. About your brother.'

'Ego, huh?' growled Charlie hotly. 'Look in a mirror, pal. Ray came further with me in six days than he did with you in twenty goddamn years! And you can't handle it! And *that*'s the truth!'

Marston and Bruner exchanged glances that spoke volumes. Then Dr Marston turned to Raymond.

'Ray, that must have been some trip with your brother. What happened?'

Without looking up from his little TV, Raymond said, 'I saw Daddy's ground. And I played cards. And

I struck out Charlie Babbitt. And I drove the car –'

'Whoa, there!' Dr Marston laughed. 'I'm getting dizzy from your trip.' He asked Charlie, 'He drove a car?'

Before Charlie could explain, Raymond interrupted. He was on a roll here, eager to talk about the last few exciting days. 'Fast! And I met a prostitute, and –'

'Tell me about *that* one.' Dr Marston's eyebrow shot up quizzically.

'That one is Iris. She's pretty.'

Charlie was getting uncomfortable. None of what Raymond was blabbing had been part of the carefully rehearsed patter. Gambling, fast cars and loose women, these were hardly the stuff of fraternal love and care for the autistic. It was coming out all wrong! That's not the way it was! But he didn't dare to interrupt Raymond; God only knew what *that* would trigger.

'Where did you meet Iris, Raymond?' Dr Bruner asked.

'Where you drink the drinks.'

'In a bar,' Bruner said, and Raymond nodded. A bar.

'How did you know she was a prostitute, Raymond?'

'Charlie Babbitt said. He said a prostitute is nice to men for money. He said money makes people nice. He gave me money to give her –'

Now Charlie was compelled to break in. 'She was just going to dance with him. It was totally innocent!'

'Do you know what Raymond would do if a pretty girl put her arms around him?' Bruner demanded.

'He'd dance with her!' yelled Charlie.

Both Marston and Bruner smiled, but Raymond said quietly. 'I danced with Susanna.'

It was difficult to tell who was the more astonished, the doctors or Charlie. Susanna? Why hadn't she told him?

'Not like Charlie Babbitt,' Raymond added.

All heads swung around to Raymond, and Dr Marston asked, 'What does that mean, Raymond?'

The question was a disturbing one. Raymond's hands reached for each other and twisted together, the sure sign that he was troubled and beginning to experience anxiety. He started speaking very rapidly, his words tumbling out now in a rush, now with frightened pauses between them.

'Charlie Babbitt . . . held me bad. He kept holding me . . . c'mon, brothers . . . *do* this stuff, and . . . it's not . . . *faggy* . . .' As he spoke, Raymond became more and more agitated, and his small body began to twitch and tremble. 'Serious injury . . . serious injury, and I'd be . . . I'd be number *one* serious injury in . . . in . . . 1988 . . . and . . .' Now Raymond turned and looked straight at Charlie. 'And . . . we're . . . not . . . we're not . . . brothers.'

Oh, Christ! I fucked up every way I could. I did it all wrong, everything! thought Charlie with a sudden sinking realization. For the first time he saw the other side of the coin, the bad effect he'd had on Raymond along with the good. Out loud he said, with profound sorrow, 'I thought . . . I was forgiven.'

'Sometimes,' Raymond said.

Sometimes. Sighing from the bottom of his soul, Charlie turned to Dr Bruner and tried to explain. 'I did it wrong. I tried to *make* him hug me. I thought I . . . was . . . the one who could break through . . . make him hug his brother . . . kiss a girl.'

'I *kissed* a girl!' Raymond said triumphantly.

A small gasp of astonishment went around the room. 'You kissed Iris?' Charlie asked incredulously.

Raymond shook his head. 'Susanna. In the elevator. After we danced.'

A small silence fell while the three men contemplated this miracle. Then Dr Marston said gently, 'So you kissed a girl. Tell me, Raymond, how did it feel?'

'It was *wet*.'

That was a show-stopper. Charlie allowed himself a small grin of triumph, which Marston saw and understood.

'Raymond's condition is seductive,' the doctor said to Charlie. 'To all of us. We all want to be the one. That's part of your charm, Raymond.'

Raymond nodded agreement.

'You liked being outside the home for a while, huh? It was fun?'

Another nod.

'But now it's time to go back,' said Marston in a soft, yet firm voice.

No way! Over Charlie Babbitt's dead body! 'Look!' Charlie was on his feet, scowling. 'We don't want the doctor's money or his fatherly advice. Open your eyes! Ray and I, we're doing fine.'

Dr Bruner, who had been silent for several minutes, leaned forward in his chair and looked piercingly at Raymond. How fine were they actually doing? It was time to find out.

'Tell me again, Raymond. How did you hurt your hand? Really.'

Raymond's eyes evaded the doctor's glance. ''Course, Daddy's *car* door was . . . and it was . . .' he babbled.

'"Course" means he's anxious,' Bruner said to Marston. 'Almost as if –'

'He's lying,' Charlie interrupted. 'For me. It was totally my mistake. It happened when I was hugging him. I held him too tightly, and I wouldn't let him go. I thought that if I just held him . . . in my arms . . . we'd connect. That he'd ... maybe ... understand that I care about him. But he went crazy. Almost bit his own hand off.' Charlie turned to Dr Marston, pleading in his eyes and voice. 'My mistake. Mine. I learned. I promise –'

But Dr Bruner stood up, shaking his head sadly, and Charlie knew with awful finality that he'd lost. It was just about over.

'You want to, Charlie, but the water's too deep.'

Bruner was right, both in theory and in practice. Raymond's condition was something that only professionals could fully understand or deal with. Even with all the good will in the world Charlie was in over his head.

But there was irony here, rich irony. The most impressive facet of Raymond's performance at this hearing was not that he'd danced, or driven a car, or played cards, or kissed a girl. No, it was that he'd lied. Lied to protect Charlie Babbitt, his brother. Because autistics don't lie. Lying implies purpose, an aim, an end to be reached, something to be gained, a reason for lying. Autistic people like Raymond, even high-functioning autistics, don't have any of those things. They don't make plans; they don't tell lies.

Both Dr Bruner and Dr Marston recognized this instantly, although Charlie couldn't know it. And both doctors realized that a genuine connection had formed between the brothers Babbitt, that Raymond had actually connected with another living human being. It was a miracle.

A miracle, perhaps, but a temporary one. Like the frog in the well in the classic algebra problem, an autistic can occasionally hop up a step or two towards the top of the well, but he's bound to fall back again. In the problem the frog does eventually get out of the well, but in real life the autistic never does. The well is too deep, the frog too disabled.

Now it was up to Dr Bruner to prove this to Charlie. Coming over to where Raymond sat nervously clutching the precious little Watchman Charlie had bought him, Dr Bruner stood over his chair.

'Raymond. What do you want?'

The reaction was swift and predictable. Raymond was instantly thrown into further confusion. His hands twisted each other without mercy. His small body twitched and jittered in the chair. His eyes rolled from side to side.

If Bruner wanted a living, breathing demonstration of a disabled person, he had it. But he wanted more. He wanted to drive the point home now and for ever, not only to his colleague Marston but also to Charles Babbitt. There was no cure for a condition like Raymond's. To think otherwise, to hope otherwise, was both futile and destructive and of no earthly benefit to Raymond Babbitt.

'Tell me, Raymond. What do you want?' More loudly now.

Raymond writhed in his private agony, unable to think or speak. He tried to look at Charlie, but Bruner had come around to the other side of his chair in order to block Raymond from Charlie's view.

Raymond was making little whimpering noises and having trouble breathing. He was disintegrating rapidly, withdrawing into that hidden world of protective rituals out of which Charlie had tried so hard to drag him.

'Look at me!' demanded Dr Bruner. 'What do you *want?*'

'Stop it!' yelled Charlie in desperation. 'It makes him

crazy! And he knows it!' Glaring at Bruner, he appealed to Dr Marston.

But Marston was regarding Raymond with scientific curiosity. 'What is it? What's doing this?'

'Asking what he wants,' replied Charlie. 'He doesn't like it.'

Dr Bruner persisted, intending to carry this demonstration to its limits, to probe the hopeless depths of Raymond Babbitt's disability and lay it bare as evidence.

'You have to tell me, Raymond,' he insisted, as Raymond began the paranoiac whisperwhisperwhisper under his breath. 'You have to tell me *now*. *What do you want?*'

Raymond was gone, totally gone, so far inside himself that nothing could reach him at this moment. He slid off his chair to the floor, still whispering, on his knees, rocking back and forth, back and forth, those dark eyes seeing absolutely nothing. And now his teeth began to chatter and his whole body to shiver, as though icy cold from the depths of the earth was penetrating through his flesh to the marrow of Raymond's poor bones.

'It's not that he doesn't like it,' Dr Bruner explained to Dr Marston. 'It frightens him. Immobilizes him. Because he doesn't know.'

Through all of this Raymond's whispering continued, but now it rose in volume a little, barely enough to be heard. But they could hear it.

'C-h-a-r-l-i-e . . . C-h-a-r-l-i-e . . . C-h-a-r-l-i-e . . .' spelled Raymond. It was a magic incantation, a protective incantation.

'He knows,' said Charlie, brushing past Dr Bruner to get to his brother. Kneeling beside him on the floor, Charlie held out his hand to touch his brother gently.

But before his hand met Raymond's face Charlie remembered and pulled it back.

'Ray. Look at me. Please!' he begged.

With agonizing slowness Raymond raised his trembling head and looked into the face of his brother. They were only inches apart from each other.

'Tell me, Ray.' Charlie spoke very gently in a near-whisper. 'Because I really want to know. What do you want?'

Raymond's eyes met Charlie's. 'What do *you* want, Charlie Babbitt?'

Charlie smiled at his brother and shook his head. 'No. What do you want, *Charlie*?'

Raymond hesitated for one heartbeat, then he said, 'No. What do you want, *Charlie*?'

'I want . . . you.'

Charlie stood up and faced the two doctors, the hustling street fighter and the men of learning. 'So,' he confessed with a small, crooked smile. 'I need my brother.' It was the first admission of need he'd ever made in his entire life. And he knew in his heart it would be denied.

'C-h-a-r-l-i-eeee,' said Raymond because that always made Charlie smile. 'C-h-a-r-l-i-eeee.'

Charlie dropped to his knees again, close to Raymond. A strong feeling of love washed over him and, oddly enough, the feeling at once strengthened him and made him give up the struggle. The battle was really over now. And Charlie wasn't the loser; Raymond was the winner. In the battle over Raymond that had taken place between them Dr Bruner had shown them Raymond at his worst, just as Charlie had shown him at his best. And they were both Raymond: the best *and* the worst. Raymond would go back to Wallbrook, where they knew his needs and would care for him. But he would go back with memories he didn't have before, experiences he could remember, take out and re-live again. The baseball game, where Rain Man had struck out the Hammer. A dance in an elevator. A kiss. The great and grand triumph at the blackjack tables in Las Vegas. And memories of a brother, Charlie Babbitt. No, Charlie.

'Look,' Charlie said slowly to Raymond, 'maybe they'll make you go away from me.'

Everybody could see Raymond thinking that over. Then he reached into his pocket and pulled out his little wallet, taking out that faded and creased photograph, now also water-stained from its sojourn at the bottom of a bathtub. It was a lovely picture – the eighteen-year-old Raymond and the two-year-old Charlie. Rain Man and Charlie. Brothers. He handed the picture to Charlie and reached over to close Charlie's fingers around it. Touching Charlie.

Charlie's hand in Raymond's. The seconds ticking by in silence. Tears rising in Charlie's eyes. Tears of sorrow and affection. Tears for the parting with a brother, even though there was the sure knowledge that this wasn't the last time they'd be together, that Charlie would be visiting and then – let the good times roll! The Brothers Babbitt, man, the dauntless duo, the unbeatable combo, would ride again!

Seeing the brothers' hands touching, seeing their foreheads pressed together, Dr Bruner smiled. The two of them had been on the road together only a week, but even in that very short time Raymond had obviously been very good for Charlie.

There's an epidemic with 27 million victims. And no visible symptoms.

It's an epidemic of people who can't read.

Believe it or not, 27 million Americans are functionally illiterate, about one adult in five.

The solution to this problem is you... when you join the fight against illiteracy. So call the Coalition for Literacy at toll-free **1-800-228-8813** and volunteer.

Volunteer Against Illiteracy. The only degree you need is a degree of caring.